ENTHRALLER

VERDANT STRING

MICHELLE DIENER

Cover Design: 100Covers

❀ Created with Vellum

ABOUT ENTHRALLER

The planet Aponi sits at the outer edge of the Verdant String.

For Wren Thorakis, working as an Aponian Special Forces artifacts consultant, it means interesting assignments and unusual discoveries. Being captured and held for ransom by a shadowy cult while working on the moon Ytla was not something she expected, though. However, while escaping her captors, she stumbles across what could be the discovery of her career—one that no artifact consultant could possibly ignore—a genuine ancestral mothership.

The mothership isn't just amazing in itself, though. Wren finds herself the recipient of crazy-powerful nanotech. It helps keep her alive and one step ahead of those trying to hide the ship's existence.

When Wren starts working out who's behind keeping her discovery secret, and why, she is plunged into a bigger plot than she ever imagined.

A shadowy organization has its eye on Aponi, and isn't shy to use the Verdant String's fiercest enemies, the Caruso, to help them take it from the Coalition.

When an Aponi Special Forces soldier, Ed Zeneri, who's existence is also inconvenient to Wren's enemies, is lured into a trap with Wren and they both come under fire, Wren's nanotech does whatever it has to to keep her safe—including enthralling Ed to protect her at all costs.

Ed knows his reaction to Wren isn't normal, or even sane, but as the compulsion to put himself in front of anything coming at her recedes, he finds he's more than inclined to do it of his own volition.

He joins forces with Wren to try to stop the takeover of their home planet, and as they race the clock to find the answers they need, he also has to convince Wren that what he feels for her is real.

As real as the enemy battleships hovering in Aponi's nearspace. As real as the deadline to bring them down.

As real as it gets.

1

———

"Why must you be so damned stubborn?" Guttra tapped a heel against the hull of the petral, managing to do the impossible—get even more on Ed's nerves than he already was.

Ed tightened the last screw on the petral's porthole window and looked sideways at the shoe doing the tapping.

It was made of the polished skin of some poor animal from Guttra's planet, Themis—so black and shiny you could probably see your face in it. Ed bent closer, and sure enough his face, weirdly distorted, looked back at him.

He shuffled his own scuffed boots on the top step of the ladder, put the laser drill back in the toolbox beside him, and carried it down.

Guttra used the scaffolding to swing down from the deck he'd been dangling his feet over and landed lightly beside him.

Ed scowled. "Get out of my workshop and leave me alone. This petral is due for pick-up in two day's time."

Guttra lost the annoying smile and the perky attitude. "Things are happening, Ed. Things you used to be interested in."

Ed raised a brow and said nothing.

He'd heard this before. And not just from Guttra. Although it had been a while since Special Forces had come knocking. He'd thought they'd finally given up.

"This isn't one of those bait and switch attempts to entice you back. This is a real, current case." Guttra shuffled on the spot, uncharacteristically graceless. "And given we're at the very end of the Verdant String, hanging off the back, as they say, there isn't exactly a large number of agents with your expertise or heritage available."

"Where's Lily?" His former colleague was the only other agent working on the Verdant String planet of Aponi with his particular skill-set, and the genes to match.

Guttra shifted even more uncomfortably. "In prison."

Everything went still inside him. Ed slowly lowered the toolbox and finally gave Guttra his full attention.

Guttra twitched under his scrutiny. "She got sent off-planet to deal with a situation for the Hathr, and they claim she participated in anti-government sedition while executing her duties, and they've arrested her."

Ed crossed his arms over his chest. "We are talking about Lily?"

"Yeah. And don't worry, you're not the only one who doesn't think that flies."

"What's really going on then?"

Guttra pursed his lips. "Word is she caught someone's eye. There are so few of you Halatians, and you're so pretty with that blue hair." Guttra mimicked chucking him under the chin, careful to keep his hands out of grabbing distance. "Lily stands out—just like you do. Too unique for your own good. We think maybe someone really, really high up on Hathr just wanted her. Trumped up a charge of sedition to have her transported, maybe hoped they'd have some say in what happened to her if she was found guilty."

Ed frowned. However far-fetched that sounded, it was possible. Lily was . . . striking. And Halatians were so few as to be almost extinct as a people.

Guttra fluttered long, elegant fingers. "Thing is, the VSC insisted they be the ones to try her, and the reaction wasn't happy. You could hear the Hathr howls practically all the way to VSC Headquarters on

Arkhor. Especially when it came out that the evidence against her doesn't appear to exist."

Ed rubbed his temple. He liked Lily. "Where's she now?"

"The VSC hired the closest Verdant String affiliated private transport crew to bring her and the others accused with her to Arkhor, so she should be safe soon. They didn't leave her in the lurch, Ed."

Unlike they'd done to him. But that was two years ago and water under the bridge.

As if he realized the place he'd led them to, Guttra winced. "Sorry. That wasn't bright of me. I need you, Ed. Yes, an incompetent, bent Defense administrator hung you out to dry back in the day. I know Special Forces have apologized, and compensated you. And that idiot is still rotting in jail."

"What's the job?" Ed leaned back against the smooth metal of the petral hull and crossed his arms over his chest.

Guttra lifted his hands in hope. "A transport came in yesterday. Scanners clocked it in as having one occupant. Sure enough, only one occupant stepped out to register." Guttra paused. "Problem was, the traveler was a Verdant String woman, average height, slim."

"What's the problem with that?"

"The occupant the scanner clocked coming in weighed three tons and was the size of a light travel pod. Which was why they were watching what got out at the docks."

Ed cocked his head. "A shape changer?" He whistled. "Thought they were all gone over a hundred years back."

"Exterminated, you mean?" Guttra raised his eyebrows.

Yeah, Ed had meant that, but it was generally frowned on to talk of extermination on Aponi. Not the warm, fuzzy, happy families image the VSC liked to project.

Not that they hadn't had cause, in the case of shape changers.

An Aponi exploration unit had stumbled on the tiny satellite moon, Nai, that was the original habitat of the shape changers. What no one back home had realized, until it was too late, was the shape changers had killed most of the explorers, shifted to replicate them, and come back to Aponi to wreak havoc.

It had been days before the authorities had realized the mild-mannered scientists who had come back from Nai were actually cunning predators who could hardly believe their luck in landing in Demeter, Aponi's capital city, with all its unsuspecting inhabitants.

It had been a slaughterhouse until the VSC Special Forces had managed to stop the killings.

"So Captain Hyt thinks the scanner will work in identifying a shape changer? What does he think it will pick up?"

Guttra tilted his head. "Given the Guan scanner your fellow Halatian created is still considered the most accurate way to see inside a ship and work out how many people and weapons are in it, Hyt thinks it's worth a shot to have you use it on the suspected shape changer."

"So he wants me to walk up to her, scanner engaged, and see if I can see by looking at her if she changes into something that weighs three tons?" Ed shook his head. "She's not a spaceship."

"I think Captain Hyt was told the scanner's been used for more than just ships in the past. This is highly classified info and we weren't given further details. Whoever it was who spoke to Hyt said it was possible the scanner could give us a reading that would let us know, one way or another."

"I've used the scanner for years, and I've never used it on anything other than a ship or building. And I haven't heard of anyone else using it any other way, either."

Guttra lifted his shoulders. "You haven't worked for Special Forces for two years. Don't worry, there'll be a full crew around you, and it'll be people from my team. Just do your thing. Like usual."

Like usual? The Guan scanner could not give an accurate reading if there was anything between it and the ship or building it was scanning, so for years that had meant free floating in space, equipment attached to his head, the readout a thin transparent screen in front of his eyes.

Standing in a hover port, scanning an individual person, was not usual at all. In fact, he doubted it would even work, no matter what some high-up had whispered in Captain Hyt's ear.

Guttra claimed this was a real case, but it smacked of the obvious ploys Special Forces had used before to woo him back into the fold. It wasn't so much that they were sorry that one of the idiots in charge had pointed him at the wrong target, then tried to lay the blame on him for the political fallout. It was more to do with the fact that Guan, the architect and engineer who'd developed what became known as the Guan scanner, made it impossible for anyone who didn't have Halatian DNA to operate.

It was why, he was sure, Guttra had kept in touch with him all this time. Ed would like to have believed Guttra was an actual friend, but he suspected he kept up a connection on the orders of Special Forces, in case they could find a way to lure him back.

And the reason for their tenacity was that Special Forces missed having accurate information on whatever ships were approaching them than they'd had before Ed left, especially as things got uglier and uglier between the VSC and the Caruso.

They were desperate to get him back, especially now they'd been so careless with Lily.

"It's not just like usual, though, is it?" Ed clenched his fists. "Even if the scanner can somehow see what's really there, if we close in, what's stopping it changing into its real self?"

"Does that mean you won't do it?" Guttra asked.

Ed considered the petral he'd been tinkering with. That had been the third time he'd taken that porthole window off and put it back on anyway.

"When is this happening?"

2

———

Guttra's idea of a full team was Ed's idea of a small army, but he wasn't going to complain. Ethan Hyt was certainly making sure whatever the woman turned out to be, she would be contained, or at least blasted into small, easy-to-dispose-of pieces.

"Just so long as I'm not caught in the crossfire." Ed eyed the armor-laden unit of thirty officers as they stood to attention in the drafty hover port warehouse near the suspect's docking station. Every one of them looked equipped to bring down a Valpa 7 gargan.

"Run fast, and you won't be." Hyt gave a cold smile.

Guttra grunted and Hyt shot him a look. "I'm joking. We'll wait until he's clear."

"Just so long as they know that." Ed jerked his head at the gathered teams. "So, I stand in front of her as she walks past? I have a feeling she's going to view that as suspicious."

"If we bring her in as she is, and then she turns into what she registered on approach, she won't fit into SF headquarters, and we don't want any structural damage. It's better, if she *is* going to change, she changes on the dock, with plenty of space around her," Hyt said.

Guttra, who was leaning against a small window, lifted the slim, enhanced visor to his eyes again, and went still. "She's coming. She's arming the security lock on her ship."

Ed gave a nod, loosened his shoulders and stepped through the small door in the side of the warehouse onto the concourse. The scanner was built into a helmet and the screen that covered his face gave him a touch of vertigo, making his movements a little jerky. He was used to free floating, attached to a cable, with nothing to do but read the information the scanner was sending him.

Walking and looking through the strangely tinted screen at the same time was close to impossible, and Ed flicked it up and away from his face to stop himself stumbling.

He walked toward the slim, dark-haired woman. She was dressed in dark green smart cloth pants and a clinging tunic, and she was headed toward the domed square at the center of the hover port. She stopped to look up at the time and weather information on a glowing board, and that allowed him to get closer without attracting her notice.

When he thought he was close enough, but still able to get away if she changed shape, Ed braced himself for the tiny sting as he pressed the tip of his finger onto the sharp sensor in his hand, drawing a tiny drop of blood.

Bio scan accepted. The tinny voice that came through his comm was a familiar reminder of past missions.

The woman turned her attention away from the info board and began digging in the bag hanging from her shoulder. She was so intent on her task, Ed didn't think she would have noticed if Hyt and all three SF teams had been out in the open, guns waving.

That alone sent the first prickly spider of uncertainty skittering down his spine. Not that he'd ever had any experience with one, but would a shape changer fuss over a shoulder bag like that?

Hey, maybe three ton monsters liked their handbags, too.

Time to find out.

He flicked the screen back down over his face and braced himself for the strangely-lit world of shadow and light. Hiding weapons, hiding extra people, was easy enough against normal scanners if you were clever and had the right materials, and most people who wanted to hide weapons or extra soldiers were and did. But the Guan scanner cut through all of the tricks.

Except, there were no tricks here.

Nothing.

Unless, as he'd thought from the start, the scanner wasn't the right tech for this problem.

He flicked up the screen to find the woman looking at him—wide eyes staring.

"What are you doing?" she asked, her gaze going to the scanner equipment that covered his head like a helmet.

"I'd like to know the same thing." He looked over his shoulder, trying to see any sign of Hyt and his team. They were nowhere in sight.

Suddenly, a flash of laz fire lit up the air around them. His suit included anti-laz protection, and he closed the gap between them, grabbing her and shielding her with his body.

He felt a few stray hits bounce off him, and he grunted at the impact.

"What . . .?" She sounded outraged, and then whoever was shooting fired again, and at last she seemed to realize what he was doing.

"Do you have any idea what is going on?" she asked him as he tucked her up close to his body.

"Someone is shooting at us." He was being flippant, but he didn't know the answer, and he wondered where the hell Hyt and Guttra were.

Where was the promise to have his back now?

"You were studying me with that scanner thing. Why?" The laz fire had stopped for the moment, and she turned her face up to his as she asked the question.

"I was trying to see if you can turn into a three ton monster."

She gave him a blank look.

And he suddenly knew. She had absolutely no idea what he was talking about. She tried to jerk away from him, as if she thought he had lost his mind.

If nothing else, her reaction clued him in. This was a screw-up.

"Listen, lady, I'm working for Aponi Special Forces. They thought you were a shape changer." He saw no benefit in keeping this under wraps. A little honesty on the table might go a long way right now.

"Special Forces?" She frowned, her confusion plain. "But *I* work for Special Forces."

Oh. Shit.

As he thought it, fighting erupted behind him, Hyt's team coming to the party at last and presumably countering whoever was aiming at either himself or the woman.

Or both of them together, because someone had gone to a lot of trouble to get them in the same place at the same time.

Laz fire came their way again, and to avoid it, Ed pulled her down to a crouch with him. He lowered his lips to her ear. "Did you tick someone off? Because back in that warehouse are three SF units, ready to take you down."

Her gaze drifted over his shoulder, her body tense against his.

She tried again to pull back, but he held on. He couldn't let Hyt's team get a good shot at her. If that's what was going on here.

He did not like it that he didn't know.

If they wanted him dead, they'd have to aim for his head or neck. But as they'd supplied him with the suit, they'd know that. And there weren't that many Guan scanners left. A head shot would destroy a precious piece of tech.

Not from the warehouse, but somewhere to his right, Ed caught sight of someone in a dark uniform lifting a laz in their direction, and instinctively he twisted, putting his back to the shooter and moving to the side.

The blast came close to his ear and now he wondered if this was someone's way of destroying the Guan scanner. That would be an interesting development.

There were certainly a number of enemies of the VSC who would benefit from leveling the playing field.

He was holding the woman like a lover now, draped over his upper thighs, her face tucked under his chin, and as she drew back a little he felt a shift in the air, and blinked as she pressed her palm over his breast bone, onto his skin where his tunic opened a little.

"I should have known they wouldn't just let me walk away," she murmured. She was still pressed tight against him, held close in his arms, and he noticed for the first time that her eyes were a mix of light green and blue. Like the sea.

He dragged his gaze away, hunting for a direction to run that looked safe, and then the shooter switched the laz from single shot to multiple, and a stream of purple light came at them.

They were dead.

Ed curled himself over her, covering the woman with as much of his body as he could, tensing in anticipation of the pain. Even with the suit, even if they didn't manage a head shot, this was going to hurt.

The sound of the laz shots smacking against an impenetrable surface behind him went on for one second, two . . . He started to lift his head to look over his shoulder, but there was nothing to see.

Nothing but Hyt's crew, finally coming out into the open.

The laz fire stopped abruptly.

"I'm very sorry about this," the woman said, drawing his attention back to her. Before his eyes she started to fade away, and Ed grabbed desperately at her, his hands closing over wisps that faded like mist.

And then he was kneeling, alone on the platform, shouting, and some small part of him understood that if he'd known it, it would have been her name on his lips.

As it was, it was a desperate, animal howl of longing for something he wanted more than anything, but could not have.

———

"You calmer now?" Hyt's face was unreadable and Ed forced himself not to struggle against the restraints. He lifted cool, hard eyes up to the captain.

With a sigh, Hyt leaned behind him and pressed the release on the clamps.

Still keeping himself under control, Ed rubbed at his wrists. The clamps hadn't been over-tight, but he'd fought them with everything in him for a while there, and his skin was red and bruised. His shins must look the same.

"Obviously, our intel was flawed." Hyt didn't look at him, turning to pace the room.

Ed watched the back of Hyt's head, and realized he'd give a body part for a heavy object to smash against the captain's skull. He took a deep, shuddering breath, his eye catching on the woman's shoulder bag, sitting on the table.

It had been emptied, rifled through, but it was just a normal bag, containing a generic comms device, a lip balm and a hair brush. "Who shot at us?" His voice was hoarse, gravelly from shouting, and he picked up the disposable cup of water on the table and drained it in a single swallow.

Hyt turned at that, and his face was as hard as Ed's. "Not one of mine."

Ed just stared at him, and Hyt slammed himself into the nearest chair. "I know. You think I don't know? If it *wasn't* one of mine, I've got the sloppiest team on Demeter—hell, maybe the whole of Aponi, and if it *was* . . ."

If it was, someone on Hyt's team had been bought. Which was very hard to do in the Verdant String, with its citizen's dividend and the ceiling limits on profiteering.

"The discharge recorders?" Ed asked for form's sake. It would have been the first thing Hyt checked.

"No one fired their weapons at you. They're all clear."

"So you have someone on your team who's dirty, and this whole thing was planned enough that they had a spare laz hidden to use, and they somehow ditched it afterwards."

Hyt rubbed a hand over his face. "With you going crazy and Guttra and the rest of the team on a hair-trigger because of the shots

—not to mention the subject swooshing away like morning mist—whoever took the shot could have taken off."

"Or one of your team could have hidden the gun, walked out with their official weapon, and their little friends could have made sure there was nothing to find once you'd gotten your head back out your arse."

Hyt dropped his hand, and the look he sent Ed was as dark as a Freo dock back alley, and just as nasty.

"The other thing I'd like to know is, how did they miss us? We were in the open, with nowhere to hide, thanks to your little set-up. They almost got us with those first few shots, but when they went multiple, it should have been easy." Ed didn't know why he'd only asked this now.

It was as if part of him didn't want to know.

Hyt's face was blank with confusion. "You didn't see?"

Ed watched him, watched his face settle into avid curiosity.

"When the shooter went multiple, it was like a shiny gray matter came out of nowhere, hovered in the air in front of you like a shield and then vanished. That's why it took me so long to get my head, as you so politely put it, out of my arse. I'd never seen anything like it. It looked metallic, and it was sure as hell impenetrable, but fluid at the same time. I thought it might have been you doing it."

Ed shook his head. "I'm just someone with the right DNA to work the scanner. It was either the woman, or something else."

"What did she feel like?"

The question was so offensive, a red mist seemed to hover instantly before his eyes. As if he would tell Hyt what it had felt like to hold her in his arms—

"Whoa! I meant, where do you think she's from, what planet?"

Ed realized he was out of his chair, his hands reaching out for Hyt's throat. He threw them up, palms out and backed up, sat down with shaky legs. He closed his eyes for a moment. "Sorry." He took a deep breath. "I don't know where she was from. She felt normal. VSC."

"Why's this so personal, Ed?" Hyt rubbed his throat reflexively. "Yes, we've been played, big time, and it has to go high for them to have fed us that kind of false data on the woman, but I'm as much a dupe as you, or Guttra. What the hell's the matter with you? What did this woman do to you?"

Ed had to hold onto his chair to stop launching himself at the captain again, a dark sweep of rage so unfamiliar, so out of his normal experience, his body felt on fire. Hands he wanted to curl around Hyt's throat, he forced to curl around the edge of the chair instead, keeping him in place. "Someone lied to me, manipulated me into being on that dock, and then shot at me. You don't think that makes it personal?" His voice was guttural as he forced himself to speak in a level tone, rather than to shout.

Hyt watched him, his gaze lowering to Ed's hands. He blew out a breath. "It's more than that. You want to kill me. You wanted to kill us all at that dock. It was as if that woman disappearing triggered a beserk rage in you and you've barely got it under control, even now."

"She said something." He realized straight away even saying that much was a mistake.

Hyt leaned forward, eyes alight with interest. "What?"

With a feeling of helplessness, Ed brought his fist up into Hyt's face, felt the impact of his knuckles against the side of Hyt's head. Watched the captain slump forward onto the floor.

He forced himself not to kick Hyt in the ribs as he passed him to get to the door, forced himself to look relaxed.

But it was just a look.

She had said she was Special Forces. But someone had sent Special Forces to kill her. There was so much going on here, he didn't know which way was up, except there was one thing he did know for sure.

He would protect her to his last breath.

He understood his feelings, his actions, were so extreme, he didn't recognize himself.

Something was going on here, and he needed answers.

He strolled out of headquarters with an easy stride, as if he hadn't just laid out the captain of Demeter City's Special Forces on his office floor, and headed for the university.

3

───────────

Wren heaved in a huge, shuddering breath and leaned, face forward, against the cool stone wall of the library with both hands. She lowered her head and let her forehead rest against the stone as she got over the shock of going from a battle ground to the quiet of the Depository courtyard.

Dissipating was getting easier, at least.

The first time she'd done it, she'd vomited for an hour afterwards. Now the mild nausea faded in a few minutes.

She straightened and turned, leaning back against the wall as she got her bearings, and tried to work out what had happened at the hover port docking station.

The courtyard she stood in was at the back of the Depository and the sound of foot traffic and the whoosh of hovers was muted. There didn't seem to be a disturbance. No small armies were searching the streets for her.

She took the few steps across the sunlit center of the courtyard to a little table with two chairs, tucked under the eaves, and sank down. She felt safe here. The Depository had become the main reason for her trips to the capital these last few months, and she had eased her tired eyes and aching head in this courtyard many times. No one would remark on her being here.

She thought back to the man.

Tall, muscular. Absolutely breathtaking.

His hair had been covered over by the strange helmet with the screen, his eyes a deep, dark blue.

He had covered her body with his.

She had seen his face when the shooting started. He'd been shocked. Then angry.

He'd been set up for something. To die with her, she would guess. She had no idea why.

And then, on top of that, she had done something to him.

She had felt the nanos in her blood surge, transfer something to him, and they never did anything without a reason.

She closed her eyes and pressed her hands over her eyelids. Breathed deeply.

What did you do? She thought the words clearly in her head.

Protected you. Us.

The answer was confusing. So many of the conversations she'd had with them had been, but she thought she'd begun to understand a bit better recently. Now she felt as if she was back to square one.

Yes, they had protected her and themselves—that was more or less the same thing since the day she had run for her life through the Ytla forest and stumbled across them. A long strand of silver beads, hanging like a trophy over the burnt out wreck of an old ship.

They had been swirling and blowing in the strong wind, drawing her eye, and as soon as she had been close enough for them to touch her, they had melted into her skin.

But they weren't beads. They were little spheres of nanotech. They had been self-aware enough to explain their nature to her. And they hadn't left her body since, except for protection. Some always stayed within her, as an anchor, some flew out to form a protective shield, and then retreated back.

"What does protecting us have to do with the man?" she asked.

He wanted to protect you. We boosted that inclination.

He had been willing to risk his body, his life, to protect her, and she'd repaid him with a compulsion.

Or the nanotech had.

She didn't control them fully.

Not yet.

She had a feeling she would, eventually.

But for now they were still somewhat independent, having spent too long outside of a person. They told her they had almost gone mad with the need for someone to protect, and that she had saved them.

Now they were dedicated to her wellbeing.

But she would rather they didn't save her in such spectacular fashion going forward.

What you did is wrong.

It was?

She sensed them thinking about it.

He was already helping us. Compelling him to do more was not good repayment for his help.

They seemed to ponder her words.

With a sigh, she stood and stretched.

She needed to find out what was going on. Why she had been shot at and whether it was her own people trying to kill her.

She was due to report to the Demeter Special Forces headquarters tomorrow, and she wouldn't be going in if they were planning to shoot her.

She straightened her clothing, squared her shoulders and walked to the brightly-painted blue door, pushed it open, and stepped into the light, airy atrium that ran the length of the building from front entrance to back.

She breathed in the sweet gyrthum-scented air, green and floral, and felt a moment of disorientation. Less than thirty minutes ago someone had been shooting at her, she had been held in the arms of a strange man in a hail of laz fire, and now she was in this most beautiful of places, her new-found haven, in the soft, golden light, standing on gleaming floors of dark purple jarram.

She put out a hand to the wall to steady herself.

"Wren? I didn't know you were coming in today." Histilo stepped out of the main depository room and stopped in surprise, then dipped in a bow, hands crossed at the wrists in front of her body in greeting, as was the Demeter custom.

"I can't stay away." Wren smiled at her, bowing back. She could not cross her hands in front of her, in the symbolic gesture that meant she was bound by the other person's wishes. Her time as a prisoner of the Har Met Vent cult on Ytla was still too vivid for her to willingly take that pose.

After she'd escaped and found the silver balls, they had helped her avoid her pursuers and find her way back to the Aponi Special Forces base on the lushly forested moon that was Ytla.

The SF team had been readying a unit to go after her—they had actually been suiting up as she arrived, and it had almost been worth all the nights dodging her kidnappers, overcoming all the dangerous terrain and even more dangerous animals on her own, just to see the look on their faces.

She moved past Histilo with another smile and made her way to the reading section, where she spent most of her time.

She came here to access the private collection the Depository had amassed on the mystery of the ancestors—the travelers who'd populated eight fecund planets across five solar systems, now known as the Verdant String.

As Aponi was the farthest planet out, the last known place the ancestors had settled down, it drew a certain type of scholar—one who liked to study the peninsula and surrounding forests of Demeter and the clifftop city of Nanganya, the two major centers on the planet, to try to work out where a ship might have landed and where it could now be found.

So far, no one had been successful.

She personally thought the travelers had dismantled the ship and used every piece of it to help them settle into a new life—pieces that slowly got replaced over the centuries, effectively making them disappear.

She was sorry about the paucity of knowledge now, though.

Because she was very sure her silver balls, her nanotech, had come with the travelers themselves. Little things they had communicated, little glimpses she had caught, had clued her in.

And the rusted hulk of the ancient spaceship they had been hanging from in the forest was an indication of how things had gone for the ancestral travelers on Ytla. Common wisdom was that Aponi was the furthest the ancestors had reached, but if they'd crashed and burned on Ytla, could they not have gone further still?

There could be a whole planet of Verdant String people out there, ready to be found and brought into the fold.

She settled down at a reader and touched the icon for the private files she wanted to read through.

Someone came in from the street entrance to the Depository and strode toward the main office, their boots heavy on the wooden floor rather than the light, slippered tread of most of the visitors to this place.

Wren turned her head to see who it was and her mouth fell open. She could only see his back, but she knew him.

The man who had cradled her in his arms. Had protected her.

Her victim.

ED STEPPED BACK out into the midday heat, leaving the cool, scented air of the Depository behind him.

Katil hadn't known anything about his mysterious lady, although she'd been interested enough.

When he'd described her, he'd sensed Katil stiffen, and she'd tipped her head, as if trying to remember something, but had let it go with a genuine shake of her head.

If something about his mystery woman rang a bell, it was a faint one.

He trusted Katil would tell him if she did know. He'd saved her son in a terrorist attack on Demeter during the Faldine War, back when he was still with the Special Forces unit, and she'd kept in touch with him ever since. She'd even been an expert witness once for one of his cases.

Ed lifted a hand and rubbed the back of his neck. It felt tight, and he had a sudden need to spin around and change direction.

He stopped.

Turned slowly.

He had intended to head back home.

Captain Ethan Hyt might well be waiting there for him with a new pair of manacles and a grievance, but until a minute ago, he hadn't cared. He just wanted a cold glass of hirtsu and a couple of hours rest.

Now?

He probed his mind. What did he want now?

The answer was, he wanted to go off on a tangent to his original course. To cross the road and walk into the narrow alley that lay between two shops, both with fronts shaded by brightly-colored awnings, their exotic wares displayed on beautiful stands.

His first instinct was to resist the compulsion.

He could, he realized. He was strong enough to fight whatever enticed him to cross the street.

He noticed that he didn't feel so full of rage, and that the thought of the woman didn't trigger a painful, deep longing for her any more. He felt loss, yes, but the feeling was back in a normal range. As if someone he loved had died or left him years ago.

Maybe psychlock wasn't in his future, after all.

So now, with choice almost fully restored, should he follow the compulsion, or ignore it?

He started across the street toward the alley.

There was always the chance she was luring him in for a top-up of whatever she had done. He remembered she'd touched his skin before he went completely off the rails, and he decided to keep his distance this time.

But his curiosity was too strong to let it go.

If she knew a little about what had led them both to that docking station, surrounded by Hyt's units and a sniper, he would like to hear it.

As he reached the entrance to the alley, he realized he was walking faster in anticipation, and forced himself to slow down. Perhaps the closer he got, the stronger the sense of longing was. It may be fading, but it was still potent enough to make him feel like a pet with his tongue hanging out at the thought of seeing her again.

He forced himself to stop completely, just to prove to himself he could.

He caught a shadow of movement a little way down the street, in the direction he'd just come from, and he pretended not to notice it. He took a step into the alley, again forcing himself to stop, to let his eyes adjust to the gloom.

He was being followed.

He didn't know when they'd picked him up. He thought he'd managed to slip out of Hyt's station without attracting any attention, but either he'd been wrong, or they'd been tracking him some other way.

He suddenly recalled the standard VSC anti-laz suit he was wearing.

His only excuse was that it had been a trying day, and he hadn't been himself for much of it.

He stripped off his shirt, bent and pulled off his boots before pulling down his pants. He ripped at the tabs, and the thin mesh suit fell from his shoulders. He pushed it over his hips, hopped from foot to foot as he tugged it off and then tossed it behind a cheerful red waste disposal. The little chip in the shoulder pad blinked green at him.

Someone deeper within the alley cleared their throat in a very delicate, very feminine way, and he lifted his head.

The woman from this morning was staring at him.

Ed followed the direction of her gaze. Down his chest, to where he was suddenly sporting a raging erection.

He looked back up at her.

"Someone was using that to follow me." He gestured to the anti-laz suit.

"I see." She kept her eyes on his, almost desperately not looking down. "Are they close?"

"Yes."

"Then come." She turned and started down the alley at a fast lope.

Ed had just enough brain capacity to scoop up his clothes and boots, and then he ran after her. Naked as a natworm.

4

Something told Wren this morning's rescuer would rather she not mention anything about their encounter in the alley.

That was fine with her.

She wasn't Aponian by birth, although her parents had been. She had been brought up all over the Verdant String, so she didn't have the same casual take on nudity as most on Aponi, but she suspected neither did the man following her.

From his blue hair, he was clearly Halatian.

The last of a people who had been visited by tragedy, compounded by cruelty, greed and inertia.

They were the walking conscience of the VSC.

She led him through the twists and turns of the back ways of the university district, places she hadn't known about before what happened to her on Ytla, but had made it her business to learn in the past few months.

She had barely spent any time back home in Nanganya since this began. She had friends there she hadn't dared visit. She had had to slip in and out of her apartment, avoiding her colleagues in Nanganya Special Forces while she did the research she needed to do.

It had been a game for a while, as she enjoyed outsmarting the best of Aponi defense, the Special Forces teams.

But when they'd followed her to Demeter, begun to trail her here, and when she realized their intent might not be just to watch her, but to harm her, it had ceased being amusing.

She had found the Demeter house, and she had started taking a different route from the Depository every time she went home to it, until there were no new ways to try, and then she'd started memorizing them all.

Behind her she heard the unmistakable sounds of someone dressing on the move, and she couldn't help grinning.

She'd have fanned herself in that alley, if she'd had a fan. She almost wished she was an Arthesian, and her hand was like a fan.

He was fine.

She had been about to step out of the alleyway and approach him when he'd stopped, turned and walked straight toward her. She'd retreated deeper into the gloom, stunned and a little afraid at how he seemed to sense her.

Then he'd begun ripping off his clothes, and she'd wondered if she should run.

She was glad now she hadn't.

She stopped at a turning point in a back alley, waiting for him, and without a sound, he was suddenly next to her, fully dressed again, and his hand clamped on her arm. "Where are we going?"

"To a place I think is safe." She stared at his hand, then up at his face. He was at least a head taller than her.

"You *think* it's safe?"

"I thought I was safe this morning, and look where that got me." She twisted her lips. "If this place isn't safe, no place is."

He released her. "Lady, after the luck I'm having today, I'm assuming the worst-case scenario."

"You have an alternative plan?"

His eyes flicked over her face, down her body, and then away. "No." He stepped back. "I think they're still behind us, so lead on."

She shivered as she started leading them again. It was as if a big, powerful beast had clamped its teeth ever so gently on her neck.

Just a reminder she had a predator by the tail.

THE WOMAN KNEW the back alleys of Demeter, that was for sure.

Whoever was following them lost them four or five turns back, but Ed kept an ear out for them anyway.

He wondered where she was leading them, but only out of idle curiosity. He would be going with her, no matter if she told him she was taking him to the Adrasten Wastes.

When she stopped in front of an ivy-covered wall, swept the fall of dark green vines and leaves aside, and pushed through a door as dark gray and mottled as the wall around it, he followed without hesitation.

The door snicked shut behind him, and he found himself in a courtyard flooded with mid-afternoon sun, a blue and yellow mosaic table set under a leafy tree in one corner.

The building in front of him looked old, and the eaves could use a little maintenance, but otherwise it was a charming setting—two steps up to a wooden door set deep in dark gray stone, with a miniature tree growing on either side.

The woman stopped at the top of the steps and looked back, as if to make sure he was following, and then opened the door, leaving it wide for him to follow.

The fact that it wasn't locked made him wary as he stepped in behind her, wondering who else might be in the house, but he sensed no one.

The Halatian in him appreciated everything about this. They were a people who loved a secret passage or a hidden room, which could only be found by solving a puzzle. The ivy hiding the door was not in the league of Guan, or Ronald Fadal, the Halatian architect of Felicitos, the tethered way station on Garmen, but it did the job.

"You leave your door unlocked?" he asked, as he looked around the cool green and gray kitchen.

"No one knows about this place, and carrying a key isn't always possible." She lifted a hand. "If I have to dissipate, my shoulder bag can't come with me."

"Dissipate? That a fancy word for you fading into a mist and vanishing?"

She shot him a quick grin. "Yes."

"And tell me how you do that?"

She hesitated, shook her head. "It's complicated."

"What did you do to me?" He did want a straight answer on that. He felt he deserved it.

She waved a hand for him to sit, and went to a cooler unit and pulled out two bottles of hirtsu and set them down, then took a seat opposite him.

She gnawed at her lip for a moment, then twisted the cap off her drink and took a few deep swallows.

He did the same, cooling his throat, enjoying the bitter, dry taste of the icy drink.

"I'm one of Special Force's expert artifact consultants." She leaned back in her chair. "I came across something in the course of my duties that has . . . altered me."

Ed remembered she'd told him she was with Special Forces, and he'd assumed she was a normal unit member, but this made more sense to him. An artifact appraiser came across all kinds of things that might bring them to the notice of dangerous people . . .

"It altered you, and now it's altered me?" He threw his conclusion on the table between them as a question but he didn't think he was wrong.

She gave a slow nod. "I'm altered for good. You, though . . ." She gave a half shrug, and he could tell she was very uncomfortable with the subject. "They tell me they simply boosted your natural protective tendencies, in order to protect me even better, but I think they misjudged the dose."

They? He let that go for a moment. "Boosted my tendencies, how?"

"I would guess hormonally, and by stimulating the specific area of your brain. It should have already faded?" She sounded so hopeful.

"It has." He didn't feel the overwhelming urge to beat his chest and stand over her like she was the beginning and end of his world, but he was uncomfortably aware he was still drawn to her.

"Good. When you came straight toward me off the street into the alley, I was worried . . ." She gnawed her lip again, and he had to force his gaze away.

"I did feel a tug in the direction of the alley. Did this mysterious 'they' have anything to do with it?"

She closed her eyes, and he had the sense she was communing with something.

If she hadn't, as she called it, dissipated, and if he hadn't been affected by whatever it was he'd been affected by, he'd have said she was putting it on.

"They say you might still be extra sensitive to my pheromones." She blushed. "I'm so sorry about this. I had no idea what they were doing, and I've been very clear with them that it must never happen again."

Ed swallowed the last of the hirtsu, setting the bottle down with a sigh of contentment. "Let's clear this up. Who are they?"

She hesitated and then extended her hand, palm up. Five silver balls rose out of her skin, and then sank back down again, disappearing completely.

"They tell me it was usual for one ball to be assigned per person, but I was all they had, and they were used to being together by the time I reached them, so they all settled inside me."

He tried not to show how freaked out he was. "So you have five times the normal amount?"

"Twenty," she said. "Two teams worth." She slid a little lower in her seat. "That's why they can fly out and form a shield to stop the laz fire. I was shot at once, just a glancing hit, and they did not like that, any more than I did. Since then, the silver balls inside me have worked out if they form a barrier outside my body as a shield, it isn't as bad as being hit through my body."

She had said she hadn't trusted him enough to tell him how she could dissipate, but she had already shared enough that he could guess.

"And the silver balls are?" he asked.

"Nanotech," she answered. Then shrugged. "I'm pretty sure."

"Who came up with something like this?" He could scarcely believe it.

"The Ancestors." She sighed. "I picked them up on Ytla. At the site of an old wreck."

And now someone was trying to get rid of her.

Ed had not wanted to get involved when Guttra came knocking because he had a few issues with Special Forces and how they'd dealt with him in the past.

This was a whole new level.

Seemed like someone in the organization was trying to wipe her out.

5

———

WREN HAD NOTHING LEFT.

She pointed her guest to the spare room and stumbled to her own, stepping into the small bathroom to have a quick shower before she fell asleep.

The sun was sinking, and she knew she'd regret the nap later, but dissipating wiped her out, and she needed recovery time.

Ed hadn't looked tired, and she guessed he wouldn't sleep, would maybe leave for a while, but she had to trust that he wouldn't betray her.

He was as much in the frame as she was. He'd been set up as surely as she had been, and he'd told her he suspected it was to make the Guan scanner useless. Only he and another Halatian could work it, and his colleague was off-planet.

She vaguely heard the kitchen door open and close, and the nanotech stirred, uneasy, but she refused to hear them. She turned over, and sunk into sleep.

She was making dinner in the kitchen, after having a good two hours of rest, when Ed returned.

He stepped into the kitchen, blinking at the sight of her preparing food, and then slumped down at the kitchen table. "Need me to do anything?"

"You can do the dishes afterward."

He nodded, gave a grunt of thanks as she passed the cooler unit and pulled out a bottle of hirtsu for him.

"Successful hunt?" she asked.

He'd slung a bag beneath the table as he'd sat down, and he hadn't had one when he left.

"Went back home to get some clothes, but my place was surrounded by SF soldiers, so I had to go shopping." He took a sip of his hirtsu. "I also tried to have a word with the head of Special Forces, Captain Hyt."

"Tried?" she asked as she slid the dish into the oven.

"He was with too many people, and he's still wearing the bruise I gave him the last time I saw him, so I reckon he hasn't had time to go to medical to get it sorted out."

"You hit him?" She landed in the chair opposite him, her own bottle of hirtsu in hand, and quirked her brow.

"He irritated me." Ed gave an almost sheepish half-shrug. "I didn't think he'd let me leave SF headquarters after what happened at the hover port without an escort, and I wanted to ask Katil in the Depository what she could tell me about a woman who disappeared like morning mist right in front of my eyes."

Wren gave him a wide-eyed stare, and realized she should have kept her expression more guarded.

"You know Katil?" He sounded surprised.

She shook her head. "I've seen her from a distance. I deal with Histilo when I'm at the Depository. I saw you walk past me while I was in there, that's why I waited for you in that alley."

"Why were you there?" he asked.

"My main source of research in the past has been the Depository in Nanganya, but I've spent enough time in the Demeter Depository as part of my job, researching artifacts and the history of various cultures, for them to be used to me there. And it's felt safer for me to work there than in the Nanganya Depository. I've been on official leave for more than three months, waiting for a transfer to Demeter SF, and I've been using the Depository to study everything anyone knows about the Ancestors in the meanwhile."

"Why do you think Demeter is safer?" Ed asked.

"Because since I got back from Ytla and started pushing for a team to go back and look at that wreck, I've been followed and watched, and I have a sense things are escalating, getting worse the closer I get to transferring over to Demeter SF."

Ed leaned back in his chair, his long legs pressing against hers, his sharp-angled face contemplative. "You said you got the nanotech at the site of a wreck on Ytla?"

"Yes."

He slid his elbows onto the table, face serious. "That's that moon with the cult on it?"

She nodded. "Special Forces were called in to rescue a small group of scientists who were being threatened by the Har Met Vent, and they came across some interesting items while they were rescuing them, so I was called in to assess them." She took a slug of her hirtsu. "I was busy recording the find, which was an interesting series of carvings in a rocky outcrop, when the two SF soldiers guarding me were ambushed and the Har Met Vent grabbed me and carried me off."

"The SF soldiers, were they killed or just knocked out?" Ed asked.

"Knocked out." She tipped her bottle at Ed. "You think someone in the unit organized the grab, on condition his team mates weren't killed?"

Ed gave a nod. "Could be. Two SF soldiers to guard you when they were already aware the cult was playing hardball seems inadequate."

She gave a nod. "Heads rolled, or so I was told, over that mistake. I don't know if that was just talk or someone actually experienced consequences." She stared into space for a while, trying very hard not to remember the three days she was held by the cult. She took another swallow of hirtsu.

"Bad?" Ed asked.

She gave a twist of her lips in answer, and he gave a nod in acknowledgement.

"They come get you? The SF?" Ed slid his empty bottle away from him.

She shook her head. "I escaped, found the nanotech, and got a turbo boost, so to speak. The Har Met Vent did manage to clip me with a laz strike near the wreck, but they obviously hadn't come across it before and they were so interested in it, they missed me lying almost unconscious in the bushes nearby. My nanos decided they most definitely didn't like being hit by laz and started working on a solution."

Ed gave a grunt at that, and she remembered he'd been saved by her nanos' solution, as well.

"When I recovered from the hit, it took me three days to get myself to headquarters. As I came in the front door, there was a team suiting up to come for me. Allegedly."

Ed was shaking his head. "So you were taken six days earlier? And they were only then heading out?" He looked skeptical in the extreme.

"There had been a massive storm from the night I was taken until the day before I arrived back, to be fair. That's how I escaped, the wind tore the roof off my prison in the middle of the night, and I managed to climb out over the wall. All signs of my captors tracks were destroyed by the weather, and I was told the SF were waiting out the conditions until they could safely come for me."

Ed's lips pursed. "The SF has changed a lot since I was there two years ago for that to be true." He stood, grabbing up her empty bottle along with his, and fetching them each another one. "The team I was in would have considered the weather a great training experience. We would never, and I can promise you this, never have left a fellow SF member in the hands of unfriendlies for six days because of a little rain and wind."

"Maybe Lieutenant Trent wasn't as courageous as your team leader." Although Wren had been disappointed with the excuses the SF had given her when she'd walked in, having rescued herself through weather they had deemed too dangerous to go out in. Admittedly, the fact that she had received, as she'd told Ed, a boost, was the reason she'd made it, but she had been a lone person with no food, water or shelter. They had been a highly equipped team of professionals who'd trained for just such a scenario.

It had soured things for her. Made her distrust all of them, when she knew logically if she had been set up to be taken, there were surely only one or two people involved. That's why she'd put in for a transfer and gone on extended leave.

"What happened with the wreck?" Ed asked.

Wren pursed her lips. Of everything, that made her the most angry. "I wanted to go back and have a look at it. It was impossible to say how long it'd been there, and while I think the nanos were left behind by our ancestors, I couldn't be sure it was an ancestral ship or not without further study. I didn't tell the SF commander that, but I did say we needed to check the wreck out."

"What was the response?"

"That it was too dangerous and they'd go back later." Wren gritted her teeth. "When I followed up after getting back home, I was told the wreck was probably an Aponian research runner that had gone down during a massive storm on Ytla twenty years ago. All those on board had managed to walk away from the accident, so there were no bodies to recover."

"And that was a lie?" Ed asked.

"I checked. No research runner has ever been recorded as going down on Ytla."

Ed set a bottle in front of her. "Someone's manipulating that team, no question. I'll get a message to Ethan Hyt, have him dig in to what went down on Ytla, who the players are."

"Will he do it, given you hit him?" Wren asked.

"He'll do it. He's got the taste for this mystery now. He'll want to know what's going on more than he'll want to stymie me. Because he knows there's someone in his team who's compromised, too."

"The person who shot at us?" she asked.

Ed nodded. "Nothing else makes sense."

She understood that impulse. It would be interesting to learn who on the Ytla team had sold her out. She knew some of them well, but didn't have any suspects. "How will you get in touch with him?"

Ed looked over as the oven chirped to signal the food was done. "After dinner, I'll go visit him at home."

Wren stood, leaning over to grab the oven mitts. "I'd like to come with you."

He said nothing, standing as she took the dinner out of the oven to get plates and cutlery for them both.

When they were seated, food dished up in front of them, he gave a nod. "It'll help focus Hyt's mind to see you in person. And you'll be in less danger from him than I will."

She felt guilty about that, because she suspected some of what had happened between Ed and the captain may be her fault. "Maybe I should approach him first," she said. "Smooth the waters, if he's still a bit angry with you."

Ed's lips quirked. "Sure," he agreed easily. "You do have a knack."

6

———

Ethan Hyt was home.

Ed watched the captain move across the window of his apartment a few times and then disappear, but the lights stayed on, and he guessed he'd sat down to eat or watch some comms.

"Does he have a family?" Wren asked, her gaze fixed on the windows above. "I wouldn't want to scare his partner or his kids."

"No. He's single." In fact, Ed had never even heard that Ethan Hyt had a romantic interest. "You ever meet him?"

She shook her head. "I was working out of the Nanganya office up until the Ytla incident. I asked to be transferred after that. I felt . . . uncomfortable in Nanganya after what happened. Distrustful. The transfer process is slow, though, and I couldn't wait for it to go through. I took all my accumulated leave and came here, staying in a hotel. Then one day when I was walking down the lane, the nanos noticed the hidden property and once I entered it, they confirmed it hadn't been occupied in over twenty years, so I moved in. I've gone back to Nanganya a few times to close up a case or give a report, but most of my work there has been wound up. I was supposed to report to Captain Hyt tomorrow."

"Wait a minute. The house was just sitting there?" Ed glanced at

35

her, astonished. They were leaning against a tree, deep in the shadows of the park in front of Hyt's apartment.

She shrugged. "I thought I was being followed and the nanos steered me in there to escape. Then we explored and the nanos could tell no one had been in the house for a long time. Something about the dust layers. It *is* pretty well hidden."

So no one could trace her to the house. That was good, Ed thought. They were truly invisible there. "And the transport you've been using to move between Nanganya and Demeter?"

"I bought it from a dealer in Demeter the first time I had to go back to Nanganya." She gave a brief shrug. "I may have been a *little* slow to submit the change of ownership papers."

Ed gave an approving nod. "Hope you didn't pay too much for it. After what happened at the hover port, it'll have been impounded by now."

She sighed. "I didn't. And I didn't leave anything onboard. I don't travel with luggage these days."

The light above switched off, and Ed pushed away from the tree. Either Hyt had gone to bed, or he was leaving to go back to work.

Beside him, Wren stood still and focused, and after five minutes, when Hyt didn't appear, they crossed the street and came to a halt beside the door into the building.

Wren reached past him, swiped her finger through the laslock, and he heard the click of it opening.

He lifted his brows as he looked at her, and she lifted her shoulders in response.

"Handy," he murmured.

They closed the door quietly behind them and took the stairs without any discussion. Hyt was three floors up, and when they stopped outside his door, Ed gave Wren room, and she did her trick with the laslock again.

Hyt's apartment smelled of seared meat, giving Ed a clue as to what he'd had for dinner. Wren came to a stop in the living room, gave a wave of her hand in Ed's direction and then pointed to the bedroom.

Ed nodded. She didn't want to be the one to wake Hyt, and Ed found himself in absolute agreement. Like every other Aponian, he probably slept naked.

The Aponi thought of clothing as an imposition most of the time, and while he'd lived on the planet since he'd been taken in after Halatia imploded, at the age of twelve, he'd found the nudist tendencies a little hard to adopt.

And he didn't want Wren getting an eyeful of Ethan Hyt.

Not on his watch.

He walked into the room, and sensed Hyt move in the darkness.

It didn't surprise him. Hyt was the captain of the Demeter SF teams, after all, and they'd barely taken ten minutes to break in after he'd switched off his light.

"It's Ed," he said.

"You going to punch me again?" Hyt asked.

"No." Ed moved back to the door. "I've got information."

"Why would I listen to anything you've got to say?"

Ed gave that statement the consideration it deserved by walking back out into the lounge without a word.

"He's awake," he told Wren. "You want some jah?"

"Sure," she said in response. "I ran out last time I was in Demeter, and what with being shot at today, I haven't had a chance to pick some up."

"You." Hyt appeared, rumpled, wearing a thin shirt and his SF pants. His gaze was laser focused on Wren.

Ed got on with making jah, putting three cups on the counter.

"That's where you got to, Ed? Looking for her?" Hyt asked.

"Looking for answers. She came to me. Sort of," Ed said. He handed Wren a cup.

Hyt shook his head when Ed offered him one, so Ed took it.

"So. What can you tell me?" Hyt slowly lowered himself onto a high stool beside his kitchen counter. "What was that shield? How did you vanish?"

"I'm supposed to report to you tomorrow," Wren told him,

avoiding his questions. "That's why I came in to Demeter today. And then you tried to kill me."

Clever redirect. Ed approved.

"Not me." Hyt dropped off the stool and stared at her, eyes narrowed. "And what do you mean, you're supposed to report to me tomorrow?"

"She's your new artifact consultant out of Nanganya," Ed said. "But I guess no one wanted her to start telling the story of her last job for the Nanganya teams to anyone else, where it might actually reach the ears of someone who knows absolute crap when he or she hears it."

Hyt slowly sat back down. "You're Wren Thorakis?"

Wren gave a nod.

"And I'll ask you again, what the hell happened today?" Hyt's gaze went from Wren to Ed. "Did you know each other before?"

"No." Ed shot Hyt a disgusted look. "You came to me, remember? Begging me to find you a shapeshifter."

Hyt's fists clenched. "I was given data direct from NearSpace Protection that she was not what she seemed. I was given advice from Planetary Administration that the Guan scanner could work to find out what she was, precisely."

"Thus handily maneuvering you into having Nanganya's problem child and the last remaining person on Aponi able to use the Guan scanner in one place for a neat double assassination."

"Problem child?" Hyt asked, and Ed could see he preferred to go in that direction, rather than admit how badly he'd been played. That was fine, Ed could always come back to the topic. And he would.

"Tell me, if you were on location, having rescued Aponian scientists from attack by unfriendlies, would you only assign two soldiers to watch your artifact consultant's back while she was in the field if the attackers were still out there? And then when she was kidnapped due to the very logical outcome of your incompetence, would you wait six days to go rescue her?" Ed drank some of his jah and watched for Hyt's reaction over the rim of his cup.

Hyt swung his head to Wren. "That happened to you?"

"On Ytla." She nodded.

"That's why you requested a transfer? You didn't trust Nanganya SF any more?"

She nodded again. "They told me heads had rolled, but they gave me no details and I didn't have to testify to anyone, and no one took a statement from me."

"Someone from Nanganya is trying to cover their ass, and they tried to use me and my team to do it." Hyt looked enraged.

"And they've bought one of your people, because I'm assuming you still have no other explanation for the shooting," Ed said.

"I don't need to look far, now I know this." Hyt was pacing. "Three weeks ago, I had two Nanganya SF soldiers transfer across to me."

"Interesting timing," Ed agreed.

"Given that my transfer only went through two days ago, and I've been waiting for a transfer for four months, I'd say that stinks," Wren said.

"Why do you think they half-assed your protection, and set you up for the kidnap?" Hyt asked her.

"The cult was running low on supplies, and they wanted a hostage in exchange for some more. They tried to get the scientists first, but the scientific team were able to hold them off and call in an SF team to help them. While I was the cult's prisoner, an Aponian supply craft dropped off a full crate of food and medicines for them, and I heard them saying they'd be able to get at least one more crate before they let the SF team rescue me."

"*Let* them rescue you?" Ed hadn't heard this part of the story. "So someone on the team, and someone in hostage negotiation, were involved. The cult needed to capture someone so their buddies on Aponi could green light the supplies they needed without too many questions. And you were sacrificed to the cause."

She'd suspected this, which is why she would no longer work with Nanganya SF, but hearing Ed say it out loud was a huge weight off her shoulders. She thought she could join the dots, but having him do it, too, with even less information than she had, was validating.

She sent him a smile of gratitude and he seemed to go still for a moment before he turned to Hyt.

"Who do you know in Nanganya that you trust?"

"I know Ferris Harden, the Nanganya teams captain. He and I have met at Planetary Admin meetings for the last two years since I was appointed. He's been a captain for at least six years longer than me." Hyt tapped his foot against the side of his stool.

"Captain Harden is the one who assured me there would be consequences for the failures on Ytla," Wren said. "And he fought my request for transfer all the way."

"There's Velda Shanïha. She's the Planetary Head of Defense, which the SF teams come under. She's got a year left on her rotation." Hyt sounded less sure of himself now.

"Have you had any dealings with her?" Ed asked Wren, and she shook her head.

"Take it to the top, Hyt. Harden sounds like he's compromised, if not completely involved. Shanïha is more likely to be straight." Ed could see Hyt didn't like it. He made a sound of annoyance. "What's the problem?"

"There's a protocol to these things. Going over Harden's head will be breaking that."

"Like he broke protocol with Wren?"

Ed saw Wren give a nod.

"We don't know he did. He might have been fed lies, too," Hyt said.

"He heard a story about how they set only two guards on her and after she was taken, waited six days to suit up, only for her to have rescued herself, and he didn't do a damn thing about it?" Ed was incredulous.

Hyt rubbed the back of his head again. "No. He couldn't but know that was ridiculous."

There was a knock at Hyt's door, and they all froze, looking toward it.

Ed turned back to Hyt. "You called someone in?"

Hyt shook his head. "I swear I didn't. I thought about it, but no. This isn't the rescue squad."

Ed hesitated, but Wren caught his eye and gave a nod, like she believed him.

"Go stand in my bedroom, out of sight," Hyt said, as the knock came again.

Ed did it, but reluctantly.

He waited until Wren was all the way inside, then angled himself so he was in total darkness, but he had a partial view of Hyt as he opened the door.

"Jenik. What are you doing here?" Hyt kept his voice easy, with just the right amount of surprise.

"Just thought we'd check you're all right, sir." Jenik's voice was a deep rumble. "We thought we saw Ed Zeneri come in here with a woman."

"You watching my place?" Hyt sounded offended.

"Just patrolling, sir. After what happened this morning." A second voice spoke up, another man.

Hyt gripped the door, his arm creating a solid barrier to entry. "Mornes, I set up the patrols, last time I looked. What I have you on roster for is keeping watch on Ed Zeneri's place. So unless you followed him from there, and your comms broke down so you couldn't call me to warn me he was on his way, I want to know what you think you're doing?"

Suddenly, Hyt was shoved into his apartment, and a large man came in, fist swinging. Hyt ducked by dropping down to his knees and then punched his attacker straight in the crotch.

The big man went down with a cry, and Hyt rose up, leaned forward and grabbed the second man in the hallway, threw him in, closed the door, and leveled a laz at him as he lay on the floor.

The soldier lifted his own laz, but Ethan got off a shot with his first.

The captain must have had the laz on him since he'd come out of his bedroom to talk, Ed realized. He guessed he couldn't blame him, after the blow Ed had landed earlier that day.

He should probably be grateful that it looked like it was on a relatively low setting, but Jenik was clearly unconscious.

"I've suspected the two of you of the attempt to kill Ed Zeneri and Wren Thorakis since I learned about the timing of your transfer to my unit, but thanks for confirming it for me," he said to Mornes, and then glanced at Ed as he stepped back out into the living area. "Secure him for me, will you?"

Ed caught the manacles Hyt tossed his way with one hand, and noted the surprise on Mornes' face. He didn't recognize the man, but then if he was recently from Nanganya, he wouldn't.

"This morning was a ploy to smoke us out?" Mornes was shaking his head, as if he couldn't believe it. His eyes widened even further, and Ed didn't need to turn around to know Wren had stepped out of Hyt's room, and was standing watching them. It was as if he had an extra sense where she was concerned.

"Sure it was a ploy," Ed said easily as he tightened the restraints and took Mornes' own manacles off his belt and used them on his ankles. "You think the captain doesn't know who his new artifacts consultant is when he sees her?"

"That's where you went wrong," Hyt said, bending to restrain Jenik, who was still out, as soon as Mornes was secure. "You waited too long, tried too hard to put her death on me, rather than on the Nanganya SF."

"You took a risk," Mornes said. "We nearly had her, and this one, too." He stared up at Ed.

"Not a hair on her head was harmed." Hyt shrugged, and Ed felt a new spike of anger at him. He forced it down.

Hyt was only following his lead on this story he was weaving.

"You know them?" Ed turned to Wren, tilting his head in the direction of the men on the floor.

She stepped closer, studied them for a while. "That one looks vaguely familiar," she said, pointing at Jenik. "Neither was on the team with me on Ytla."

"What possible reason could you have to do this?" Hyt asked Mornes. "You'll be going to prison, your careers are over."

Mornes pursed his lips, turning away from them.

"You going to call this in?" Ed asked.

Hyt nodded. "This needs to be official now. And I need to speak to Velda Shanïha as soon as possible."

At the way Mornes reacted to the mention of Velda Shanïha's name, Ed guessed that wouldn't suit them and their fellow plotters at all to have the Head of Defense involved.

"What will you do?" Hyt asked.

"We'll be in touch," Ed said. "I'm not sure we're willing to trust the whole of your team just yet."

Hyt nodded, looking pained but resigned. "I have more questions about what happened this morning."

Ed glanced at their prisoners, then back at Hyt, and he nodded in recognition that nothing would be said in front of them.

"Thank you, Captain Hyt. For obvious reasons, I won't be making my appointment with you tomorrow." Wren headed for the door.

"Understood. I'm sorry about what happened at the hover port. I will get to the bottom of it."

Wren inclined her head in acceptance of the apology, and then edged around the unconscious Jenik. "Coming?" she asked Ed.

"Always," he said. And then followed her out.

7

———

The word repeated in Wren's head, little hammer strikes of guilt. She felt sick at what the nanos had done to Ed, and she wondered if he even realized what he'd just said.

She glanced sidelong at him, but his attention was on their surroundings, watchful and alert.

Ethan Hyt lived on the edge of the city hub, along the west side of the peninsula, and they skirted the busiest sections to get back to her hidden house. There wasn't much they could do until Hyt asked his questions and got some answers, and they both needed sleep.

"I've been thinking of contacting one of my friends who works as an artifacts consultant for the Verdant String Cooperation Initiative." Wren hooked an arm through Ed's as they approached a group coming the other way.

They had both changed after dinner into casual clothes, and they looked like any other couple, walking home from a night out.

"But you haven't yet?" Ed murmured, nodding to the group as they passed each other.

She wondered if he realized his hand had tightened slightly on her arm until the group had passed.

"No, I've been too nervous," she said. "I couldn't think of a way to ask her what I needed without raising all kinds of flags. Anything that's remotely connected to the Ancestors is a hot topic right now, after what was found on Faldine and Fynian. Not to mention the spaceship Tally Riva discovered in Raxia's Outer Boundary."

"There does seem to be a sudden influx of findings, doesn't there?" Ed said.

"I've wondered about that. In the case of Faldine, the expansion after the war led to someone finding the ruins. Fynian had a whole legend built around the mysterious signal that was only detectable when the solar flares abated, which on Fynian is hardly ever, and the Raxians finding the ghost ship floating in their Outer Boundary was expansion again, like on Faldine."

Wren felt a spike of excitement at the idea that the wreck she'd found on Ytla was another such discovery. It was probably being stripped right now by the cult of the Har Met Vent. The spike of rage she felt at how her request to return to study it had been dismissed hammered at her again. And the fact that the thugs in the Har Met Vent were probably planning to sell off invaluable historical artifacts only rubbed salt into the wound.

"Where did you go?" Ed asked, and she lifted her head to look at him.

"Brooding about that wreck, and how those assholes in the cult that kidnapped me have probably stripped it bare."

His lips twitched with amusement. "I know it's not funny, but you look like you want to take someone apart."

She found her lips curving upward. "I wouldn't mind."

"Let's wait for what Hyt has to say, but if he doesn't get a lot of cooperation, then contact your friend," Ed said. "Tell her about the wreck. At the very least, official eyes will turn in Ytla's direction. And if you tell her the whole thing, and ask her to pass it up the Initiative chain, hopefully Aponi will be asked to explain what's going on, and some hard questions will be asked."

That made sense. She'd prefer to give the Aponian government the chance to do the right thing, rather than rat them out to the Initiative and get the whole VSC involved in their business.

The way the government was run, there could only be a few people who were acting illegally, but it would still be very embarrassing for Aponi. Wren felt she should give them a chance to clean up their mess before they admitted to it to the rest of the Coalition.

Aponi had taken her in when her parents had been killed on Faldine, in a surprise attack that was part of the escalation of violence that had eventually led to the war. She felt a sense of obligation to the planet that had educated her and supported her since she was eighteen. The birthplace of her parents.

"Look lively," Ed murmured, and she hugged a little closer to him and focused up ahead.

Two men were walking toward them.

"Special Forces?" Wren whispered, looking up at him with what she hoped was a loving smile.

"Maybe. But the SF trains us to blend better than this. These two think a lot of themselves." Ed bent his head as if he were nuzzling her neck as he whispered his reply.

She had to fight a shiver at the feel of his lips against her pulse.

The men had slowed fractionally at the sight of them, and she could feel them sizing her and Ed up.

These two were on the hunt, and she had a bad feeling she and Ed were the prey.

"They wouldn't know we've joined forces, would they?" she asked softly. "They have to be looking for us individually."

"I would have thought so, but this has been a sophisticated operation, and strings have been pulled at the highest levels, so I just don't want to bet on it." Ed had slowed them down a little, mirroring the men's movements.

Her nanos were busy inside her. She could feel the fizz in her blood, and time seemed to slow. She analyzed the men approaching them with quick glances as she played the role of loving couple with Ed, and worked out the best way to attack.

No dissipating, she told them. *We don't leave Ed on his own.*

Plus, she couldn't keep doing that. Hyt had questions about it. So would others. It was as obvious as a brightly lit sign over her head that there was something very strange going on with her.

The point of no return was fast approaching. They were steps away from the two men, both groups pretending to just be members of the public, out for an evening stroll.

Ed steered her a little to the side, as if to give the two men room to pass, and she caught the man closest to her lunge for her out of the corner of her eye.

She dropped to a crouch, so his hands closed over empty air, and Ed lifted something out of his pocket that extended out into a long stick and struck him, hard and fast.

He went down with a faint cry, and then Ed spun, getting behind the second man. He struck again, and the man went down on one knee.

Wren rose up, slapped an open hand against the man's neck, and he went down in a faint.

"That might be even handier than the laslock trick." Ed looked down at the unconscious man, flicked his stick so it retracted, and stuck it back in his pocket. He crouched, searching under their coats for identification. He moved quickly, and she stood guard, looking up and down the street.

"A couple of people are coming," she murmured, and he stood, slipping what he'd found in a pocket, and then joining her in the shadows.

They moved to the closest side street, keeping out of sight, and kept off the main roads on their way home.

"Who are they?" Wren asked.

"They've got ID that says they're Arkhoran. But look at this . . ." He held out a tiny crystal square.

"What's that?" she asked.

"A crystal chip. The Breakaways used to use them to store funds. No VSC member would have one, they're absolutely useless here. I think they may well be born on Arkhor, but I think they're more recently from Garmen or Lassa. I think they're Cores thugs."

She was so surprised, she stopped. Looked over at him.

He shrugged. "I've got a friend on Arkhor, Nyha Bartoli. Her parents and mine were close on Halatia. The Halatian Interests Association connected all surviving Halatians with each other after we'd been settled on other planets of the Verdant String, so those of us who were left could keep in touch."

"And she told you something about the former breakaways?"

"She told me that Arkhor suspected that some of the Core Companies from the breakaway planets were developing new tech in partnership with the Caruso, and they tried to use her and four young Halatian girls as hostages to get hold of some ancient tech."

"You're talking about Cepi," Wren said, astonished. "You're talking about the Cepi incident. That was your friend?"

Ed nodded. "She's fine, and so are her wards, but that's thanks to Arkhor SF. The people who were behind the Cepi incident were ruthless."

"And the crystal chip tells you these two aren't VSC residents? They're working for the Cores?" Wren asked. "But the breakaways were taken back by the VSC. You think they're mercenaries for hire now?"

Ed paused. "That's actually a possibility. But more likely, they're with the Cores execs who ran from Arkhoran and Baldivas authorities when they took back Garmen and Lassa. At least four of the top owners of the Core Companies got away when things got out of control on both those planets, and the Caruso were caught up in both incidents as well."

"The VSC thinks the Caruso have been hiding them?"

"If not hiding them, at least giving them information. I can't see there being too much trust between the two groups, given the Caruso looked like they were planning on double-crossing the Cores on both breakaways in the end." Ed grimaced. "I still have a few friends in the SF, and I heard what went down on those planets. But since then, both sides might have found it suited them to let bygones be bygones for the moment."

"But why are they after us?" They were close to home now, and Wren stepped away from Ed a little.

"Either they don't want you talking to anyone official about that wreck, or they want to kill the only person left on Aponi who can work the Guan scanner." Ed lifted his shoulders.

"More likely you," Wren said after thinking it through. She pushed aside the vines and pushed open the door into the courtyard.

"Why do you say that?" Ed asked, closing up behind him.

"I told Captain Harden I barely got a good look at it and I couldn't say exactly where it was located." It had been close to the truth. She'd been running for her life at the time.

"Someone suspects that's not true," Ed told her, hooking his jacket behind the kitchen door. "And you gave them every reason to think they're right and that you not only know where it is, but that you took some tech away with you, after that display this morning."

Wren closed her eyes, rubbed a hand over her face. "Damn."

"If it helps," Ed said, gently taking her own jacket off her shoulders, and hanging it beside his own, "I think they're after me, too. Two for one. That's what they tried this morning. Someone thinks they're too clever by half, planning something like that."

"Should we split up?" Wren asked, looking up at him as he turned to her. "Make it harder for them to get us both?"

Ed tilted his head. "That would probably be the clever thing to do," he admitted. "But that's not going to happen."

She reached out and took both of his hands, felt a sinking feeling weighing down her gut. "Why not?"

"Because I'm not leaving you." He curled his fingers around her wrists, neatly reversing her hold. "We're more of a target together, but we're more of a threat, too."

Neither of them brought up the obvious. Ed obviously refused to go there, and Wren was too much of a coward too broach the subject of whether he was still under the thrall of her nanos.

They promised they'd reversed it all, but she couldn't see how.

Always, he told her.

He'd known her less than a day.

8

Ed woke to the sound of Wren moving around in the kitchen.

He lay still, comfortable and at ease in a way he hadn't been for a long time.

He tested his mental faculties for any overwhelming desire to rush to Wren's side, any feelings of desperation for the sight of her.

He didn't think he'd really felt that way since before he'd entered the Depository yesterday, but he had disturbed her at Hyt's. Perhaps he shouldn't have said he'd always come with her, but the word had escaped on its own.

Maybe he was still under the influence in some way. Perhaps the nanos had rewired his brain.

That was possible, but he decided not to worry overmuch about it.

Getting involved with Wren Thorakis was surely not the worst thing to ever happen to him. By a long way.

He'd go as far as to say he'd do it all over again, even knowing he was being manipulated.

Her distress at the thought of him being entranced was real. That told him more than anything that what had happened was more an accident of fate than a self-serving plan to save her own ass.

He rolled to his feet, used the shower off his room, and was in the kitchen in under ten minutes.

Wren must have heard him moving around because she was just setting breakfast on the table as he walked through.

"I thought you were low on supplies," he said, looking at the freshly toasted bread and the sammab, the small dishes of toppings the Aponi spread over their toast each morning.

"I was." She slid into a chair and raised a cup of jah to her lips. "I did a quick shop this morning."

He raised an eyebrow. "Any sign of danger?"

She shook her head and lifted a delicate, bare foot to push his chair out for him in invitation.

He sat with a nod of thanks and dived into the food. "You're good at this," he said.

"This?" she asked, on a laugh.

"Feeding me."

She spread some fruit compote over her bread. "I've been on leave from the SF for nearly four months. I found cooking was something I liked doing."

He'd been out of the SF for two years. He'd started making personal use spaceships, otherwise known as petrals.

Her way was probably a lot less frustrating and a lot more delicious.

"Any news out there on what happened yesterday?" he asked.

"Oh yes." She grinned. "On all the screens. Not the dissipation, thankfully, not even the nano shield. But the sound of laz fire and a whole lot of soldiers tramping around, looking grim. Most people were talking about it. Apparently there was a mix up by the SF, and they opened fire on an innocent bystander. Most people are of the view that the captain will be lucky not to be sanctioned."

"Someone is trying to damage Ethan Hyt's credibility." Ed thought about it as he sipped his jah. "My guess is it's whoever up the chain of command set him up yesterday."

"We need to speak to him after that attack last night." Wren set down her cup. "I'm assuming he'll be at headquarters."

"I don't like that we've been forced into hiding." Ed voiced the unease he'd felt since he realized the Cores were involved in this. "I know we don't have much choice, but it was a clever move on their part. They're restricting our information, our ability to get to the bottom of this."

"I've been keeping a low profile for the last four months," Wren said. "I've got a few tricks we can use."

"Got a way for us to get into SF headquarters unseen?" he asked.

She gave a serious nod. "As a matter of fact."

THE DEPOSITORY HAD BEEN the main venue for her research, but Wren had known there was information in SF headquarters that would be equally useful, and she had found a way in by the second week of her time in Demeter.

She had also wanted to keep her ear to the ground for any murmurs about her, the Nanganya SF office, or what had happened on Ytla.

She hadn't had any success on that front, but the artifact database had proved to be useful enough that she'd kept coming back to see what she could find.

She led Ed through the back alleys to the tall building that contained the government offices, the Protection Unit headquarters, and Demeter's SF central office.

It rose pale pink and orange in the morning light, the design resembling a gate, the pillars on either side were Protection Unit and SF offices and the bars joining them made up the various government departments.

It was practical and symbolic. A neat visual depiction of the cooperation between the administrative and protective branches of government.

Hyt had hopefully had easy access to Velda Shanïha as a result. The Planetary Admin's Head of Defense oversaw both the Protection

Unit and the SF, and her office was on the third bar of the gate from the ground.

Wren had seen her on screen a few times. She was young for her position, but she had worked in both Protection and SF and there had been a vacancy in the Head of Defense role when her two years of compulsory service came up. She could have declined and been assigned something else, or the council could have vetoed her stepping into the position based on her youth, but neither of those things had happened.

She had done a good job, by all accounts.

Wren stopped on the street at the top of a flight of stairs leading downward. They were set beside an older building, one of the behemoths from the pre-Coalition days. Some of them had been declared planetary treasures, and this was one of them.

The stairs looked like they were part of the building—an access to the basements—but they were not.

"Down here?" Ed asked.

She nodded, running lightly down and swiping her finger through the sophisticated laslock on the door at the bottom.

Ed followed her in without question, then raised an eyebrow when as soon as the door closed behind them, a light bloomed to life, illuminating a long, narrow corridor.

"It's the emergency exit for the Gate," she said. "I found the plans in the Depository."

Ed shook his head. "I worked in the Gate for five years and I never knew about this."

"I think someone got a Halatian architect to put this in. And I don't know who knows about it. The person who commissioned it might not work in the Gate any longer. It certainly seems to be completely unused."

Ed smiled, apparently delighted. "Do you know which architect?"

Wren shook her head. "You're loving this."

His smiled widened. He lifted his hands. "I'm Halatian."

She led the way, smiling herself, finding his excitement at the secret passage charming.

"Where does it come out?" Ed asked.

"Into a bathroom." That seemed to be what he'd expected her to say, because he gave a nod.

"That's common?" she asked.

"Bathrooms are good because you can access the passageway in private. Sometimes the architect will create a few interesting kinks in a common passageway, where someone could duck out of sight and activate the opening."

"So there may be more secret passageways?" Wren asked. "Ones that aren't on the plan?"

He lifted his shoulders. "Depends on how paranoid the person who hired the architect was."

"You could find them, maybe, if they're there?"

He gave a cautious nod. "Maybe."

They reached the end of the passage and took the stairs that led upward to a small landing four floors up. There was no door in front of them, it looked like the stairs ended in front of a solid wall.

Without her needing to show him, Ed brushed a hand over a section of wall and a door shimmered from opaque to transparent. They peered through it into an empty bathroom.

"So far it's been empty every time," Wren told him.

Ed touched a button on the side and the door swung inward.

She was impressed. It had taken the combined skills of both her and her nanos to find that button the first time. The Halatians obviously had a way of doing things, and Ed knew the secret code.

They stepped into the room, closed the door behind them, and Wren moved across to open the bathroom door cautiously.

As she peered out, she saw a woman walking away down a passageway, her back to Wren, heading toward an open plan area with fast, efficient steps.

"Which way?" Ed asked, plastering himself up against her back to peer out, too.

She stilled, liking the feel of him. "The opposite way." She pointed right, and slipped out, with Ed on her heels.

"Slow down."

She turned back to tell him that wasn't a good idea, but he was looking at the walls of the passageway.

He had said another trick was to create kinks and turns in a passage to give someone privacy to slip into a secret room or corridor, and there *were* strange kinks in this one.

He took her hand and guided her into a little dead end offshoot of the passage, his fingers dancing over the flowers, leaves and trees carved into the richly-decorated enamel wall.

"There." He pressed something and she heard the faintest click. He grinned in triumph, pushed the wall with his shoulder, and there, beyond, was another corridor.

They stepped inside, and Wren gasped.

They were standing in what looked like a transparent tunnel. She could see the passage they'd just come from to her right, and to her left, a series of private offices and conference rooms, all occupied.

"Suddenly, the Guan scanner makes sense," she breathed. "They can't see us?"

"That would rather be the point," Ed murmured back.

"No wonder your fellow countryman built something that can see through walls. This is common on Halatia?" she whispered. "These secret tunnels?"

"Was common," he corrected her, moving the sentence from the present tense to the past.

She patted his arm in a ridiculous effort to comfort him on the loss of his entire planet while she wondered how anyone had operated on Halatia, knowing they were probably being spied on. Now was probably not the time to ask.

"There's Ethan Hyt," he said, pointing a little way down the passage, and she followed him to stand directly in front of the office where Ethan paced, alone, as if waiting for someone.

"Is there a way in?" She kept her voice as quiet as possible.

Ed began to look, shook his head. "It'll come out in an office somewhere. Probably the office of the person who ordered this built. But I'd rather see what's going on with Ethan before we go looking for it."

She agreed. She was too afraid to lean against either wall, so she sat down, cross-legged. Ed shot her an amused look and leaned against the wall with his shoulder, arms crossed.

The office Ethan was in, like all the others down the line, let out into a corridor which consisted of a massive window all along one side, looking out onto the city. Each office door was also a window, letting in the natural light from the exterior window, although it could be made opaque for privacy.

Whoever's office Ethan was in, they had chosen transparency, and she caught sight of a woman approaching, holding a cup in each hand. The door was slightly ajar, and she pushed it open with her shoulder and stepped into the room.

Velda Shanïha.

Ethan took a cup with a murmur of thanks, and Wren saw a flash of something on his face as Velda moved past him to sit behind her desk.

He'd been reluctant to approach Velda when they discussed it last night, and he'd told them it was a break in procedure, but now Wren would guess it had more to do with the fact that Ethan Hyt had feelings for the Head of Defense.

Strong feelings.

"So, tell me what's going on, Captain Hyt." Velda lifted her cup and took a sip of jah.

Ethan didn't sit, although Velda surely meant him to. He kept standing, cradling the cup in his hands, as if warming them. "Two men transferred from the Nanganya SF office a few weeks ago. They tried to kill me last night."

Velda set her cup down carefully. "You know why?"

"I think it's got something to do with my new artifact consultant out of the same office. She was supposed to come in today for her first day on the job. Instead, someone in Planetary Admin set me up to take the fall for her murder by the same two men yesterday, along with the murder of Ed Zeneri."

Velda stared at him for a long moment, tapping her finger. "Who in Planetary Admin?"

"Henry Nostrada."

Velda drew in a quick breath. "Henry." She gave a slow nod. "Why?"

At last Ethan sat down, took his first sip. "Wren Thorakis worked out of Nanganya, and when a group of scientists gathering data on Ytla got into some kind of stand-off with the cult there, SF was sent in to check out the situation. They found some culturally significant carvings while they were protecting the scientists, so Thorakis was called in to consult." He scratched the back of his neck. "Seems to me, someone there set her up to be kidnapped by the cult. They assigned only two guards to her while she was in the field, and then when she was inevitably captured, they left her with her captors for six days. Someone used that time as an excuse to drop off supplies to the cult, signed it off as part of the ransom demand, and Thorakis said she overheard the cult members saying she should be good for at least one more supply drop before they let the SF team rescue her."

"Let?" Wren noticed Velda honed onto the same word Ed had the day before. "You're saying more than one person on Aponi is sympathetic to the cult, and set Thorakis up to be taken to give them an excuse to supply their friends?"

Ethan pointed a finger at her in approval, then drank more of his jah.

"Why try to kill her now, though? She served her purpose." Velda slid her elbows onto her desk, her gaze locked onto Ethan's face.

"There was a big storm on Ytla, which the SF team used as their excuse for not rescuing her right away. It was so handy, I'm going to go back and check exactly when they found the carvings and when they called her in to consult, and see if it was before or after they got a storm warning. Problem was, the storm ripped the roof off the hut where she was being held and she escaped. She made it back to the SF base by herself, no rescue needed."

Velda slowly got to her feet. "I didn't hear anything about this. Not even that an SF consultant was taken prisoner." After a moment, she sank back down. "But even so, why kill her?"

"She complained about how the SF didn't have her back.

Requested a transfer to Demeter. Which they slow-walked over four months. They don't want her talking about it to her new colleagues, is my guess. Because when I heard the story, you had better believe I thought it stank. Someone is compromised on the Nanganya teams, and in fact, more than one person. A single individual could not have pulled this off."

"Someone is covering their ass. But *kill* her?" Velda shook her head.

"Only thing that makes sense is that whatever is going on is bigger than just someone using Thorakis' kidnap to supply the Har Met Vent with the medical supplies and food they needed. And given Ed Zeneri was maneuvered into being on the dock with Thorakis when the two Nanganyan SF soldiers tried to take her out, I'd say that's a certainty."

"Again, why?" Velda twisted her fingers together.

"Because now that Lily Jacine is in prison on Hathr, Ed Zeneri is the only one left on the planet who's trained to use the Guan scanner."

"Ed wasn't working the scanner for us anyway," Velda pointed out.

Ethan gave a nod. "But I had planned to meet with him. That's why I pushed so hard for him to help when we were sold that absolute nonsense about Wren Thorakis being a possible shapeshifter. I was determined to bring him back into the fold. We'd uncovered a few massive smuggling rings by pure chance over the last two months, big enough to make me wake up in the night in a cold sweat as to what we might have missed. We need him, and I mentioned that in more than one briefing to the whole team."

"So they infiltrated your team and tried to make it look like one of yours lost their nerve and shot Zeneri and Thorakis by mistake." Velda did not sound friendly. "They don't want someone with a scanner watching what's coming into Demeter."

Ethan gave a nod. "They want us blind."

"What about the other stuff I heard went down yesterday?" Velda asked. "Silver shields appearing out of thin air. Someone vanishing in a puff of smoke."

Ethan lifted his hands. "I tried to ask Ed and Wren when they came to see me last night, but then the Nanganya transfers tried to kill me, and it cut things short."

"Ed Zeneri and Wren Thorakis came to visit you last night? Are they working together?" Velda asked, tilting her head.

Wren glanced over at Ed, saw he was looking at her.

"Are we?" he mouthed.

"Yes," she murmured, at the same time Ethan said it.

"I think we need to get into that office," Ed said. He gestured down the passage and she followed him.

The opening was only three offices down from Velda's and it was into a storeroom. Clever, she supposed. Offices changed, storerooms rarely did.

They stepped into it and Ed moved to the door, looked out.

"Clear," he said.

They made their way to Velda's office without seeing anyone else, and Ed opened the door, held it for her.

As they stepped in, both Ethan and Velda stared at them in shock, with Ethan surging to his feet. Ed turned and activated the opaque function on the door as he closed it, making it impossible for anyone to see in. Unless they were in the secret passageway, of course.

"Wren and Ed," Ethan said. He half-turned to Velda with a wave of his hand. "I'm assuming you know this is Velda Shanïha."

"We do," Ed said by way of greeting.

"How did you know about this meeting? How did you know where my office is?" Velda slowly rose to her feet as well.

"I have an inside source," Wren said, catching Velda's eye and giving a nod of greeting. "I made sure to do my homework before I transferred here, in case I was jumping from one problem straight into another."

Velda watched her for a beat in silence. "Who?"

"I'm not going to answer that until I trust you a good deal more than I currently do." Wren didn't even know herself if she was lying. It was possible she would tell Velda about the passageway at some point.

Velda and Ethan exchanged a look, which Wren interpreted to mean they would work on finding out who might be passing her information by themselves.

It was an unfortunate waste of their time.

Ed made a sound of irritation, flicking a look at Ethan. "Worry about who told who what later. Wren has more information on what happened on Ytla than she told you last night."

"More?" Ethan asked. He sat down again, sinking slowly into his seat and indicating she take the one beside it.

Wren didn't want to sit, but she did it anyway, more to keep things cordial than any other reason. "There's a wreck there. I saw it."

"A wreck?" Velda frowned. "On Ytla?"

"I think it might be an ancestral ship."

There was a moment of silence.

"Oh," Ethan said. "This explains a *lot*."

9

____

ED REALIZED ETHAN HYT OBVIOUSLY KNEW MORE ABOUT ANCESTRAL ships than he did.

"What does it explain?" he asked, leaning against the wall and crossing his arms and his legs.

"Two men were found unconscious in the street last night. Facial scans show they're wanted by the VSC. They're both accused of crimes on Lassa while they were working for a Core Company operating there." Ethan leaned back in his seat and propped his right ankle on his left knee and wiggled his foot. "I've been trying to work out where they fit. This information slots in nicely."

Ed fished in his pocket, tossed the crystal chip he'd taken out of one of the men's pockets last night to Ethan. "Found this on them before we left them."

"They attacked you?" Ethan asked, catching it deftly and studying it on his palm.

Ed nodded. "They were hunting us. I think they were working with Mornes and Jenik. They couldn't have known we were together and near your apartment any other way."

"Mornes and Jenik are the two Nanganya special forces transfers?" Velda asked.

Ethan nodded. "I've got them in holding. I thought I'd discuss how to deal with them with you before I contact Ferris Harden, the Nanganya SF teams captain. Wren here thinks he's complicit."

"Is that so?" Velda asked her.

Wren hesitated, glanced over at Ed, and then nodded. "I think he lied to me a few times, and he definitely tried to stall my transfer to Demeter."

"He'd have been the one to sign off on the supply drop, too," Velda said. "No one lower on the chain could have done that."

Ed should have thought of that. It made things very simple, suddenly. There was no question Ferris Harden was involved.

"What will you do?" Wren asked Velda.

"I'll have him brought in for questioning." Velda tapped her lips. "I'll have to ask the head of the Nanganya Protection Unit to do it. That will be a difficult duty for Pamela Ingot. She and Ferris are friends, or at least cordial, as far as I'm aware."

Ethan shrugged, as if to say too bad for her, and because it was exactly how he was feeling himself, Ed found himself liking the captain more.

"What about the Lassian thugs?" Velda asked. "Will they talk?"

"They were only just coming out of whatever Ed and Wren here did to them this morning." Hyt eyed them both. "What exactly did you do?"

"Ed knocked his one out the usual way. I know a trick on how to pinch a neck nerve. My one grabbed me, and unfortunately for him, I was able to reach his neck. It renders the person unconscious," Wren said, with a shrug. "Some people take longer to come round than others."

Ethan looked at her as if he was offended at the level of shit she was shoveling his way, but Velda simply looked surprised and a little impressed.

"Better than killing them," Ed said to Ethan with a grin. "They were armed, we weren't. We didn't have much choice."

"You didn't stick around to explain, either," Ethan grumbled.

"You can't blame us for that," Wren said. "We had no idea how many friends they'd brought with them."

"Good point." Velda looked over at Ethan. "Do you think there could be more of them, Ethan?"

Ethan nodded. "Possible. If those two got in, more could have. We'll need to try and find out where they were staying, see if there's evidence of more of them."

"Who were they after, do you think?" Velda asked. "Ed or Wren?"

Ed glanced at Wren, and she lifted a shoulder. "Both?"

"Yes." He didn't know if it were true or not, but if it was both of them, the chances were higher they'd stay together. And he wanted to stay together.

He hadn't had this much fun in a long time.

"But you don't know each other?" Velda sounded skeptical.

"Never laid eyes on each other before yesterday morning," Ed said, cheerfully. "Thanks for that, Ethan."

Ethan Hyt watched him with narrowed eyes. Ed could see he was wary of his answer.

"Getting back to the ancestral wreck." If Velda Shanïha was aware of the undercurrents, she obviously decided to ignore them. "Who did you tell about it?"

"I didn't report it as an ancestral wreck, just a wreck." Wren lifted a hand, checked off the names. "Captain Harden, Lieutenant Trent, the head of the SF team with me on Ytla, and my boss, Demilla Garrett, the head of support services in the teams."

"And?" Ethan asked. "What happened?"

"Harden called me into his office and told me the wreck was a research runner that had gone down on Ytla twenty years before." Wren leaned back in her chair. "He said everyone on the runner had made it out alive, so there was no incentive to spend the time and effort going back to find it, especially with the Har Met Vent nearby."

"Maybe what you saw *was* this research runner," Ethan suggested.

Wren shook her head. "I didn't believe him, so I looked it up. There was no research runner that wrecked on Ytla twenty years ago, or any time, for that matter." She hesitated. "And then, there was also what the Har Met Vent members said while they were looking through the wreckage for me."

Ed turned to her, surprised that there was even more to this than she'd already told him. "What was that?"

"It was hard to hear everything. There was a massive storm raging. But it sounded like they had found another part of the wreck somewhere else on Ytla, and I'd led them to exactly what they'd been looking for for months. It sounded like the cult was a front for a group specifically hunting for the wreckage."

"Just like on Cepi," Ed murmured.

Velda pressed both palms down on her desk. "This is getting bigger with every revelation. Ethan, this is another question Pamela Ingot must put to Ferris Harden."

"I'd like to fly to Nanganya, be with Ingot when she questions Harden. And it wouldn't hurt to talk to Lieutenant Trent, either. He's either the most useless teams leader I've ever heard of, or he's in this up to his neck." Ethan looked offended at the thought of Trent and his actions.

"What about Demilla Garrett, the head of services?" Wren asked.

Hyt flicked a hand. "Maybe she was shut down by Harden, maybe she's involved. I'll speak to her, too."

Velda gave a slow nod. "Agreed. I'll speak to a few people on the Council. You say Henry Nostrada is the one you think set up the confrontation at the docks? I'll need some backing to go after him."

"What about you?" Ethan Hyt turned to Ed. "What are your plans?"

"If you can give us some guards, people you really trust, then maybe what Wren and I should do is what they're trying hard to stop me doing."

"Which is?" Wren asked him.

"Using the Guan scanner to check incoming ships." It had the benefit of getting Wren up in nearspace on a teams runner with him. She would be relatively safe up there.

Ethan was nodding. "That would be useful."

"Wouldn't you need me in Nanganya?" Wren asked Ethan. "It will be harder for Harden and Trent to deny things when I'm there to contradict them."

Ethan eyed Ed. "Maybe. But it could also be dangerous."

Ed acknowledged the lifeline Ethan had thrown him with a tiny nod. "Let's try and work out what the bigger picture is. What they're trying to hide. You can always go to Nanganya later, when Ethan has a better idea of who exactly is involved in this. Right now, we don't know who we can trust."

"If something's coming in to Aponi that those criminals who used to own the Cores are trying to hide, we need to know as soon as possible," Velda said. "And I'd rather have you alive and safely tucked away for the moment, Wren. Let Ethan and I work out how far this conspiracy has spread, while you and Ed see what's coming in that someone is so desperate to make sure we don't know about."

Wren gave a slow nod. "Alright. For how long?"

Ed would have felt slightly insulted, but he knew he'd feel the same way. They were all maneuvering her into doing nothing, when for four months, all she'd done was hide in the shadows and fight.

"Give me three days to see what I can find out in Nanganya. When I come back, we can talk," Ethan said.

"I should know what Henry Nostrada's deal is by then, as well." Velda leaned forward, focused and serious. "You're our main witness, Wren. Now they've failed at setting up Ethan to take care of you for them, they'll need to go after you directly. A lot of their problems go away for them with you gone, which is why they targeted you in the first place."

Wren sighed. "I'll stay with Ed."

He didn't smile, but he wanted to. He wanted to a lot.

10

———

"I heard you laid the captain out." The SF soldier who spoke, Hatch, was eyeing Ed with dislike, and Wren felt a sickening clutch of guilt in her chest.

"That's on me." She leaned forward and Ed sent her an amused look from his place beside her in the runner. He was leaning back, ankle propped up on his knee, totally relaxed.

Hatch—young, male, extremely buff—glared at her. "You weren't there. I saw you dematerialize into a gray mist."

"I was still responsible."

"How so?" The soldier's partner, a woman around the same age, face sharp with angled cheekbones and long, thickly-lashed eyes, glanced over at her. She'd been introduced as Bailey. She was piloting the small craft taking them up to the observatory, although she'd put it into auto after they'd reached the edge of nearspace.

Wren glanced at Ed, but he continued to look slightly amused at her coming to his defense.

"Ed thought the captain had set me up. Set us both up."

"I can see how that might have happened, given what we know about Mornes and Jenick, but all the shooting was over by the time you hit him," Bailey said.

"He wasn't going to let me leave. And I needed to find Wren." Ed lifted wide shoulders. "I apologized. We're good."

Hatch blew out a breath. "I get that. The captain wouldn't have put us here otherwise. But I don't like that you did it."

Ed gave a grunt of acknowledgement, and that seemed to be that.

Hatch settled down, but Bailey kept watching her.

"How did you do it?" she asked.

Wren knew was she was asking. "Smoke and mirrors," she answered.

"Hmm." Bailey finally looked away, back to the control panel in front of her, but Wren didn't think she'd convinced her. Nothing she could do about that. And she certainly wasn't going to explain, even though Ethan Hyt had assured them that these two were loyal through and through and squeaky clean into the bargain.

The loyalty certainly seemed to check out.

"How long until we reach the station?" Wren asked.

Bailey tapped her wrist. "Half an hour. You should see it soon. Out the left window."

Wren turned and sure enough, the sunlight touched the large, dark gray nearspace observatory. It wasn't big enough for anything larger than a runner the size of the one they were using to dock, but it looked like it could comfortably house twenty or more people. She had assumed they would be the only ones on station, but looking at the size of it, she wasn't quite sure where she'd gotten that impression.

"How many are in residence?" she asked.

"Eight," Hatch said. "Five academics on some research project, and the usual three maintenance staff."

"We've checked them all out," Bailey said. "They seem clean, but the captain has let us know this goes very high up, so someone could have scrubbed anything dodgy out of their file."

Everyone was still a suspect, then. Wren didn't sigh, but she felt like it. This was how she'd been living for the last four months.

Things were finally happening, though. She could live this way a little longer. And now that she had people around her who believed her, it was actually better than before.

"What project are the academics involved in?" Ed asked.

"Signal identification, I think." Bailey waved a hand, like it didn't matter.

"Signal identification." Ed said it slowly, and everything in Wren came to attention, including her nanos.

Signals.

She had spent every moment she could since she'd escaped the Har Met Vent on Ytla researching ancestral spaceships, and signals kept coming up.

It was a signal that had led the criminals who used to run the Core Companies to the ancestral spaceship on Fynian. A signal that had led the Raxian Expeditionary Force to find the ancestral ghost ship floating in space. If there wasn't such a problem on Faldine with magnetic fields, most likely they would have found the ancestral spaceship via a signal there, too, rather than having one of their military pilots more or less crash next to it.

Had someone detected a signal from the downed wreck on Ytla?

She looked over at Ed and he gave a tiny nod, as if his mind had gone to the same place as hers.

They would need to watch their new neighbors.

The information suddenly made her feel better about coming here.

She'd wanted to confront Harden with Ethan Hyt but she understood why he preferred her to be out of it for now. So while they were up here, with Ed scanning incoming freighters for whatever it was that someone was trying to hide, she could snoop around and see what the academics were up to.

The observatory was now a massive structure hanging above them and Bailey focused fully on maneuvering them up close to it.

Wren felt the thump as they connected to the dock and saw mechanical arms come out to clamp them more securely.

"The runner's staying here?" Ed asked.

"Yes. It's for our use. Captain Hyt wanted us to have a way off the station whenever we need it." Bailey sounded pleased about that, and Wren had to agree.

If she wanted to get back to Aponi, she didn't want to have to wait hours for a runner to come up and get them.

When they stepped through the connecting tunnel, each carrying their own bag, she was surprised to find no one was there to greet them.

Everyone looked around for a moment, and then Bailey shrugged. "I have the bunk arrangements already," she said, pulling out a small screen. She held it out to the rest of them, and then pointed. "You and Ed are here, Wren."

They were sharing a suite, Wren saw. They had their own bedrooms, but with a shared lounge and bathroom. Bailey and Hatch each had a single room, smaller, with hardly any seating area, but with their own bathrooms. They were on either side of Wren and Ed's suite.

They found the section they'd been assigned, dumped their bags, and then met out in the passageway. Ed was holding the scanner and its attachments, and had stripped down to the thin bodysuit most space walkers preferred under their suit when they were out on the line.

"We're starting straight away?" Hatch asked, sounding pleased.

"No reason to wait, is there?" Ed asked.

"The captain said one of us has to be out there with you when you're on the line, and one in the control room," Bailey said.

"Fine with me."

"You happy for me to wander around, poke my nose into what's happening on the other side of the station?" Wren asked.

Bailey hesitated, then gave a nod. "Shout if you think there's something off about anyone." She handed out tiny comms that attached to the back of their ears. "Just brush a finger over it to activate," she said. "When you're in the suit, you can sync it to the comms system inside the helmet," she told Ed. "I'll show you how."

They moved to the control room first, as Wren wanted to see where it was, and what it looked like.

It was a pleasant space, with two couches set on either side of a low table, and a wall with space suits hanging from it on hooks, along with large screens to watch what was happening outside.

"Be careful when you do your tour of the station," Ed said to her, setting down his scanner.

Wren snorted. "I'm the one staying inside. *You* be careful."

His lips curved. "I'll be out on the line. No place like it."

She had never been out on the line herself, but a few of the consultants she'd worked with through the years had had to examine artifacts that were floating in space, and they had said the same. Something about having nothing tethering you to safety except a thin cord made a deep impression on the psyche.

"I'll see what's for dinner, and check out our not-so-friendly friends," she said.

Ed's eyes laughed at her. "Feeding me again."

She lifted a shoulder. "I've heard line work burns up the calories."

Hatch and Bailey had been watching the byplay, and Hatch suddenly handed Ed a suit. "Flirt on your own time. Let's go."

Bailey gave a chuckle, and Wren left them to their shenanigans.

If her cheeks were burning, well, her nanos could take care of that in a moment.

11

———

THE CONTROL ROOM FOR THE LINE WAS AT THE FRONT OF THE observatory, and she and the others' bedrooms were situated on the right hand side of the station, so Wren wandered left, peering into a gym, a smaller comms room that looked like it was used more for relaxation than serious talks with the administrators on Aponi, and finally came to the doorway of a lounge and dining area with a large kitchen at the back.

There were other rooms up ahead, and she guessed they were probably more sleeping quarters and perhaps labs or workstations for the academics, and a work room for the maintenance crew, but she was sure this was the place to meet her quarry.

She stepped inside.

"Who are you?"

She heard the question at the same time her nanos alerted her to the presence of someone in the room with her.

A head had risen from one of the couches in the lounge, and she stepped closer to see a young woman lying across it. She'd pushed up onto her elbows, and she was frowning at Wren in an unfriendly way.

"Wren Thorakis. And you are?"

The woman's frown deepened. "What are you doing up here?"

Wren tilted her head. "SF teams business. What are you doing up here?"

"SF teams?" The woman swung her legs off the couch and stood. She pulled a comm from her pocket and tapped it. "There's a strange woman on the station. Says she's Wren someone or other."

Cool eyes watched her, and Wren watched her right back, slightly taken aback at the hostility.

Whatever she was told, the woman's face flushed, and her eyes narrowed even further. "So I was just left in the dark, is that it?"

The answer was obviously not to her liking, because she shut the comms off, and put it back in her pocket with a vicious movement.

"Apparently you're expected."

"I don't think it's possible to get a lock on the docking station unless you've been given the codes," Wren said helpfully.

The woman's lips thinned and her cheeks flushed, then she walked away, stalking out of the room.

Well.

Wren could feel her nanos go into a higher level of alert. "Not-so-friendly was more right than I knew," she murmured.

She walked over to a notice board next to the kitchen and saw that a person named Banks was down for making dinner for the maintenance crew, and that someone called Ludlow was down for the five academics.

Looked like they were on their own when it came to meals.

She accessed the inventory, saw that aside from special items one of the academics had brought up with them for their own use, the stores were open to everyone, and she set about perusing what was available.

She was just putting a cake in the oven when a man came in, stumbled to a stop at the sight of her, and then squared his shoulders slightly as he approached.

"Hello, I'm the head of station maintenance, Terry Banks." He gave the Aponi greeting, and Wren gave a cool nod from the other side of the kitchen counter.

"Hello."

"Ah," he rubbed the back of his neck. "Were you the one who met up with Trish earlier?"

"If Trish is a medium height woman with dark hair and a charming personality, I think so."

Banks winced. "Sorry we weren't there to welcome you when you arrived. It was a last minute communication that you were coming, and I honestly forgot about it after I sent through the sleeping quarter arrangements. I've been trying to upgrade the minor space debris detectors for the last three days, and I'm not making a lot of headway."

Wren felt at a loss as to a response. "I'm sorry to hear it," was what she managed to come up with.

"Was Trish . . .?" He glanced at the door as if expecting Trish to appear, and lowered his voice. "Rude?"

"She was," Wren confirmed. She walked over to the jah machine and programmed some in. At least this kitchen was well equipped and well stocked.

"Hello, hello, who's this then?" A man appeared in the door, and Wren thought Banks relaxed slightly when it wasn't Trish. She obviously loomed large in his mind. "I'm Dr. Jens Ludlow of the Demeter Higher Learning Institute." He extended his hands in greeting, and Wren gave a smile and a nod in exchange.

"I'm Wren, with Demeter Special Forces." Captain Hyt had confirmed she was now on the team, and on the clock, as far as he was concerned. It had eased something in her when he'd given her a final contract to approve and she had received all the necessary access to the Demeter systems that she needed to do her job.

"Special Forces? As a soldier?" Ludlow asked.

"An artifact consultant." They had decided to tell the truth as much as possible. Ed was walking the line with the scanner. She was an artifact consultant. They'd leave it to the occupants of the station to draw their own conclusions. And if they got it in their head they were looking for a smuggled artifact or something of that nature, so much the better.

"When did you get here? We usually have a welcome committee."

"Just a couple of hours ago. I must admit we were slightly surprised when there was no one to meet us."

Banks blew out another breath. "That's my fault, Jens. I was too caught up in my work, and I forgot to mention we had an SF team coming up."

"A team? How many of you?" Ludlow asked. She wondered if she was imagining the nerves she thought she could hear in his voice.

"Just the four of us." Wren took her jah and leaned on the counter. "I had a look around and worked out we all have to fend for ourselves when it comes to the canteen. I see you and Ludlow are down for making dinner for your groups tonight."

"Yes. The kitchen's big enough that there's no need to schedule a time to cook unless you want to, we can all cook at the same time, no problem." Banks shook his head. "I really am sorry I wasn't a better host."

"So this is who has Trish all worked up." Another man stepped through, short and stocky, but he could probably give Hatch some competition in the muscles department.

Banks made a gesture with his hand, which Wren guessed was a desperate attempt to get whoever it was to shut up, but the man either didn't see it, or deliberately ignored it.

"I'm Juller." He sniffed the air. "Do I smell cake?"

"I'm Wren." She ignored the cake question. "Are you also part of the maintenance crew?"

Juller gave a nod. "You knew we had visitors coming?" he asked Banks.

"I did. It slipped my mind, and I forgot to tell anyone. I'm sorry." Banks was starting to sound a little irritated. "It's no big deal, is it? There's plenty of room, and they've got their own job to do."

"No. No, of course not. Always nice to get someone new up here. We're on a full three month shift, so visitors are always welcome." Juller walked into the kitchen and went to grab a bottle of hirtsu from the cooler. He waggled the bottle and both Banks and Ludlow lifted their hands in a silent request for one.

"Where are your colleagues, Wren?" Ludlow asked, taking his

bottle of hirtsu with a nod of thanks and sitting down on one of the high stools in front of the kitchen counter.

"Out walking the line," Wren said. "We only need three on at a time, so I decided to work out dinner arrangements."

"Walking . . ." Juller sent a glance Banks's way. "Didn't you just get here?"

"Yes." She finished her jah and set her cup in the washer. "It's only a one hour trip from Demeter. It didn't make sense to hang around."

"No." Juller looked at Banks again. "You obviously know what you're doing."

Wren simply smiled at him. Everything in her wanted to run to the control room and make sure there were no maintenance problems. Because Juller and Banks were freaking her out.

Instead she leaned casually against the counter. "You are obviously an academic, Dr. Ludlow. Are your colleagues up here all in the same field?"

Ludlow had been watching them all, sipping on his hirtsu. He set it down and gave a nod. "I'm here with two members of my department and two research assistants."

"What're you looking into?"

He spun the bottle, as if giving himself time to answer. "High frequency signals left in the wake of spaceships that pinch to the black. We're trying to see if the sound waves give a clue to where the ships are pinching to."

"That would be useful," Wren said. "In the rare case of a spaceship trying to evade authorities by pinching to the black, you could read the sound waves and work out where they'd pinched to. Follow right behind them."

"Exactly. I shouldn't be surprised a member of the SF would realize the value of it so quickly." He sounded far more enthusiastic than her nanos said he was.

His face seemed to struggle to hold an expression.

"Are you asking ships to give you their destination and then trying to work it back, or do you try to decode it, and then ask them where they went and see if that matches your information?" she asked.

"We aren't that far along with the methodology. But for a start, we're asking them where they're headed, to see if there are similarities in the frequencies of ships going to the same pinch point." Ludlow tipped up his bottle and finished his drink in a few swallows.

"Sounds fascinating. My colleague, Ed, is the technical expert of our group. I'm sure he'll be fascinated by your work."

"Ed?" Banks asked. "Ed Zeneri?"

"You know him?" Wren gave another smile, pretending she couldn't see the utter dismay on Banks's face. "Oh, maybe he's walked out on the line here before?"

Of course he would have. This had been a major part of his job before he left the teams.

"He's scanning?" Banks asked.

"It's what he does," she said.

"Yeah." Banks shifted in his seat. "That's what he does."

12

———————

There was tension in the common room, but Ed didn't much care when he first arrived.

All he and Hatch wanted was food, and as usual, Wren had come through. She'd sent a message through to Bailey that they had to see to themselves as a group, and coordinated the timing with when they came off the line.

They had caught four freighters with illegal loads, although nothing that looked too dangerous. More in the line of undeclared goods, more crates than the manifest showed, and other efforts to reduce the transporter's excise bill.

The administration had most assuredly been robbed blind since he and Lily had stopped using the Guan scanner.

He would have to remember to ask Hyt when Lily had last used it, and whose idea it had been to send her to Hathr.

He and Hatch had cleaned their plates and got up for another serving before he felt like he could hold a reasonable conversation.

"This is really good, Wren," Hatch said.

Bailey had been watching them with amusement, but she nodded in Wren's direction. "Agreed. Thanks for taking first shift."

"That was a long time out on the line." Juller spoke as he passed the table. "I thought standard procedure was two hours max."

"We've all got our higher level certs." Bailey leaned back in her chair to eye him. "Six hours max."

"Six hours?" One of the women in the academic team who was on cleanup duty in the kitchen put a bowl down. "I didn't realize it went that high."

"That's the SF for you," Banks said. He didn't sound enthusiastic. "Top of the food chain, right Ed?"

Ed glanced at him. Wren had told Bailey via her hidden ear comm that Banks had seemed unhappy to hear he was on the observatory, and that both Juller and Banks got nervous when they heard the team was walking the line.

After hearing that, Bailey had spent the whole time they'd been on the line nervously looking through all the technical safety mechanisms in the control room for a potential issue.

So far, nothing. But Wren hadn't been overestimating the nerves here. They were clearly on display.

"It's been, what? Two years since I was last up here? I see you're head of maintenance now, Banks. Congratulations." Ed scraped the last of his second helping up and savored the stew Wren had made.

"I thought you'd left the teams, Ed." Banks wrote something on the schedule and then turned back to them. "Heard you'd quit."

"No." Ed smiled at him. "Just took a break. Polished my tech skills and took it a little easier for a while."

Banks jerked a nod, but he was deeply unhappy.

Ed tried to remember what had happened the last time he was up here, other than the situation that had ended his career. An administrative manager had told him they had a tip that an incoming ship was smuggling in a criminal, and sure enough, he'd found a tiny room that could well have been a hidden compartment with the scanner, along with a heat signature that was roughly the size of a person.

He'd been up here on the observatory with the usual team of three to support him, and they'd boarded the ship on his order, kicked down doors, only to find out the person in the compartment was a rare wildcat, extremely sensitive to shock, held in a padded cage, on its way to Demeter to be given a full medical. It belonged to the ambassador from Rnnali, one of the handful of non-VSC planets that did business with the Verdant String. Those planets had set up a loose coalition of their own, but it was bound by trade and security concerns, rather than a shared common ancestry, like the VSC.

The wildcat had died a day later, and Planetary Services declared it a critical incident.

Ed hadn't been worried. He'd received notification from someone on the SF admin team, and he didn't think he could have done anything differently, given the information he'd had.

Until the manager concerned denied ever talking to Ed.

His official comms device showed no such communication, and the SF comms installed on the station hadn't either.

Unfortunately for the manager, the maintenance staff on the observatory had been conducting a full tech scan at the time of the call, and it had been recorded on the obs station's main system.

It had taken nearly two weeks to get the information, and during that time, fingers had been pointed and voices had been raised. The fallout had led to two resignations and the prosecution of the manager, who couldn't or wouldn't say if anyone had in fact given him the tip-off, and whose motivations for the whole incident had never been uncovered. Neither had they found the person who'd erased the comms on both ends of the SF comm system.

Ed had walked away.

He understood now why he'd felt so strongly, despite the apologies. It had felt like another betrayal, like the one he'd lived through as a child when Halatia had imploded, and the VSC had dithered and bickered over who was going to take the survivors, while those survivors suffered and died at the hands of the pirates who'd scooped most of them up as they were escaping Halatia.

Had Banks been the maintenance worker responsible for the scan that had saved his name? And if so, why was he so bitter about seeing Ed again?

Maybe Ed was supposed to have stayed gone.

In fact, given the attempt on his life a few days ago, and the similarity in the set up—this time using Ethan Hyt as the recipient of the dodgy 'tip'—to the one that had ended his career, he wondered now about the motivation behind what had happened two years ago.

If someone hadn't wanted him up here, scanning, then they got their wish, even if Ed hadn't ended up taking the blame for the 'critical incident'. The end result was still his leaving the teams, taking the number of people able to work the scanner down to one.

And now Lily was off-planet and in trouble.

His return had to be extremely frustrating to whoever wanted a clear sky to bring in whatever they wanted to.

And it also begged the question, what had they needed clear skies for last time?

That was two years ago. What mischief could they have gotten up to in that time.

Ed felt a sudden leaden weight in his gut.

He had a feeling whatever it was, he'd helped it along in some way by walking off like a hurt child.

It was time to try to put it right.

13

———

He had done nothing but refuel since he came in off the line, and Wren had to admit she admired that kind of focus.

"The others definitely watched us leaving the canteen with it with longing expressions," Bailey said. She had brought a small bag in with her to the small sitting room between Wren and Ed's bedrooms, and she dug inside it and brought out a small device. She turned it on and held it out as she slowly made her way around the room.

Hatch swallowed, his gaze tracking Bailey, suddenly understanding what she was doing. "Do you think—?"

"Yes. They definitely *were* angling for a slice," Ed said, sending him a warning look. "But there's nothing stopping them from making their own."

"The thing that's stopping them is they don't have a team member who's made baking and cooking her hobby," Hatch said cheerfully, still eating, but chewing slower now as they all watched Bailey do a full circuit of the room.

She held up a single finger.

One listening device.

Wren felt her nanos go on full alert. She had to force herself to lean back in her seat as they directed their focus on any signal they could find.

She watched as Ed pointed to his room, then Wren's, and Bailey nodded and headed off there.

They needed to keep the conversation going or whoever was listening would know something was up.

She forced herself to participate.

"Banks seemed a good enough cook."

"Very focused on his job, though, isn't he?" Hatch said. "Didn't even tell anyone we were coming."

Bailey emerged from Ed's side, held up another finger.

Wren wrestled enough control to stand and she offered everyone more jah, all the better to keep the conversation light. Bailey stepped out of Wren's bedroom, with yet another finger up.

"So, what's next?" she asked, careful to keep her voice calm.

It was a generic enough question, but everyone knew what she meant.

She could kill all three devices now with a single touch, but she didn't want to give herself away to Hatch and Bailey, and they probably had equipment to do that, anyway.

"Let's sort out some kind of schedule for the next few days," Ed said. He stood and walked over to the first device Bailey had indicated, crouched in front of it, and lifted up a sleek metal cylinder. It was the kind of thing that looked vaguely practical but was clearly there for aesthetic purposes.

He set it on the low lounge table and waved Bailey into his room while Hatch and Wren kept up a conversation about schedules.

When they came out, Ed set a lamp down on the table and then the two of them went to her room, came out with another lamp.

Ed looked at the three items for a long moment, then went to his room and came back out almost immediately, carrying a bag. He carefully put the items inside it and closed it up.

"Can you fly down to Demeter and back tonight?" he asked Bailey.

"Sure." She gave a nod. "It'll take me three hours end to end."

An hour to fly down, an hour to hand off the devices, an hour back. Wren approved. The make and tech of the devices should tell Hyt something about who was listening in.

"Talk to Guttra at headquarters once you're on your way," Ed said.

"Agreed." Bailey hefted the bag. "Let me check Hatch's and my room before I go, just in case."

She walked out, closing the door behind her.

"They'll know we found the bugs," Hatch said.

"Sure. But we couldn't tolerate them in here," Ed said. "And this way, we'll find out where those devices came from. Plus, we can see who looks edgy among the crew now they've been uncovered."

"Even more edgy, you mean," Wren said. "They already look like a loud noise would spook them."

"Do they?" Hatch cut himself another piece of cake.

"You were too busy refueling to notice," Wren told him with a grin. "And my welcome was not warm, either. Plus, Banks seems to be very unhappy to see you, Ed."

"I picked that up." Ed sat down, nudged Hatch aside and cut himself some cake. "I was wondering about it. He might have been involved with what happened to me two years ago."

"I heard about that," Hatch said. "You were set up?"

"Just like Captain Hyt was set up. Almost exactly." Ed picked up his cup of jah. "A little too exactly. Someone made a mistake there. Although, to be fair, their plan worked well enough last time. I wasn't blamed in the end, but I still left the teams."

"And as soon as you were about to come back, they tried it again." Hatch nodded. "So there is definitely something they're trying to hide."

"What's going to happen to incoming traffic while you're resting?" Wren asked. "You can't be on the line more than six hours a day. Are we just doing spot checks?"

"No spot checks. Every ship will be scanned. The freighters will have to wait. They're probably forming an orderly queue out to the moon cluster as we speak."

Wren snorted out a laugh. "I guess there will be some very unhappy skippers tonight."

Ed shrugged. "I guess there will be."

"We should also check the control room for listening devices before Bailey leaves," Hatch said. "I'll take the dishes back to the canteen while I'm about it." He patted his stomach. "Thanks for the cake and the dinner, Wren. Best station food I've ever had." He scooped up the plates.

"I think we can assume the gym and the canteen are bugged too," Ed said. "Don't say anything outside the rooms we've checked that we don't want them to hear. I'll go with you to check the control room."

He and Hatch left, and as soon as the door closed behind them, Wren stood and let her nanos rise to the fore.

She had held back, waiting to be alone.

She closed her eyes and slowly turned in a circle. For the last ten minutes her nanos had been telling her something was off.

She let them scan the space.

There.

She angled her body, her eyes focusing in on a tiny wink of light.

She walked over to the corner and snatched up a scuttling creeper.

It was a miniature lens on eight legs, all black, including the glossy lens face.

Her nanos tasted it through the skin of her fingers.

She knew tasted wasn't the right word, but it felt right. They probed it.

They had gotten her to pick up numerous pieces of technology since Ytla, and she had walked through numerous tech stores in both Demeter and Nanganya since, picking up items and holding them while her nanos learned the tech of the new world they found themselves in.

Sudden, sharp pain bit at her, and she threw the bug, swearing.

An electric shock, her nanos told her. They would know better next time.

She hunted for the device, found it tucked between a chair and wall in the corner of the room.

It darted away, and a long, thin silver spike shot from her fingertip and impaled it.

Bemused, a little freaked out, she stood, staring at it, and at the silver extension of her finger.

The door opened and she turned.

"Bailey found some more," Ed said, then he stopped dead.

The silver spike retracted, and she cupped her other hand, let the creeper drop onto her palm. "So did I."

14

"I say we confront the bastards." Hatch glared at the creeper on the table. "There were listening devices in our rooms, and in the control room, but if they're using creepers . . ."

Ed knew if they were using creepers, the team could scan for electronic ears all they liked, someone just had to drop another creeper down, and let it scuttle inside their living quarters.

"I've got a way to disrupt creeper signals." Wren was focused on the creeper as well. "I only have one device that can do it, but I'll spend some time tonight making more and we can have one in each room."

"Serious?" Hatch lifted his gaze, frowning. "What tech is that?"

"Secret tech," she said.

Nano tech, Ed guessed. And probably learned in the last ten minutes.

Not that he was complaining.

"What equipment do you need?" he asked. "There's some stuff in the maintenance room you could probably use, if I remember from the last time I was up here."

She gave a nod. "Let's go see."

"What about me?" Hatch asked.

"Get some rest," Ed told him. "You're walking out on the line again tomorrow."

"So are you," Hatch pointed out.

"One of us might as well be rested," Ed said, and Hatch gave a shrug, shot another hard look at the burned out creeper, and followed them out.

"You should go rest, yourself," Wren said, walking beside Ed as they made their way past the control room and up the corridor that led to the maintenance room.

"I'd feel better if someone was there to watch your back," he said.

"I more or less have that already," she told him, voice soft.

"So I noticed."

She shot him a look, as if to gauge what he meant by that.

"It's a good thing, Wren. Better than not having it." He knew he wasn't the one with the nano tech inside him, but it had saved her numerous times, so it seemed beneficial to him. "Better than the alternative."

She gave a nod. "I'd have been dead a couple of times over without it, so yes. But that silver spike . . ." She lifted her shoulders. "That's never happened before."

"Because of it we have the creeper, and you have a way of shutting them down," he said. "I'm assuming that knowledge is newly acquired?"

She nodded. "It feels out the tech, learns it, and adapts."

They had been talking quietly as they walked, but when they saw one of the academic team turn into the canteen up ahead, they stopped speaking altogether, moving past the room and further down the passage.

There was another comms lounge, and then a large room with benches and various pieces of equipment set up.

Ed did a quick scan before he stepped inside, but there was no one here, even though the maintenance crew would surely have someone on duty around the clock.

"Maybe they're off somewhere, complaining about losing all their spy tech," Wren said.

She probably wasn't wrong.

He watched as she walked over to a long work bench, touching the items on it with delicate fingers as she moved down the length of it. She was doing the same to the next bench along when Ed sensed someone behind him.

He turned to find Banks looking at Wren with a strange expression.

"She's a looker, your new colleague."

"So she is."

"You together?" Banks flicked a look up at him.

"That's why we've got the shared accommodation," Ed said. He didn't feel even the slightest twinge at the deception.

"Separate rooms, though." Banks's attention went back to Wren.

"Teams policy," Ed said with a shrug. "Every person gets their own room. Whether they sleep in it or not."

"Huh." Banks lifted a shoulder. "That figures." He stepped into the room. "What's she doing?"

"Looking for some things she needs to make a jammer." Ed leaned back against the wall, crossed his arms over his chest.

"A jammer? What for?" There was an intensity to the question that told Ed a lot.

"We found listening devices in all our rooms, and a creeper. Bailey's taken them back to headquarters to see if the techs can trace where they originated." He kept his gaze focused on Banks when he spoke.

"Headquarters?" Banks seemed to relax a little.

So he had someone in headquarters running interference, maybe. Ed would shut that down with a call to Hyt.

"Yes, Captain Hyt and Head of Defense, Velda Shanïha, are very anxious to get to the bottom of a series of events that they think endanger the safety of Aponi. So I expect they'll make sure the tech trace will be done with full oversight."

Banks swallowed. "That's good."

"Is it?" Ed couldn't keep the humor out of his voice.

"You think it's me? You think this is a joke?" Banks turned on him in an instant, fists clenched.

"Who else could have set the devices but you? You're the one who allocated our rooms, and you said yourself over and over at dinner that you forgot to tell anyone we'd be coming up." Ed lifted both hands.

"Shit." Banks lifted his hands and cupped the back of his neck, biceps bunching. "I didn't set them."

"Then you have nothing to worry about," Ed said. "Just like last time."

"And what's that supposed to mean?" Banks hissed.

"It means I've been thinking about your attitude toward me since I got up on station, and what happened last time I was here, and I've got to wondering what your role in all that might have been."

Banks shot him a horrified look and began to back away. "You leave me alone. And make sure you account for all the equipment you use. SF headquarters needs to replace anything you take."

Ed looked back at Wren, who was standing, head bent over her work, at the far end of the room. "No problem."

"You should have stayed away, Ed. You should have kept your head down."

Ed turned all his attention back to Banks. "What do you know about it? Who's pulling your strings?"

"No one." Banks was already in the corridor, and he shook his head. "Don't say I didn't warn you."

He strode away.

"What's got him so het up?"

Ed stepped into the corridor and looked toward the canteen. The academic they'd seen going into the kitchen earlier stood in the passageway. She was holding a bowl of fruit.

"Laschka, right?" he asked, recalling the introductions they'd exchanged at dinner.

"Yes. And you're Ed. Easy to remember." Laschka nodded down the hall. "Why's Banks looking like he's lost home leave privileges?"

"He and I have a history." Ed leaned against the door jamb. "He didn't like being reminded of it."

"That sounds like a story, but I'm guessing you're not going to tell it?" Laschka said. She was a tall woman, only a little shorter than he was, and she was wearing soft lounge clothes, had her hair, which had been twisted up in a neat coil at dinner, tumbling loose around her shoulders. She lifted a carda, a small, round fruit that was a shade or two redder than her lips, and popped it into her mouth suggestively.

Ed grinned. "I'm afraid not. I'm here with Wren."

He made it clear the 'with' had many meanings.

"Ah well. Pickings are slim up here," Laschka said cheerfully. "Can't blame me for trying."

"How long have you been up here?" Ed asked. That would be an interesting piece of information.

"Almost three months. It was a real scramble. Jens—that's Professor Ludlow—said he'd got data from some freighters that looked promising, and there was a grant going, and suddenly we were up here." She blew a strand of hair out of her eyes, her hands full of the over-large fruit bowl. "But unfortunately, I'm going to have to withdraw soon."

"Are you needed at home?" Ed asked.

She paused, then blew out another breath. "I'm feeling strangely inclined toward honesty with you," she said. "I'm going because Ludlow's premise is crap. I've tried to go along to get along, but if I stay here much longer, my professional reputation is going to be tarnished. There's nothing to his claims. It's a dead end."

Well, well.

"He won't accept that?" Ed asked, keeping his tone conciliatory.

She shook her head. "I don't understand why not. I've never known him to be so unwilling to see the facts in front of him."

Unless of course he had a completely different agenda.

"What'll you do?" Ed asked.

"I'm working up to a final confrontation. Depending on how things go, it'll happen either tomorrow or the day after." She grimaced. "I've known Jens for twenty years. It's going to be a hard conversation."

He nodded, wondering if she was playing him, trying to take him into her confidence, or whether she was genuinely struggling with the integrity of the project.

"You're obviously taken, but what about Muscles?" She gave a sudden, naughty grin. "I tried to catch his eye at dinner, but he was all about the food in front of him, sadly."

"Hatch?" Ed asked on a laugh. "He was walking out on the line. It sucks you dry. Can't blame a person for needing to refuel."

"You were out on the line, too, but I saw you had plenty of focus to spare for little Wren."

"What can I say?" Ed shrugged. "She draws the eye."

"Your eye, anyway." Laschka popped another carda in her mouth. Sighed. "I'll give Hatch another chance tomorrow. Why not?"

She wandered after Banks down the passage.

Ed watched her go, surprised to realize he was as suspicious of her as he was of Banks. He'd warn Hatch to be very careful what he said if he chose to let Laschka catch him.

He looked up and down the passage, but there was no one else lurking around, and he stepped back into the room and walked over to see if Wren needed any help.

Probably not, he decided when he saw the neat line of devices in front of her.

Creepers beware.

15

Bailey had come back in the night, and Wren bumped into her in the canteen.

"Are you walking out on the line today?" She waited to ask until they were leaving the canteen with the plates of breakfast they'd made for themselves, heading for the small lounge in the control room.

Neither were prepared to talk about anything in the communal lounge and dining area. Not after finding listening devices and creepers.

Bailey nodded as she scanned her finger through the control room laslock and stepped inside. "I'll do three hours, Hatch will do three. It means we'll both be more alert the rest of the time. There's no such break for Ed, but at least when he rests, between the two of us, we'll be rested enough that we can keep an eye."

Wren could keep an eye, too, but she knew they didn't see her as dangerous, and she was happy to keep it that way for now. She set down her plate and her cup of jah. "What do you need me to do?" She activated one of the creeper detectors she'd made last night, and set it on a side table.

Bailey glanced over at her, taking a seat on a small couch. "Be ready to consult. We caught numerous freighters sneaking stuff in yesterday, but it was minor infringements, just more of their declared goods than they'd admitted to. We might come across something more juicy today, even if it's not specifically what we're up here looking for."

"After yesterday's haul, word is probably out that every freighter's being scanned," Wren said. She sat down herself, picked up her cup. "If someone has something I'd be interested in, they've probably decided to wait this out before they try to come back in."

Bailey lifted her shoulders. "Maybe, maybe not. I've seen people do the damndest things because they just don't think they'll get caught. Or they have a deadline or a client they don't want to disappoint, and they somehow convince themselves they've done the work they need to keep it hidden." She gave a wicked grin. "Besides, they don't know we're using the Guan scanner. Lily's been gone six months already, so they probably think it's a standard scan."

"The people we're trying to catch know, though," Wren pointed out. "That's why they tried to kill Ed."

Bailey frowned. "Good point. It would be interesting to see who suddenly changed their minds about coming into Aponi nearspace, wouldn't it?"

"Very."

Bailey leaned behind her, snagged a comms unit from the desk behind her and tapped it. "Guttra, it's Bailey. Wren's pointed out the people we're after will know the current checks are being made with a Guan scanner. So maybe we should ask the military to take an interest in any freighters who've had a sudden change of plan about entering Aponi nearspace."

Wren couldn't hear the other side of the conversation, but Bailey gave a grunt of satisfaction, and set the unit back down.

"He's on it." She bit into her toast with relish.

The door to the control room opened, and Hatch and Ed, each carrying a plate of food, appeared in the doorway.

"Morning."

There was a short, sudden beep, and then the acrid smell of burning circuits.

Wren stood, saw the creeper that had followed the men in through the door curled into itself, smoking gently.

The others followed her gaze.

"Your creeper detector doesn't just detect," Hatch observed.

"I didn't realize it was that . . . vigorous." Wren felt faintly embarrassed. Her nanos, in contrast, preened.

"Nice." Bailey walked over and picked it up. "It'll be hard for the lab to work out where it came from if it's too damaged, but I'd rather it be dead than recording us."

Wren reached out to take it and Bailey handed it over. She studied it, felt the nanos considering the burned out husk in her hand. When she lifted her head, Ed was watching her, and she shot him a smile as she sat back down, and moved over on her seat so he could sit next to her.

He ambled over, his shoulder and thigh rubbing against hers as he lowered himself down and made himself comfortable. Hatch found a seat and Bailey caught them up on Guttra agreeing to ask the military to stop and search all freighters backing away from nearspace.

"It's a good idea," Ed said. "And speaking of being extra cautious, Hatch, I think you need to be wary of Lashka."

Hatch looked at him with a blank expression. "Who?"

"One of the academics on the research team, right?" Bailey said.

Ed nodded. "I ran into her last night while Wren was building the creeper destroyers, and she gave off a strange vibe. I don't know if she was trying to play me or not, but she voiced an interest in sleeping with Hatch, so I'm just saying, if you allow yourself to be caught, be careful not to give anything away."

Hatch stared at him in horror, and Wren found the blush that stained his cheeks adorable.

"No problem," he eventually managed to get out.

"That's what she was doing at dinner last night," Bailey said, snapping her fingers. "Trying to catch Hatch's eye. I wondered why she kept looking our way."

"But Hatch was too focused on his dinner," Ed said. "Which made her feel a trifle put out."

Hatch cleared his throat. "Moving along. Who's out first on the line?"

"Me," Bailey said, "you were out for six hours yesterday. Get used to the control room, and I'll go out."

The comms unit signaled an incoming call and Bailey got up to answer it.

"We're about to go out," she said, and there was an edge to her voice. "Scanning will begin shortly." She fidgeted, clearly impatient to be off the call.

"Complaints?" Ed asked when she finally murmured a polite goodbye and signed off.

"They're backed up. More than eighty freighters waiting." She blew out a breath. "Tempers are running high."

"Then let's get to it." Ed set his plate and cup down.

"I'll deal with the dishes, you go do your thing." Wren began collecting the crockery, and Ed put a hand on her arm.

"Be careful. Those creepers are coming from somewhere, and that means there are enemies up here with us."

She nodded. "I'll be careful."

He looked like he wanted to say more, but stepped back instead. "Lashka and Banks are both suspect. Ludlow definitely is. I've already spoken to Hyt about him. His project is bogus. Lashka told me as much last night."

"You still suspect her after she told you that?" Wren was curious as to why.

"A good way to get someone's ear is to pretend to be confessing something you think they already know or suspect."

Hatch had turned to listen in on their conversation while Bailey suited up. "You think she was pretending to be honest so we'd take her into our confidence?"

Ed nodded. "There was something a little too pat about her 'honesty' for my liking. And I don't think Ludlow would have included people on his team who could expose his experiments as unworkable. They're either out of their depth, or they're with him all the way."

"What do you think he's really up to?" Hatch asked.

"I suspect he's looking for an ancestral spaceship signal. That would be easy enough to hide in a signal experiment project." Ed just wondered why they needed to find a signal if they already knew the location of the ship.

"I don't think I'm wrong about the wreck being an ancestral spaceship, but the men who were hunting me said something about a partial wreck." She wished she'd heard more. "I was injured, only half-listening, but I think they'd already found some of it, and that's why the cult is on Ytla to begin with, as cover for their search. If a massive mothership broke up on entry to Ytla's atmosphere, there could be sections of it all over. They might not have found the part with a working signal yet."

Ed gave a slow nod. "Maybe the site you stumbled on doesn't have anything interesting enough for them. They're looking for tech." He gave her just the faintest hint of a smile, because he knew she had gotten the most interesting tech of all.

The nanos acknowledged his nod to them with a wave of humor.

Wren couldn't help smiling as they fizzed with joy. They liked being seen by someone else, she realized. They liked the connection.

"Ready when you are." Bailey turned, all suited up.

"Happy hunting," Wren said, and, arms full of dishes, went to observe the enemy in the canteen.

16

———————

The question came from Cora, who had been introduced to Wren last night as a research assistant on the academic team. She was slight and moved like she didn't know what to do with her hands.

She stood beside a pile of dishes, gripping those hands together in a tight hold.

"Not wonderful, but that's how it always is for me the first night I stay somewhere new." Wren stacked the dishes in the washer, and then stepped back to let Cora stack hers. "I travel a lot for work, so I'm used to it."

"I'm still not used to it," Cora said. "There's something about the air pressure, and the faint hum of the environmental system, that just won't let me relax."

"How long have you been up here dealing with it?" Wren asked, although she knew from Ed the team had been up here three months.

"Two months. Some of the team have been up here longer, but they decided they needed more people and I volunteered." Cora shook her head. "I'm putting in early for home leave. I can't stand to be here for the full three month rotation, and we're not having a lot of success with the project, anyway."

Wren made sympathetic sounds.

"How long are *you* up here, then?" Cora asked.

"We're not sure yet." Wren smiled. "At least two weeks. Maybe longer."

Cora nodded. "What are you doing? I didn't catch that part of the conversation last night at dinner."

"We're scanning the incoming freighters."

"Oh." As if suddenly understanding something, Cora looked up at her, eyes wide. "Ohhh. That's why there's a line of freighters stretching past the moon cluster?"

"That's why," she agreed.

"You're scanning them all?"

"We're being thorough," Wren said with a shrug.

"I can't imagine anyone's happy about the delay."

Wren gave a laugh. "No."

"She doesn't care." The tone was spiteful, and it was no surprise to Wren to find Trish had stepped into the canteen.

"It's true. I don't," she said cheerfully. "We found so many reporting infringements yesterday, it looks like a thorough check is long overdue."

"Don't turn your back on any of those freighter captains, if you happen to bump into one," Trish said. "The chatter I'm picking up is vicious." There was an element of glee to her voice, and Wren had to wonder about what was driving it.

"You sound almost pleased about it," Cora said, her surprise obvious.

Wren tilted her head. "Yes, you do. I wonder why that is?"

Trish turned away without answering, as if she realized she'd shown too much, and with a friendly nod of goodbye to Cora, Wren left the canteen, her nanos on alert.

She'll attack, they told her. *If she gets a chance, she'll attack. From behind.*

That sounded right. Although Wren was still unsure of the reason for it.

"Wren, you're needed." Hatch's voice came through her comm. "Ed found something suspicious."

"Yay." She meant it. She was looking forward to something to do.

She made it to the control room in minutes, and as she stepped in, there was another beep and the smell of burning, and then a crunch underfoot as she stepped on something metallic. Her device had zapped another creeper.

She flicked it away with the toe of her boot.

"Must have been waiting outside the door," she said.

"Or it followed you from the canteen." Hatch picked it up and tossed it on the table next to the other one.

Her nanos would have picked that up, but she gave a nod of agreement. "Could be."

There was a hollow thunk, and then the air lock opened and Ed and Bailey stepped in, already lifting their helmets off their heads.

"Bailey, you stay in the control room and rest up. Ed, Wren and I will take the runner out to the ship." Hatch took Bailey's helmet from her and hung it on the wall.

Bailey nodded, her gaze catching on the second creeper on the table. She lifted her brows. "I figured that would be the best plan." She started stripping out of the suit.

Ed already had his off, and he accepted the slim package Hatch handed him. He opened it and took out a warm, damp cloth from inside, rubbed his face and neck with a sigh of enjoyment.

"Sweaty work?" Wren asked.

He nodded. "I'm beginning to remember why I stayed away so long."

He left to change and they were in the runner, heading for the freighter, in under ten minutes. Wren studied the ship with interest as they approached.

"It looks like it's VSC-built."

"It is. From Raxia." Ed tapped the screen he was holding, showed her the schematics. "I think there's something off in here." He showed her a narrow chamber that looked like it ran along the length of the bathrooms in the crew quarters.

They reached the freighter in minutes, and landed inside the hold, nestling between large storage units and two small runners similar to their own.

A very irritated man met them as they disembarked and introduced himself as the purser.

"This is an imposition."

"Then let us check what we need to check and we'll be on our way." Ed sounded calm and practiced. It may have been a while since he'd done this, but he clearly still knew how to play the game.

They followed the purser down passageways, getting curious and sometimes hostile looks from the crew, and eventually Ed pulled up short.

"Here." He had set up the scanner while they were traveling across to the freighter, and he had attached the clear screen in front of his eyes as they walked. He pointed. "There's a door."

Hatch went over, running his hands over the wall.

"There is no door there," the purser said, "I have the ship's schematics. There is nothing—"

Hatch pressed something and a narrow door popped open.

Wren studied the purser with interest. He was speechless, and she believed he hadn't been aware of the door.

"This is where things sometime get dangerous," Ed said.

Hatch nodded, pulling out his laz. "I'll go first."

Ed put a hand on his own laz, sitting at his waist and he gestured to Wren. "I'll take up the rear."

She shot him a look. Although she wasn't armed, she was far from defenseless. Hatch might not know it, but Ed did. Still, it was good to keep up the fiction she was the most vulnerable member of the team.

She looked over at the purser, but he was already leaving at a fast clip.

"Gone to inform the captain, is my guess." Ed nudged her into the secret passage. "Best to keep the door closed behind us."

"Does that work?" Wren asked.

Ed shut the door. "Sometimes. If they open it, it shows they know about it. So usually they try to pretend it's all a big mystery to them. But if they really can't afford to lose whatever it is we're going to find in here, then they'll come after us, no matter what that reveals about their culpability."

Hatch was waiting for them a little way along. He'd turned on a powerful light he'd clipped to his jacket.

"Can you see a light fixture anywhere?" Ed asked him.

"There has to be, right?" Hatch played the light along both walls. "There." He touched something and lights flickered on.

"What have we got?" Ed edged past her, standing shoulder to shoulder with Hatch, which just about blocked the way completely, and Wren had to go on tiptoe to look over their shoulders to see for herself.

"What *is* it?" Hatch asked.

"Let me see, and maybe I can tell you," Wren said, voice dry, and Ed shot her a grin over his shoulder and flattened himself against the wall to let her through.

She had to press past him, and then she saw the shelving running down most of the narrow space, with only room for one person to access it.

She stepped closer, and then stilled.

"What is it?" Hatch lowered his voice to a whisper as he repeated his question.

"If these boxes are genuine, then they were stolen from Cepi." She reached out and brushed a finger over one of them reverently. It was cold, a stone surface that would fit with what she knew about the artifacts from Cepi, the now-destroyed moon that used to circle Kalastoni.

She picked the box up, and found it was heavy, but even in the poor lighting, now she had it in her hands, she could see the ridge of a mold along one side.

"Are they genuine?" Ed asked.

She set it back down, tapped the surface with her fingernail and then lifted the lid. "No." She pulled out a neat package from inside, hefted it. "From the weight of it, I'd say this is bonami." She looked over at them, eyes wide. "The most I've ever seen in one spot."

She turned back to the shelf, and counted twenty five boxes all in a row.

"Someone's been sampling the goods," Ed said, nodding to the package she was holding. It had clearly been opened, the side neatly sliced open and then taped back up.

"Or checking the purity," Hatch guessed. "This looks like more than all the bonami users on Aponi could even get through."

"This trader's going on to Arkhor and a few other planets in the VSC. My guess is that only some of the product is being offloaded here." Ed moved to stand next to her, and picked up a box. "Interesting they chose a fake Cepi artifact to transport their drugs in."

"You're thinking about the Core Company execs who are still on the run? They were responsible for the Cepi disaster, and it was their people we bumped into in Demeter."

Ed lifted his shoulders. "Seems a little coincidental."

"Why would they give themselves away like that?" Hatch asked.

"We've connected the dots, but to most people, it's just a fake tourist item from Kalastoni," Wren said. "It might be a handy way for them to identify themselves to their partners, or a way to pass along a message—"

Before she finished speaking, they all heard the sound of someone entering the passage.

Ed moved from beside her to in front of her, next to Hatch.

Frustrated, she crouched down, where she got a better view of someone moving nervously down the corridor.

"Yes?" Ed snapped the question.

The person stopped, then moved again, and Hatch reactivated the light on his jacket, making the space even brighter so they could finally see who they were dealing with.

The man was wearing what Wren guessed was a captain's uniform, although this was a private freighter, not a military ship.

Most likely the freighter was part of a transport company, but she hadn't thought to ask Hatch about it beforehand.

"I'm Captain Masin. My purser showed me where you went in," Masin said, and Wren gave him points for at least trying to sound like he didn't know about the secret passage. "I wanted to see what you found, and feel you should have waited for me before you entered."

"That's not how it works," Ed said. "This is an undeclared space, and I certainly don't think you've registered twenty-five packages of bonami on your manifest."

Masin was silent for a beat. "Twenty-five?" His voice shook a little.

"Someone told you it was less, or more?" Hatch asked.

"No one told me anything!" Masin drew himself up.

"Then you did this all by yourself?" Ed asked, politely.

It was at that point that Masin went a little mad.

Later, Wren wondered if it had been him who'd been sampling the product, and he had become addicted. Or maybe it was just that he realized there was no getting out of the situation without consequences.

He gave a shout and lunged at Hatch and Ed, and they both deployed their laz at the same time.

Masin went down with a strange, animalistic cry, and lay, convulsing, on the ground.

"Two medium strength hits at the same time," Ed said, looking down at him. "Next time, we should work out which of us goes first."

Hatch gave a nod, also standing over Masin, calmly watching him. "Agreed. First time working together always requires a learning curve."

"Got a reviver?" Wren asked them, straightening up from her crouch.

"Yes." Ed pulled a slim cylinder out from one of the many pockets in his jacket and handed it to her.

Wren bent over Masin and punched the needle into his upper arm.

He stilled, closed his eyes, and his breathing evened out.

"So what now?" She'd never been involved in the pointy end of discovery. She was always brought in once the dust had settled.

Hatch tapped his ear. "You got all that, Bailey?"

"Got it," Bailey said in Wren's ear, and she realized they had been transmitting since they arrived. "Protection has been informed, and they will be arriving shortly with two Ports and Excise officers." She paused. "Maybe stay where you are until they arrive. The rest of the freighter's crew seems unhappy."

Ed glanced back at Wren. "Will do."

"Not on my account," Wren said.

"Humor me." Ed sent her a charming smile. "I'm easily stressed."

Hatch snorted out a laugh, then tried to cover it with a cough.

Wren rolled her eyes, but she supposed dragging the semi-comatose captain out into a ship full of his crew was probably not the wisest choice. "What will happen when Protection get here? Will they arrest him?"

Hatch lifted his hands. "Protection and Customs and Excise might fight it out as to who takes him away."

"So it's best we ask him what we want to ask him now?"

She didn't know if he'd have anything useful to say, but the fake Cepi boxes were a definite connection to the former Cores Companies, who were also very interested in ancient tech, and that was worth a question or two while they had the captain to themselves.

She could get him to talk.

The thought popped into her head unbidden, and she hesitated. She could, but should she?

It was crossing a line. She knew that. She had felt guilty about the repercussions of what had been done to Ed, but this would be deliberate. Her making the choice.

Her gaze snagged on the row of bonami, and her lips firmed into a thin line. Bonami was a terrible drug, dragging its users deeper and deeper into a sleeping state, punctuated by wild, violent forays for more of it, as the addiction tightened its hold.

After a certain point, there was no going back. The addict simply lay, incapable of movement, skin tight as they starved and dehydrated, unable to accept anything but the drug that had destroyed them.

And Masin was bringing in enough to swamp two whole planets, at least.

Decision made, she crouched beside him and lightly tapped his cheek. "Captain Masin."

He stirred, and she felt her nanos prick against her fingertips.

"Who are you working for? Who gave you the boxes of bonami?"

Ed and Hatch stepped a little closer, very interested in what she was doing.

"They made me." Masin rubbed his chest where Ed and Hatch had hit him with their laz.

"Who made you?"

"I'm too low down to know the main players." Masin sounded bitter. "I deal with someone called Rhen."

Ed made a sound, and she looked over her shoulder at him.

"That's the name of one of the Lassian mercenaries we encountered on the street a couple of days ago," he said.

"Rhen's in custody?" The captain lifted his head. "Is that how you knew about the stash?"

Ed gave a shrug, not saying no, but not confirming it, either.

Masin shook his head and then lay it back on the ground, looking sick.

"Why would you do this?" Hatch asked him, waving a hand at the line of boxes. "What could possibly be worth it?"

"They had proof of some . . . mistakes I made." Masin turned his head away. "Mistakes my family might have been unwilling to forgive."

So they'd caught him being unfaithful, or perhaps worse.

Wren guessed there were plenty of people who had secrets they were desperate to hide.

"How many times have you done this?"

He looked like he didn't want to answer, but she knew her nanos were in his system, making him more uninhibited.

"This is the second time."

"Did you drop off the whole lot on Aponi?" Hatch asked.

"Some here, half the load on Raxia. One final box on Arkhor."

"What's the process? Who receives it?" She had a feeling the details were important.

"I give everyone dock leave, and then I get the boxes, put them in big containers, and wheel them out. I take the load to the warehouse where we get our food supplies, leave them in the numbered bay Rhen gives me, and when I come back, the containers are full of our supplies, and the boxes are gone."

"The same set up in Raxia and Arkhor?" Ed asked.

Masin nodded.

"Protection is here, with Customs and Excise on their heels. They want you to let them in." Bailey's voice came through.

Wren got to her feet. "Slow walk it, will you, Hatch? So I can get some images of the boxes." She moved to the shelf, picked up the first box and took out the package of bonami. She flicked on her small handheld light and carefully went over every inch of the box's surface, looking for any clue as to where it was made.

"You seeing this, Bailey?" she asked.

"Yes. You want me to try to find out where it comes from?"

"Please." The material it was made from was a type of resin. It felt close to stone, and the patterns and glyphs molded into the sides and lid were exact matches to those found in the now destroyed alien ruins of Cepi. "Whoever created these boxes was working with images from Cepi itself. These aren't just similar, they're exact matches."

"So someone likes to get it right, has pride in what they're doing, or these glyphs have meaning." Ed picked up the lid and studied it.

"No one has worked out the meanings." Wren was sure of that. "So it's probably someone who's a perfectionist."

Hatch stepped closer. He hadn't gone down to let in the protection team yet. "Or they've assigned their own meanings to the markings," he suggested. "As a sort of secret code."

Wren looked over at him, and she saw Ed had done the same.

"Not just a pretty face and abundant muscles," Wren said in the end. "You've got a brain, too."

Ed laughed, and Hatch lifted a hand in a rude gesture as he turned to go down the passage, but she caught a glimpse of his red cheeks.

"Saved by the Protection Unit," Ed called after him. "And you don't hear that every day."

17

Customs and Excise were predictably annoyed by everything they had done.

Ed smiled. He hadn't enjoyed being back walking out on the line, but he didn't mind irritating the crap out of C&E.

"This is his second time bringing in this quantity," he said, cutting off the officer who was muttering about the open box. "So you haven't just fucked up this time, you've fucked up twice. Do you see how much bonami is here? Your inability to find this has to have led to a massive increase in bonami on Aponi."

The officer turned, eyes hot. "Hang on—"

Ed cut him off. "So instead of muttering and complaining, how about a thank you to us for using our special equipment to find what you were not able to find, and let us go back to dealing with the backlog that has to be building up."

"That's you?" the other officer asked. "You're the team holding up the works?"

"You could put it that way, that we're holding up the works, or you could say we're finding massive quantities of bonami and large amounts of undeclared goods." Wren said. "It's interesting how you frame it. Are you on the take here?"

Both C&E officers stared at her, mouths open.

"The lady asked you a question," Ed said.

"I'd like to know the answer to that, myself." The Protection Unit's team leader, Violet Fann, had been standing near Ed, observing the set up, but now her full attention was on the C&E officers.

"No," the one who'd been muttering managed to get out. "*I'm certainly not.*"

"Me, either." The second one almost spoke over the first.

They both looked a little wild-eyed.

"Then what's it to you if there's a back up? It's not your cargo on the line. And I don't know about you, but to me this is a significant bonami haul." Violet Fann tilted her head. "Or have you seen bigger?"

"I've never found bonami before," the second C&E officer said, stiffly. "I don't know what's a big haul and what isn't."

"Maybe we need someone a little more senior here." Violet walked away, dismissing the C&E officers with a flick of her hair, talking urgently into her comms set.

"If that's all, I think we'll be off." Ed glanced over at Wren, and she sent him a quick, bright smile in acknowledgement of their double play.

He grinned back, stepping aside to let her go ahead of him.

Captain Masin had already been hauled off, and when they emerged from the secret passageway, Violet Fann and two of her team were standing near the door.

The crew had been sent back to quarters until they could all be questioned, and Ed guessed that was where the rest of Violet's team were, gathering statements.

He gave a nod to her as he and Wren passed her, heading for Hatch who was up ahead, talking to another Protection Unit officer.

"Ed, wait." Violet held up a hand, and Ed slowed, letting Wren go ahead of him.

Violet spoke for a few more moments into her comms set and then strode toward him. "You off?"

"Seems there's a back up," he said.

She gave a low chuckle. "Apparently. But seriously, backed up or not, are you going to scan every ship out there? There's over a hundred, last I looked."

Ed nodded. "You heard about any trying to leave?"

She nodded. "Got word this morning that the military is rounding them up. That was your suggestion, was it?"

"It was Wren's, but yes, it came from us."

"Five ships have so far broken out of the line and tried to leave. The military have boarded each one and done a thorough search, but looking over at the set-up here, I don't think they'd have found this. Neither would anyone in the Protection Unit. I'm thinking maybe we need to liaise and get the military to bring them close to the obs station where you can scan them more thoroughly."

"Fine with me." More hours out on the line, but if the freighters were trying to run, they may be exactly the ships he should be scanning.

"Is that Wren?" Violet asked, looking down the passage to where Wren had stopped beside Hatch.

"Yes. Our new artifacts consultant."

"Ah." Violet nodded. "You're looking for something specific in these scans. I wondered."

Ed didn't answer, but his silence was answer enough.

"You could tell us what you're looking for. We could help," Violet said.

Ed lifted his shoulders, to convey that wasn't up to him, and she gave a grunt of understanding.

It was what it was.

And Protection wasn't immune to corruption, either. Whoever they were dealing with had been exercising their influence since at least Wren's capture on Ytla.

Keeping it to a small group was best, even if the knock-on effect was some delays to the freighter industry.

18

———

Wren had never seen a battle cruiser before today.

She'd been in one, when she'd been taken off Ytla, but she'd been in the med bay the whole time, recovering from her ordeal.

Now she could see two. The Aponian military behemoths hung, intimidating and lethal, with the recalcitrant freighters between them.

Wren could see six ships herded into a group, not five, so a sixth trader had obviously tried to duck out of line.

The freighters varied in size, from small, private runners to larger commercial ships. The only thing they had in common was that they'd ditched the queue and cancelled their Aponian entrance permissions.

Ed and Bailey were out walking the line, and she and Hatch stood together in the control room, observing it all. Above and a little behind the obs station, out of sight of the front viewing panel where she stood, was the Protection Unit's runner, ready to assist if Ed found something interesting in his scans.

"Freighter Two," Ed said over the comms. "Freighter Four and Freighter Five."

"Shit." The military captain who'd led the first round of searches, Captain Trin Darnell, broke into the transmission, clearly annoyed.

"No shame in it, Darnell," Ed said cheerfully. "They've been tricky."

"And the other three?" Captain Violet Fann of the Protection Unit asked.

"Clear."

"There you go, Darnell, only a fifty percent fail rate," Violet Fann said.

The comment seemed particularly inflammatory to Wren, but Hatch laughed softly. "They never pass up a chance to needle each other, the military and Protection. It's built in."

"I thought the competition was between the SF teams and the military. And Protection." Wren thought about it. "And C&E."

"Yes," Hatch said, shrugging. "We're the envy of everyone."

"Or the problem," Wren said, and Hatch turned to give her a sour stare.

"It's never us. It's them."

"That's what someone who's the problem always says," Wren told him.

"You're part of the teams, too," Hatch reminded her. "So you're part of that same problem."

He had her there.

They waited for Ed and Bailey to come back in, and then, just like last time, she, Hatch and Ed went over to check out Freighter Two. The Protection Unit runner and a military runner containing Captain Darnell and his hand-picked team joined them, so they had to juggle to find space for three runners to land in the small loading bay.

A military officer, left on board after the initial search to watch the crew, met them.

He saluted Darnell as he stepped out of the military runner. The military captain turned out to be of medium height, wiry, with sharp cheekbones and brows that slashed upward like dark wings, his hair cut brutally short. Next to him, Violet Fann, with her curly hair pulled back in a loose bun, with her curves and her plump lips, looked like his complete opposite.

Wren wondered if their differences fueled their game of one-upmanship.

Whatever was between them, there was a crackle of tension in the air when they nodded to each other in greeting.

"Report," Darnell snapped to the officer who met them.

"As ordered, I didn't mention that the Guan scanner had picked up an anomaly," the officer said, his gaze flicking to Ed. "I said we'd chosen some ships at random for a second search."

"And the response?" Darnell asked.

The officer shrugged. "Unconcerned."

That meant most likely this freighter was not the one they were looking for. Wren was sure whoever they were hunting knew Ed was using a Guan scanner, and they would also know she and Ed were stationed on the observatory.

They would have understood what was about to happen when they were ordered forward to the obs station.

She felt a sudden wave of relief at the thought of the massive battleships on either side of them. Even if the people they were hunting knew what was about to happen, they could do nothing about it while the might of the Aponi military looked on.

Ed lowered the visor in front of his face.

"Which way?" Violet Fann asked.

"Out the loading bay and to the right." Ed glanced back at Wren, as if to make sure she was all right, and when she gave a tiny nod, he turned back and walked through the doors. Darnell and his three soldiers, Violet Fann and her two officers, and Hatch and herself, all formed a loose protective formation around him.

The military unit flanked him on one side, the Protection officers took the other, leaving her and Hatch to take up the rear.

Wren studied the ship with interest as they moved down a passage.

This was a medium-sized freighter, gray and utilitarian, but clean and neat. The crew looked out at them from a few doors as they passed, with Wren catching glimpses of bedrooms, and a small lounge.

One thing she noted was that all the crew she could see were men. It stood out as unusual. Wren didn't think she'd ever encountered that before.

Ed led them all the way to the back of the ship, to the captain's suite, and they found the freighter captain standing outside his door.

He frowned at the sight of the scanner.

"What's this?"

"I suspect it's your downfall," Ed said, his voice going grim as he stared at something on his visor only he could see. He turned to Darnell and Fann. "You'll need to restrain him."

Ed looked . . . dangerous. Like he could slide into violence at any moment. And all his attention was focused on the captain.

Whatever it was that he could see, it was bad. Wren felt the hairs stand up on the back of her neck and her breath caught.

Violet Fann flicked a look at Ed, and seemed to be about to ask him for more information, but one look at his face and she suddenly moved, grabbing the captain and shoving him up against the wall.

"What's the charge?" the captain asked, voice going higher as Darnell joined her, pulling out wrist restraints.

Violet's two officers took charge of him, pulling him back.

Wren studied the man, and he glanced her way. The look he sent her was . . . wrong. Disturbing.

As soon as he was secured, Ed walked through the door, and Wren followed directly behind him, with Hatch on her heels. Like her, Hatch must have felt the tension, because he pulled his laz from its holder as they moved into the room.

"Move that cabinet," Ed said, pointing, and Wren made her way to it, leaving Hatch free to hold his laz two-handed in readiness.

She found the one side of the cabinet was attached to the wall with hinges, and felt a prickle of anticipation and dread. She went to the other side, found a tiny lever at her eye level at the back of the cabinet, and flicked it up.

There was a click and the cabinet swung free—silent and smooth.

Wren pushed it away from the wall, using some muscle as the cabinet was much taller than herself. As she did, she saw faint marks on the floor where it had made a path from regular use.

The cabinet was made with a material she wasn't familiar with, and she guessed it would block a normal scan.

Once the cabinet was out of the way, she found a low sliding door she had to crouch down in front of to open.

A noise came from the room hidden beyond—a clink of metal.

She glanced back.

"I hear it," Hatch said. "Let me see."

"Wait." Wren crouched lower and slid the door open, angling her head to see into the space while still giving herself some cover.

"They're tied up," Ed said, voice soft and strained. "They're no danger to you."

He sounded . . . too calm.

Wren sent him a quick look, then ducked into the room, with Hatch right behind her.

The reason she hadn't been able to see anything before, she realized, was because they were indeed tied up. Two women, chained to the wall, only visible once you were fully in the room.

They were sitting on thin red cushions, legs pulled up, arms around their knees, peering at Wren through greasy locks of hair, thick metal collars around their necks. They were attached to the wall with heavy chains.

Wren stumbled to a halt.

Behind her, she felt Hatch do the same.

He began to swear under his breath, and then he turned, ducking out as he called for medical help.

Two sets of eyes fixed on her.

"It's all right," she said, keeping her voice gentle. "We're here to get you out." She moved toward them, both hands out, and crouched between them.

They both flinched away from her, and she shuffled back, hands up in apology.

She had been in captivity herself, on Ytla. She understood.

"I'm Wren," she said. "My colleague Hatch is going to help me free you."

Hatch came back in holding a cutting tool for the chains, but the women both cringed at the sight of him and Wren got up, herding him back a little, and took the laser tool.

"Get Violet Fann in here." She kept her voice low and didn't say why, but he gave a nod, ducking back out.

Violet Fann crawled in, face set and blank.

"This is Captain Fann, of the Protection Unit," Wren said. "She's going to help me get you free."

Violet Fann helped her slice through the chains that connected the women to the wall, but that wasn't an option for the collars around their necks.

"Do you know how he got this on you?" She was crouched in front of them again, and both women stared at her, one a little less glassy-eyed than the other.

"I woke up with it on," the woman said, voice hoarse. "It feels seamless, I don't know how he got it on."

"Can I?" Violet asked, sinking down beside them, hand out to the collar.

The woman gave a nod.

Violet ran a finger around it. "Electromagnetic lock," she said. "We need to look for a small device with the right frequency to open it. Probably in his room."

She crawled back to the door to let Ed, Darnell and Hatch know, and Wren thought she heard a faint cry of pain from the freighter captain.

She wouldn't have been surprised if Ed wasn't asking him where he kept the device.

We could work it out, her nanos offered.

It was comforting that they could, but she declined.

Only if there's no other choice. Making him hand it over, he condemns himself further in the eyes of the law, and we don't give ourselves away, she told them.

They settled, accepting her logic, and Violet came back in, holding the device in her hand.

She was obviously familiar with locks like these, because she had the collars off in moments.

It was a rush after that, getting the women out of the room, and then off the ship into the hands of the Protection Unit medic. Darnell took responsibility for the captain, so the women didn't have to be on the same runner as their tormentor, and Wren thought he and Fann parted on more cordial terms than before.

"What happens now?" one of the freighter crew asked, as they stood in the bay, watching the military runner leave with the captain in restraints.

"You'll be towed down to Demeter and all questioned. If any of you had any idea what was going on, prepare for a life in prison." Ed had lifted the visor back up, but the scanner still sat on his head and shoulders, giving him more height, emphasizing his size and making him look even more intimidating than usual.

"They knew," Wren said.

"We did not." The crew member turned to her, eyes hot, fists clenched.

"There isn't a single woman on board this ship. Have you ever heard of such a thing?" she asked Ed.

"No." He gave a slow shake of his head. "I have not."

"I asked about that when I took the job. The captain said it wasn't from want of trying, but some of the older crew told me women won't work with him. They last one planet hop and then they leave. I thought it strange that he had such poor dealings with women. I had already put in for a job closer to home, but I had no idea he was … doing whatever it was he was doing." The man backed up as he spoke, his voice getting higher.

"The ship's out of Kalastoni?" Ed asked.

"That's what I was told when I joined the crew, but I joined up in Raxia. This freighter doesn't have an actual home port. We take on abandoned freight and find new buyers for it. The captain owns this ship outright; he isn't under contract."

That's how he'd managed to keep anyone in authority from noticing too much. He never stayed anywhere long enough.

Wren turned away in disgust. "You ready to go?" she asked Ed.

"Very ready." He sounded closer to himself now.

Hatch was talking to the soldiers who were staying behind to fly the ship down to Demeter, but he broke away when he saw them heading for the runner.

"We going to take a look at Freighter Four?" he asked.

"I think Protection and the military need a little time to organize themselves after this. We'll keep scanning the other freighters, and wait for them to give us the backup we need to board the other two ships." Ed sat in the runner, lifting the scanner carefully off his shoulders.

Hatch slid into the pilot's chair and reversed out of the bay.

Wren knew of only one other place she'd been as pleased to see the back of, and that was her collapsed prison on Ytla.

"I need a shower," Hatch said. "And some cake."

"I need to bake a cake," Wren told him. "So you're in luck."

19

———————

"DO YOU KNOW WHY THERE ARE TWO FREIGHTERS WAITING RIGHT OUT front, with battleships on either side?" Jens Ludlow hailed Wren from the entrance to the canteen, stepping in to the room with a look back over his shoulder, as if he could see the view right outside the door.

Which he couldn't.

The best view was from the control room, although there would be other viewing windows throughout the observatory.

"Logistics, I think." Wren made her reply as vague as she could.

"Logistics?" Dr. Lashka Garde, the woman who had spoken with Ed last night, raised a beautifully shaped eyebrow and strolled in behind Ludlow. "What's logistics got to do with battleships?"

"Protective overkill, probably, but I've never seen one before, so I'm enjoying getting a close up view of two." Wren kept her voice cheerful as she mixed up the topping for the cake.

"I haven't either, actually." Lashka gave a hum of interest. "I wouldn't mind a tour of one."

"I'd love that, as well. If you have a way to make that happen, count me in." Wren shot her a smile. Her nanos actually sat up and took notice at the possibilities. The tech they could explore on a big battleship was an exciting thought to them. They had lost their

119

chance the first time, when she'd been in the med bay, but if they could have a tour . . .

She can't get us on, Wren told them. *She's just digging for information.*

She almost smiled at the sense she had of their disappointment.

"I saw in the news that C&E confiscated a massive haul of bonami this morning. Was that your team?" Lashka asked.

"It was." Wren met her gaze. "It makes the inconvenience pale into insignificance, doesn't it?"

"There are rumblings about the queue, are there?" Lashka looked amused. "I can imagine the administrators are getting a lot of angry comms."

"Probably." Wren spread the topping over the cake. She glanced up, saw Trish in the doorway. "Trish here thinks I shouldn't turn my back on any freighter captains any time soon."

Ludlow and Lashka Garde turned to look at Trish, and she sneered at them all and then whirled away, stomping off.

"Well done." Lashka gave her a quick, sidelong glance. "You chased her off. That woman has very strange anger issues. I'm not sure she should be up here."

Wren agreed. She couldn't understand why someone as unstable as Trish was allowed to remain on station. "Banks should have already sent her down," she said.

"Yes." Ludlow was looking at the door with a sour expression. "She is obstructive in every way."

That was interesting. Wren had assumed Trish was in on whatever Banks was doing, hence her hostility toward her and the rest of the team, but if she was obstructive to the academics as well, she might only be tolerated because her instability allowed Banks to get away with whatever it was he was up to.

Someone thinking straight would have reported him by now. Trish was definitely not thinking straight.

Juller—the other maintenance team member—she couldn't read well enough. He was polite and friendly when he did speak, but he didn't say much.

She had to believe he knew what was going on here, unless he was someone who put their head down and simply refused to see what was right in front of them.

"You said protective overkill, does the military think those freighters are dangerous?" Jens Ludlow was watching her, but she pretended total concentration on spreading her cake topping and didn't look up.

"They wouldn't be wasting two battlecruisers otherwise, Jens." Lashka's voice was a little sharp. "But I don't like how close they are to the observatory, if so."

There was a flick of sound from Wren's comms link, and then Bailey's voice was in her ear.

"Captain Darnell and Captain Fann are ready for us again."

"Coming," she said. She gave the cake one last smoothing with the thin metal spatula she'd found in a drawer, and picked up the plate.

"Feeding your team?" Lashka asked.

"Hatch is a bottomless pit," she said with a grin as she headed for the door.

"He and Ed are heading back in?" Jens asked.

"They are."

His question sounded reasonable, but he seemed a little too interested, and it made her wary. Still, anyone who was watching the obs station could see they were coming in, so she wasn't telling him anything he couldn't work out for himself.

She made her way to the control room and then waited outside the door for a moment, scanning to see if her nanos could pick up a creeper waiting to dart inside with her.

There.

She touched the laslock and stepped inside, finger to her lips as she did.

Bailey had turned as the doors began to open, lips parted to speak, but she pressed them shut and waited for the creeper to crash and burn first.

Wren set the cake on the table and then picked up the smoking bug.

"They must have a whole box of them," she said.

"It has to be Banks," Bailey said. "He's got access to all the electronics."

"The academics could just as easily have brought them up disguised as equipment," Wren said. "But it is getting tiresome. After we check the last two freighters, I'll go looking for the motherlode and take them all out at once."

"Can your device do that?" Bailey asked.

Wren froze for a moment, then lifted her shoulders. "Even if I have to do it one by one."

As she spoke, the internal airlock door opened and Hatch and Ed came through, helmets already off. Hatch let out a whoop at the sight of the cake, and was out of his suit faster than Ed.

Ed glanced at the cake, lifted his gaze to hers, and gave a nod, as if the beautifully decorated cake confirmed something for him.

The look he sent her was thoughtful.

It made her want to back out of the room, to find some privacy, but she forced herself to give him a nod of acknowledgement. Of what, she wasn't quite sure.

Probably that she knew he knew what had happened to her on Ytla had come roaring back today in Freighter Two. He must have sensed how hard the women's trauma had hit her, even though what had happened to her was not even close to what she suspected had been done to them.

It was Bailey's turn to come with them to conduct the search, and as soon as Ed was out of his suit and had gotten dressed, they left Hatch happily eating cake as they headed for the runner.

"Which one of the two freighters is more likely to be the one we're looking for? Is one more obvious than the other?" Bailey asked.

Ed was leaning back in his seat, sipping water and taking bites of a piece of cake Wren had cut for him to eat on the way over. He hummed a no, his mouth full.

She thought he looked thinner. She knew walking out on the line was hard, but she was seeing with her own eyes just how hard.

"I didn't have a bad vibe about Freighter Two until I saw the two prisoners chained to the wall," he said. "I just chose it because it was the farthest to the left and I thought we'd work left to right."

"You want to keep to that method, then?" Bailey waved a hand at the freighters.

"Might as well. Whatever they're hiding, given the fact that they tried to leave the line, let's just assume it's bad," Ed said.

Wren hoped it wasn't going to be as bad as Freighter Two. She tried to suppress a shiver. If all it was was extra cargo or drugs, even weapons, she'd be happy.

She'd managed to keep memories of her time on Ytla at bay for a while, but this morning had brought them all rushing back.

"Did they find out where the women were from?" she asked Bailey.

"They were from Lassa." Bailey glanced at her from her place at the runner's controls. "Since Lassa was taken back under Verdant String control, as a vassal planet to Bodivas, some of the population who were forced to work there have stayed on, free to set up businesses or do what they want. But some were so traumatized, they just wanted to leave. It sounds like the captain of Freighter Two offered the women work on his ship, with a promise to let them off at whichever planet they chose, and then drugged them. When they woke up, they were in that room you found."

"And because they're Lassian, they probably didn't have family checking up on them. It's possible no one knew they were missing." Wren knew about that all too well. She had no family—her parents had died in a bombing on Faldine—and the long trips she took for work meant her friends were used to her being away for months at a time. When she'd gone missing on Ytla, only Nanganya SF had known she was gone.

She shivered.

The now-deposed leaders of Lassa, the former breakaway planet, had gone through their people with horrifying regularity, leaving many survivors alone, with no family ties. Wren tapped a fist on her knee. The captain had chosen his victims carefully. Had chosen not to set up a home base for the same reason.

"He organized everything in his life to make him able to do what he did," she said. "His whole business setup was designed to allow him to indulge his fantasy life."

"He's done it before," Ed said with a nod. "No question. They need to see if there've been any bodies found along his route that could be his former victims."

Wren shivered. She remembered jerking awake at every noise in the small shack the Har Met Vent had locked her in. She had been imprisoned in that room, but not shackled.

They hadn't thought it necessary, as they didn't think she could get far, even if she managed to escape and run. As it was, she'd only gotten out because the storm that had swept over them had ripped the flimsy roof off her prison, and she had managed to climb out.

She looked up, saw Ed watching her.

Her nanos soothed her, but she had made a deal with them early on not to soothe her too much. She had a feeling that suppressing the feelings of fear and helplessness she felt when thinking of her time in captivity would only make it harder in the long run.

Her nanos must have agreed, because they did not intervene as much as they could.

"You all right?" Ed asked.

She gave a nod and a fake smile. "Fine."

He didn't believe her, but he inclined his head, giving her privacy.

"Coming up on Freighter Four," Bailey announced.

Darnell and Fann had not yet entered the freighter, their ships were waiting just outside the bay, so Bailey passed them, going in first and settling in as far forward as she could to allow both ships room to come in behind her.

Both the military and Protection had brought considerably more people this time. Teams of six, it looked like to Wren.

They all looked a lot more alert than they had last time, too.

Ed was ready to go by the time they stepped out into the bay, and he oriented himself, levering the visor down over his eyes and standing quietly for a few beats.

He walked toward the wall to the left of the doors of the bay. "It's right here." He slapped the wall with a hand. "But I think to get to it we need to go through the bay doors and gain access from the passage."

There were no members of the crew around, and Wren guessed that the military had sequestered them in a room somewhere. Perhaps, unlike last time, there was more than just one officer on board to oversee the ship. The horror of Freighter Two clearly weighed on them all.

There was a tension radiating off everyone—and no one wanted to be unprepared a second time.

Ed walked out of the bay, with everyone following behind him.

"There," he told Bailey, pointing to a lever that looked like part of the fire control system.

She pulled it down, and a panel popped open.

She pushed it aside, and it kept sliding, opening wider and wider.

The hidden cache was a long, narrow space, with lights that flicked on as the panel opened. Weapons were sitting in individual holders all along the wall, their dark metal gleaming in the bright light. They all looked the same, and were all completely foreign to Wren.

"Jarnaks." Captain Darnell breathed the word from behind her.

Wren turned slightly to look at him. "What are they for?"

"For hunting usinian on Faldine." Darnell shook his head. "Jarnaks are completely illegal. Some hunters think they can get away with it because Faldine is so sparsely populated and the Protection Force is spread so thin. Also, since the end of the war, the military has largely withdrawn."

"Things must be busier now that they found those ruins and the downed ancestral ship," Wren said. It had been more than eight years since she'd left Faldine, but she'd put in a request to be part of the artifacts team sent to study the ruins. She thought the fact that she'd spent a lot of time there as a child would work in her favor, but she had a feeling Captain Ferris Harden, the captain of the SF teams in Nanganya, had scuttled that application, or never submitted it in the first place. He wouldn't have wanted her so far out of reach.

Darnell inclined his head. "That's true, but it still leaves a lot of planet, and actually the increase in tourist and academic traffic means the big game hunters can slip in a little easier now. Before, they stood out because there were so few visitors."

"Are we sure this is meant for Faldine?" Captain Fann asked. She was studying the weapons with interest. "I didn't notice Faldine as a stop on the manifest."

"No, but they are going to Arkhor, and Faldine's on the way. My guess is they were planning on meeting someone in Faldine near-space to hand these over to."

"Is this everything?" Wren turned to Ed, hoping desperately the answer was yes. This was by far an easier find than the women.

He was turning in place, sweeping the area slowly and methodically.

"This is it." He lifted the visor.

Wren wasn't sure if she was projecting, but he seemed as relieved as she was.

She exchanged a smile with him, and was taking a step toward him when she was suddenly thrown to the floor.

There was a strange roaring sound, and people were shouting all around her.

Everyone here was trained, and despite their inter-agency rivalry, everyone was trained well.

No one panicked.

"A laser strike," Darnell was saying. He seemed very confident about it. "We're under attack."

"We need to get to Freighter Five." Ed was crawling toward Wren, and when he reached her, he put out a hand to help her to her feet.

As she took it and he hauled her up, the import of what he was saying sunk in. "Freighter Five is the one." It must be. And someone didn't want them reaching it.

"Shit." Bailey had overheard them, and she tapped her ear. "Hatch, make sure someone knows not to let Freighter Five go anywhere."

Something on Bailey's face made Wren reach out to grab her. "What did he say?"

Bailey shook her head. "Nothing. The comms are dead."

"Ours, too." Violet Fann made a sound of frustration. "You think this laser fire is coming from Freighter Five?" she asked Ed.

Another shudder ran through the ship. Wren slammed back against the wall but managed to keep her feet this time. Ed turned to her, hand out, but she shook her head. "Focus on keeping yourself and the scanner safe, not me. That's what they're trying to destroy."

She needed to break him of the habit of always thinking of her first.

She was sorry her nanos had imbedded that in him, and she felt a jolt of guilt at every indication of it.

The whole ship shuddered again, but not the way it had when it was under fire. This felt more like it was grinding against another object.

Darnell and Fann exchanged a look and then ran to the bay.

Everyone else followed, and Wren stumbled to a halt when she saw the bay was blocked from the outside by the dark metal of a massive ship.

"They're shielding us," Ed said, and Wren could hear the surprise in his voice. "Something is stopping them from returning fire, so they're using themselves as a shield."

The battleship shifted, just a little, and a tiny one-person pod slipped through the space it made, and landed in the bay.

Darnell was beside it in a moment, and the woman who got out spoke to him in low, urgent tones, then handed him something, got back in, and flew out.

"Direct comms," Darnell said, waggling what turned out to be a comms device. "They can't return fire, because the ship that's shooting is doing it between the freighters in the line. It keeps moving, too fast to track until after it shoots again."

"We've seen this before," Ed murmured.

Darnell looked over at him and gave a nod. "On Cepi, on Parn, and on the breakaway planets. Possibly on Faldine and Fynian, too."

"Rogue former Core Company owners?" Violet Fann asked. "I heard something about a fast cruiser that was hard to track."

Darnell gave a nod. "They got some of the tech from the Caruso." He shook his head. "We would love to get hold of one but every time one has been close to our grasp, it gets away or it's destroyed."

"Can we ask the battleship to shield us all the way over to Freighter Five?" Ed asked.

"Freighter Five is nothing but a field of debris." Darnell's words brought silence to the whole group.

"Shit," Bailey said. "They would rather destroy their own people and ship than let us have a look at what they're smuggling in."

"I don't know about you," Violet Fann said, "but that doesn't give me a good feeling. At all."

20

———————

HATCH WAS WAITING FOR THEM AS THEY DOCKED AT THE OBSERVATORY.

Ed liked the young officer. He was straightforward, and he seemed to have gotten over his unhappiness at Ed for punching Ethan Hyt.

He opened the door for them, forming a welcome party unlike they'd gotten on the station so far.

"It was amazing to see," he told them as they walked back to the control room. "Incredible." He waved his hands.

"Did you see where the laser fire was coming from?" Bailey asked.

Hatch shook his head as he swiped his finger through the laslock into the control room. "Somewhere behind the freighter queue, moving back and forth, so it was impossible to guess where the next shot was going to come from." He stepped in, half-turning to them as he spoke.

"We were worried when we couldn't get you—" Bailey stopped talking, and started to reverse.

Wren was about to protest. Bailey's sudden halt forced Ed to stop abruptly and Wren ran into the back of him. Her words died as she felt the nudge of a laz on the nape of her neck.

"Keep moving forward, people." Banks's voice had a slight tremble to it.

Wren finally had a view of the control room, and there was Juller, a laz pointed toward them, standing by the control panel. Banks was herding them in from behind.

Ed turned back to look at her, and she flicked her gaze to the scanner, which he was carrying under his arm.

This was bad.

"Quite a blow to your side, losing all those weapons," Ed said. "And by your own hand, too. Not to mention the crew."

"Not by my hand, Ed." Banks had moved past her and was standing with his body angled to keep them all in view. He looked over at Ed, mouth twisted in a snarl. "I didn't aim and fire, and I wouldn't have, if it were my call."

"But it's not your call, is it?" Ed said. "Just like last time, you're the lackey who takes the fall when it's all over."

Banks made an explosive sound at that, and Wren realized Ed had scored a direct hit.

Banks knew he was being used, and he didn't like it.

"What have they got on you?" Hatch asked.

Banks gave a quick shake of his head, but not because he was denying they had something on him, Wren decided, but because he didn't want to go into it.

"Where's your little ray of sunshine?" she asked him, because Trish was nowhere in sight.

Banks glanced at her, but it was a dismissive flick of his gaze. She was the non-combat team member who made cakes in her spare time. He wasn't worried about her at all.

"I've never seen one of these," Juller said, speaking for the first time as he lifted the crawler catcher. "They're effective."

"More SF toys no one else gets," Banks said, bitterness dripping from every word.

"Did you try to join the SF?" Ed said it as if it had suddenly occurred to him. "And they wouldn't let you in because of what happened when I left." He said the last bit slowly, as if things were finally making sense. "I'd have thought your masters would have preferred you to stay up here, keeping watch. Are you sure it wasn't their interference that didn't get you the job?"

"I didn't try to join the SF." Banks shook his head. "But when I ask for equipment, I have to practically beg. Then you lot prance about up here, dripping gadgets I've never even seen. It rubs me the wrong way."

"No, they wouldn't have let you join, would they? They've already got enough moles and spies in the SF, and they needed you up here."

Banks glared at him. "Well, they did."

"And who, exactly, are they?" Bailey asked, voice cool.

"We're not here to answer your questions," Juller said. "We're here for the scanner."

"What good will it do you?" Ed asked. "It only works for me."

"We don't need it to work," Juller said. "We need it to not work."

"Freighter Five is destroyed, but you're still worried about the Guan scanner. So that means there is more to find," Ed said. "Good to know."

"You won't know it for long." Banks's words were angry, but as soon as the words were out he looked unhappy he'd allowed Ed to goad him into saying it.

"Bragging about how we'll be dead, and it won't matter what we know?" Wren asked, sure she was right about his moral distaste for what was planned for them.

He flicked her a look, and she saw both fear and defiance in his eyes.

He didn't like being associated with their death, but he'd do nothing to stop it.

She stepped forward, bringing herself closer to Banks, and then leapt at him, swinging her arm so her palm came down on the nape of his neck.

He stumbled forward, and as he did, Juller shot at her, but she didn't need the silver shield her nanos had used at the docks on Demeter, she slid behind Banks and the laz strike hit him full in the chest as he went down.

Hatch took the initiative when Juller turned the laz in her direction and a second after Juller got off his shot, Hatch had him in a headlock and Bailey had him disarmed.

"I feel like I'm just a pretty face," Ed said, still standing exactly where he had been, with the Guan scanner under his arm.

Wren flashed him a grin. "I wasn't going to say anything, but..."

He laughed.

"Good work, Wren." Bailey adjusted the setting on her laz and shot Juller in the chest, and he stopped struggling against Hatch and went limp.

Hatch lowered him to the ground and began restraining him. "Yes. That was just the distraction we needed."

They thought the laz hit from Juller had taken Banks down, she realized. They didn't know he was about to collapse anyway.

It was an excellent outcome.

"I do what I can."

Bailey restrained Banks and then they laid both men against the wall.

"So," Bailey lifted her hands. "Trish. What are we thinking?"

"She's obnoxious and unhelpful, so whether she's involved or not, I wouldn't count on her talking, either way." Wren couldn't see how she wasn't involved, though.

"Agreed. Though chances are high she's in this up to her neck." Ed set the scanner down on the table. "Let's contact headquarters and let them know what's going on."

Hatch went to the control panel, tapped something, and then drew in a deep breath. "While they were waiting for us in here, they cut us off. Comms are down."

"Comms are down on the whole station, or just from here?" Ed asked.

"That's a good question." Hatch turned away from the control panel and checked the setting on his laz. "Want to go find out?"

21

———

NERVOUS AT HOW CLOSE THEY'D COME TO LOSING THE SCANNER, ED made the decision to lock it safely away in their runner before they did anything else.

Hatch came with him to watch his back, and held the crawler killer out to make sure they weren't followed by anything mechanical, either, but the short corridor between the control room and the docking station was empty, and they were gone less than ten minutes.

"Good to go," Hatch said as they reentered the control room. "No more crawlers. Makes me think we either got them all, or Banks called them off because he thought we were under control." He glanced across at their two prisoners, both of whom were coming out of their unconscious state.

"Let's be cautious anyway," Bailey said. "No sense letting our guard down while we're ahead."

Hatch gave a scary smile at that. "I like being ahead."

Ed did, too.

He gave a tiny nod of approval when Bailey and Hatch kept Wren in the middle of the group as they headed for the canteen. When they stepped in, they found Cora and Laschka, who were sitting on the comfortable couches in the lounge area, sipping jah.

They moved like the military unit they were, and Laschka, at least, picked that up.

"What's wrong?" she asked.

"Banks and Juller attacked us," Ed told her. "We're clearing the station of threats."

Laschka lifted both hands and wiggled her fingers. "No threat here."

He didn't believe that. At all.

He flicked his gaze to the comms unit and Bailey moved over to it and tried to patch in.

With luck, Banks had disabled the comms in the control room to stop them reaching headquarters, but he wouldn't want the whole obs station out of the loop.

Bailey evidently got through, because she spoke for a minute in low tones to someone, then stepped back.

"Protection is on their way," she said.

"You weren't joking?" Cora blinked at them. Her initial lack of reaction had stirred Ed's suspicions, but now he wondered if she was really just that oblivious.

"What's happened to Banks and Juller?" Laschka asked.

"They're safe where we put them," Ed said. "Ready for Protection to scoop them up."

"And Trish?" Cora asked.

"Have you seen her?" Wren's tone with Cora was friendly, and Ed realized she must have spent some time chatting to Laschka's assistant.

"In that big room they use for repairing the equipment," Cora said. "She was there when we walked over to the canteen."

"Thanks." Bailey took point again, standing by the door.

"What about us?" Laschka asked.

"Stay here, out of the way, and you're good," Ed said.

She stared at him for a moment, tipping her head back a little to meet his eyes. "That's not completely true, now is it?"

"I can't help you with whatever you've got yourself involved with,"

Ed told her. "But whatever you've done, physically attacking us will just make things worse."

Cora looked over at Laschka, as if finally understanding there was a lot more going on here than she realized, and the look Laschka sent her back was pitying.

Laschka raised her hands again. "I never do anything that might break a nail," she said. "You're safe from me."

Again, Ed didn't believe it for a moment, but he jerked his head at Bailey to keep going, and they left without another word.

The corridor was silent, but there was definitely someone in the work room. Bailey and Hatch flowed through the door, timing and movements fluid and confident.

"Did you—?" Trish was working on something, but she broke off when she looked up and saw who had come through the entrance.

"Did they get us?" Bailey asked. "No."

Trish dropped what she was holding and reached back to grab something at her lower back.

Bailey shot her with her laz.

She collapsed, falling sideways and disappearing from view.

Ed walked over, saw it was indeed a laz Trish had been going for.

"Almost too easy," Hatch said, and Ed could hear the nerves in his voice.

He agreed. "Yes."

"Shooting a freighter is one thing, shooting the obs station is another entirely." Wren said almost exactly what he had been thinking. "But these people haven't seemed to be afraid to go big."

"You think capturing us was just something they gave Banks and his friends to do, to make them think they were useful?" Bailey's voice was soft with awe.

"If they were freaking out after the freighter was shot, maybe," Ed said. "It would certainly help keep them quiet and give them no time to consider selling their masters out."

"Wait a minute. You think they're going to shoot the *obs station*?" Hatch held his laz out to his side.

"Any minute." Ed lifted Trish up, hefted her over his shoulder. "Let's get everyone off."

"Why don't I contact Protection and tell them to back away while you load Banks and Juller into our runner," Wren said. "We don't want Violet to put herself and her team in the firing line."

"What about the scientific team?" Hatch asked.

"They have their own runner. I'll make sure they know they have to leave." Wren's gaze caught his, and she gave a nod. "I'll be right behind you."

Ed didn't like it, but they didn't have a choice. He really believed they were right. The obs station could come under attack at any moment. He jogged out of the room, holding Trish behind her knees.

Bailey and Hatch followed him, heading for the control room to grab the other two members of the maintenance team.

He was aware of Wren behind him, running to the canteen, and he caught the sound of her urging Lashka and Cora to get their colleagues and go as he turned the corner.

It took the others five minutes to get Banks and Juller into the runner, so all three maintenance workers were laid out in a line.

Banks was awake and aware, and he lifted his head. "What's happening?"

"We think your friends might have the same plan for the obs station as they did for the freighter." Ed glanced at him and saw the real fear in his eyes.

Banks didn't claim there was no way that would happen.

He knew who he was involved with.

"Where's Wren?" Bailey was sitting at the runner's controls, and she was fidgeting. "I don't like that she's still in the station."

Ed didn't either. He took out his comms unit. "I'll go get her—"

The words were barely out of his mouth with the whole station shuddered.

"We're hit." Bailey touched the panel in front of her and he felt them break free of the coupling.

The runner dropped down, going under the station, Bailey using the only cover they had, although the hit had caused major damage to the orbital, and bits were falling off. She had to dodge around the debris.

"Wren!" Ed shouted her name into his comms unit.

"I'm alright." The whisper she sent back did not reassure him. "I'm trying to get to the scientific team's runner—"

The obs station took another hit, and the comm cut off.

"We've lost signal." Bailey kept moving under the station, headed, Ed was relieved to see, toward the runner coupled to the station on the opposite side to their own.

He would have been forced to take the controls if she hadn't.

"How are we going to get her out?" Hatch asked, expression tense as he looked out of the narrow window at the debris floating past them.

"Any way we can," Ed said. "Any way we can."

22

———————

Wren crouched in a darkened corridor near the canteen, listening for any movement that would signal an attack from members of the academic research team.

She couldn't go back the way she'd come—the corridor leading to the SF runner and her room was blocked by a large portion of the ceiling, which had fallen when the station had been hit. She didn't feel safe to go forward, either, as Jens Ludlow had attacked her when she'd gone back to warn Cora and Laschka, and while she'd dealt with him, she didn't exactly trust the rest of his colleagues.

His attack on her hadn't shocked Lashka, Wren had noticed as she'd stepped to the side to avoid his fist, but Cora had stared at the head of the academic team with utter horror as he'd thrown his punch.

Wren didn't need to use force to bring her opponents down, but she had the sense it was more believable as a method if she chopped down on Ludlow's neck with the blade of her hand than if she touched him with her fingertips.

As he fell, she looked down at him, then back up at the two women. "It seems our suspicions about your project were spot on," she said to Lashka.

"So the delightful Ed has already intimated." Lashka grimaced as she stared at her colleague. "This is most annoying and will likely stain my reputation. How can I improve the outcome?"

"What's going on?" Cora asked, her gaze fixed on her boss.

"All you need to know is that someone is going to try and destroy this obs station with all of us in it. Get your people, drag Ludlow with you, and get off this orbital. Everything else can be worked out later."

Lashka gave a resigned nod, and grabbed one of Ludlow's arms. "Take the other one, Cora."

Wren left them to it, aware she'd been gone longer than she'd planned.

She'd been jogging down the corridor when she was thrown against the wall. The sound of alarms and the smell of burning had engulfed her, and she lay, dazed, until Ed's shout in her ear piece revived her.

She forced herself to her feet and that's when she realized the way was blocked. There was really no choice but to head toward the academic team's runner, danger of attack or no, and when she could hear no other signs of life, she began to move.

She glanced quickly into the canteen, but it was empty, although she didn't think Cora and Lashka could have gotten too far, especially if they were still dragging Ludlow.

The air was thick with smoke, and before she could lift her shirt to cover her mouth and nose as a filter, she felt the tickle of her nanos as they covered her lower face. It was suddenly a lot easier to breathe again.

Her boot hit something soft, and she saw it was Ludlow himself, abandoned in the passageway.

Leave him, her nanos told her.

He'll have useful information, she told them back.

They accepted that, and she grabbed the back of his shirt and kept going, dragging him behind her.

The whole station trembled again under another hit and Wren fell to her knees.

Is the information he has worth your life? the nanos asked her.

Cora appeared out of the smoke, stumbling toward her, blood dripping from a cut across her forehead.

The tickle over her lips told Wren her nanos had sunk back out of sight and she started to cough.

"Wren, I thought you'd already gone."

Wren shook her head, eyes watering as she straightened up. "No, the way to my runner was blocked. Why are you coming back this way?"

"I got turned around. Lashka is dead. A piece of ceiling fell on her and crushed her." Tears welled in her eyes and spilled down her cheeks. "I haven't seen Garner or Kailis, the other two in our group, since this started." She glanced down at Ludlow. "You're trying to rescue him?"

"I found him in the corridor, didn't think I could leave him," Wren said. "Will you help me drag him to the runner bay on your side?"

Cora gave a nod, and Wren flipped Ludlow over, grabbing one of his hands. Cora held the other and they pulled him along behind them.

Better, her nanos said. *Faster*.

There was no sign of anyone else anywhere along the route to the runner. When they got there, it was clear there would be no safe exit for them, though.

"The runner is . . . gone." Cora peered through the small porthole set in the air lock door, and then moved aside for Wren to get a look.

The runner was more than just gone. It was a tiny debris field all on its own.

As she stared at it, another runner rose up from beneath the obs station, and she inhaled sharply. Her team.

"Your friends?" Cora asked, catching sight of the small craft. Her voice was full of relief.

"Yes. Hopefully they can get us off of here." She waved, and the runner edged closer, looking for a place to dock.

"What's wrong?" Cora tried to look over her shoulder.

"I think the docking equipment was destroyed along with the runner."

Bailey got close enough that the runner ground against the station with a shriek of metal, and then she was forced to pull back.

Wren eyed the air lock. They would have to walk the line. And to do that, they'd need air masks at the very least, but preferably suits.

She moved to a door set in the side wall, opening it up, and found there was a small change room that contained hooks for three suits, but only one was left.

She looked at the empty spaces for a beat and then glanced over her shoulder. "I think I know what happened to Garner and Kailis," she said.

Cora stared into the space. "Bastards," she breathed. "They left us." She looked from the suit, to Wren, to Ludlow, lying on the floor, and bit her lip.

"You get in the suit," Wren told her. "I'll look for air masks for myself and Ludlow."

She didn't wait for an answer. Time wasn't on their side.

There was nothing inside the small change room other than the single suit, so she ran out of the bay and down the corridor, looking for any hint of a cupboard or room which might have masks and other equipment.

She had just entered a small control room when the world went strangely silent, and then she felt a whump in her very bones.

She was thrown upward, spinning as she went, and suddenly she noticed there were thick, silver bracelets on her wrists, and something crawled over her forehead, like a band.

She reached up to touch it, and felt the smooth, cold slide of metal. She blinked, lifting her arms to get a better look at the cuffs that had appeared on them, and then something hit her, hard, and she spun.

The obs station was below her. She looked at it in surprise, trying to work out what was going on.

And then, as if a cosmic hand reached out and yanked her back to reality, she sucked in a terrified breath, and spreadeagled her arms and legs.

They had been hit again, and she wasn't walking the line. She was out in space with no tether whatsoever.

How?

Save your breath, her nanos said. *There is only so much air we were able to trap in with you.*

She looked down at herself, and saw she was covered in a filmy, body-hugging suit. *You?* she asked.

Us, her nanos agreed. *We are stretched to our limit.*

She saw something floating lazily below her, and the shape of it had her turning her head sharply to focus on it.

Ludlow, skin coated in ice crystals, spun slowly past her.

The others? she asked.

She was starting to feel lightheaded. Breathing was harder, and she looked around for any sign of the runner.

Dread gripped her at the thought of it being ripped apart like the bay had been.

Behind you, her nanos said, and she could hear satisfaction in their tone.

She tried to spin around, finding it difficult with nothing to leverage against, and then arms came around her.

She felt a tingle as the nanos covering her face retreated, and a mask was fitted over her head.

She was turned, but before she saw who was behind her, she knew it was Ed. He was holding her gently, his big body taking up her entire view, and he drew her up to his chest, his arms around her back and under her knees.

His lips moved, and she guessed he was talking to Bailey or Hatch, because they suddenly began moving backward, pulled on the line.

The nanos held in place over her skin until just before the air lock hatch opened, and as Ed drew her in, they sank into her body, leaving her shivering with cold in the icy chamber.

"You're still wearing your crown," Ed told her, and the band around her head melted into her, too.

"Is Cora alive?" she managed to croak out.

"Don't know." His gaze went to her wrist and she saw one cuff remained.

A thin probe rose up out of it, a slender, silver stem. It bent toward him.

Ed watched it. "Unnecessary," he said.

Wren frowned, trying to work out what he meant. The silver stalk dipped down, as if giving a nod, and fell back into the wrist brace, then the whole thing disappeared into her skin.

A signal sounded, and the moment it did she could hear someone spinning open the air lock.

Ed carried her into the small runner, and she shuddered at the warmth.

"Your lips are blue," Hatch said. He was holding a blanket, and he tucked it around her while she was still in Ed's arms. He put her down on the bench, stripped out of the thin emergency space suit he was wearing, and then hauled her back into his lap, so she could feel the heat of his body.

She forced herself to move her head closer to his ear. "What was unnecessary?" She kept her voice a whisper.

"Don't worry about it," he murmured back.

She looked up, saw Hatch was staring at her.

"How did you survive that?" he asked, and he sounded freaked out.

"There was only one suit left for walking the line," she said. "Garner and Kailis, from the academic team, were gone. Cora said they'd disappeared, and as two of the suits were missing, they might be floating out here. I told Cora to take the last suit, and I was out of the bay, looking for masks for myself and Ludlow, so we could all get to you. That's why I survived. I wasn't in the bay when it was hit." She looked up at Ed. "If she got into the suit in time, she might be alive."

"We're scanning for all signs of life," Hatch said. "What happened to Ludlow and Lashka?"

"Ludlow was unconscious." She decided not to say who had made him unconscious. "Cora told me Lashka was dead. Part of the ceiling fell on her." She shook her head. "Ludlow was in the bay with Cora. We dragged him there with us."

Someone made a noise, and she turned her head, saw Banks, Juller, and Trish laid out together, restrained but awake.

"Got something to say, traitor?" Bailey's words were cold, and she was looking at Banks. "Other than thank you to us for saving your behinds."

Wren angled in Ed's lap so she could see her, sitting in the pilot's chair. She looked hard and sharp.

"You haven't saved us for long," Trish spat. "We're dead as soon as we're anywhere 'official'."

"Boohoo." Bailey's eyes glittered as she moved her gaze to Trish. "You chose your path. Did you like how your masters gave you the busywork job to imprison us while they set up their shot to take down the whole observatory?"

Trish looked away, and Juller closed his eyes in impotent fury, but Banks turned to look at Bailey. "You don't know what you're talking about."

"Really? Enlighten me." She turned fully in her chair to face them.

But then Banks turned away like Trish and with a snort of derision, Bailey turned back to the controls.

"Didn't think so," she muttered. "Didn't fucking think so."

23

HE HAD HER, SAFE AND RIGHT IN HIS ARMS.

Ed suppressed a shudder at the memory of when he'd seen her floating in the debris of the station, and for a moment . . .

But her nanos had done their job, and he would put up with a lot from them for it.

"Ed." Bailey glanced at him over her shoulder. "It's Violet Fann."

Ed reluctantly set Wren down on the bench and settled in next to Bailey at the controls. "Captain Fann."

"You and your team alright, Zeneri?" Violet Fann sounded concerned.

"We're all alive. So is the maintenance crew, who we have in custody, but the whole of the academic team is either dead or missing. We have reason to believe Dr. Lashka Garde is dead, and her body is in the station. I saw Professor Jens Ludlow's body with my own eyes. He's floating in the debris near our current position. One of the research assistants, Cora, may or may not be alive, and Dr. Garner and his research assistant, last name Kailis, are missing, possibly alive in full suits, floating near the station."

"The maintenance crew is in custody?" Violet Fann sounded

bemused. "Wren said something about them when she told me the station might be under attack but I don't understand."

"We take a dim view of people who hold weapons on us and try to restrain us." Ed left it at that. There were no doubt ears listening in.

"Right." She let the word hang, then carried on. "The battleships are doing a full life scan sweep, and they'll scoop up whoever they find, so you can head back to Demeter."

"Will do." Ed stood. "Let's get back to headquarters."

He felt Bailey and Hatch's relief at his order, and caught the opposite on Banks's face. The head of maintenance was more than a little unhappy with being brought in.

"Who are you afraid of?" he asked. "Protection, the SF teams, the Department of Defense? Where do you think the group you work for is likely to have their plants?"

"Everywhere." Trish was the one who answered.

"Everywhere?" Hatch stretched out his legs as Bailey dropped them through the atmosphere. "That just can't be true. I'll allow they could have a few plants, promising I don't know what, or black-mailing their marks, but I just don't believe they are as all powerful as you think. They've played a mind trick on you all."

No one had any more to say about that, although Ed mulled it over as they plunged through the sky toward Demeter.

He agreed with Hatch. The chance of corruption and betrayal was almost non-existent in the Verdant String. Everyone had to take a turn at working in the government—public service duty was compulsory unless you joined the military or the Protection Unit. It was three years of your life, although if you liked it, you could stay for five. You could choose an area that aligned with your education, and while you could defer your service for a while if it didn't suit you when your time was called, no one got away with not doing it.

It kept people from forming corrupt power structures and it meant there was little chance of people cooperating in a corrupt endeavor, because of the short tenure of their stay. Chances were people with corrupt intentions would be hard-pressed to find someone of like mind, and the penalties were swift and severe.

That wasn't to say it didn't ever happen, but it was rare.

For this shadowy criminal organization operating out of the former breakaway planets to have seeded a vast number of cronies through the many arms of government on Aponi not only stretched credulity, it just didn't seem logistically possible.

Which probably meant the people they did have in place had enough reach to pretend there were more of them than there really were.

Which meant they were high up on the chain.

Ed didn't like it.

He'd been played before, and he was just beginning to see it was probably by the same people.

He heard Bailey talking in a low voice to ground control, and then the higher rev of the engines as she settled the runner lightly onto its landing pad.

A Protection Unit was waiting for them, as well as an SF team out of Ethan Hyt's office.

"Know them?" he asked Hatch, who checked the feed and gave a nod.

"They're good."

"We hope." Bailey sounded tired and strained, and she and Hatch shared a look, as if they'd been talking among themselves and he'd missed it. They probably had, while he was out walking the line to grab Wren.

The door opened, and they handed the three maintenance crew over, walking them across the landing pad to where the Protection and SF units were waiting in front of a large hover.

Ed stepped up to the Protection unit officer and tilted his head at the prisoners. "They claim they're in danger of being killed in custody, and that's not completely out of the realm of possibility, so if I were you, I'd watch them, and whoever comes in to see them, very closely. Even if those visitors have been cleared. Even if they work in your unit."

The woman gave him a look he couldn't quite interpret. She straightened her uniform, mouth pursed. "Noted."

"Just so you're aware, my team and I are recording this hand-over for our files." He wondered if that was a tightening of the skin in the corner of her eyes. "There will be no denying I didn't warn you later." He had a bad feeling about things, now that Banks, Juller and Trish were being settled into the hover. Like they were spot on in their assessment of their chances of living.

He studied the PU officer carefully, and she hunched a shoulder and glared at him. "Understood."

"We'll be escorting the hover to the Department of Defense," the SF teams leader said, his voice cheerful in the face of the clear tension between Ed and the Protection Unit officer. "Hatch has filled me in, we know they're targets."

The SF team stepped away from the hover for a moment, leaving the prisoners under the watchful eye of the Protection team, to have a quiet talk with Bailey and Hatch.

Ed started back to the runner, headed toward Wren, who was standing at the bottom of the stairs watching the proceedings with interest. He needed to get his scanner and his and Wren's bags, and then they could finally catch up with Ethan Hyt.

Just before he reached her, a strange sizzling sound filled the air. Ed was watching Wren as the air seemed to boil overhead, and she *moved*, reaching out to grab him with a strength he hadn't realized she had, and taking him with her as she dived beneath the runner.

The world exploded around them.

He felt a wave of secondhand heat, but there was a barrier between him, Wren and the wall of laz fire. He looked back at a distorted image of himself, as a thin, mirror-like shield wrapped around them.

The Protection Unit hover exploded, and the debris flew up and came crashing all around, burning as it fell.

A moment of silence came and went and then the shield was gone and it was just him and Wren, tight up against each other, lying in the shelter of the runner.

Ed raised his head to look at the chaos, and saw one of the Protection team looking at them, eyes wide.

"Bailey and Hatch," Wren murmured into his neck, and he could feel the racing of her heart.

He pulled her up with him and then levered into a crouch, trying to find the Protection Unit member again.

"They're down." Wren had also risen to a crouch, and she ran, bent double, out into the open, heading for where their friends lay, surrounded by burning debris.

Ed followed behind her, looking upward for any sign of the ship that had hit them from above, and then sweeping his gaze around the wreckage.

The Protection Unit officer who'd been watching them was tending to a colleague lying on the ground. Had he seen the silver shield? Ed had a horrible suspicion that he had.

Ed headed toward him, sidestepping a piece of the hover, and came to an abrupt halt at the sight of Banks, lying face down and dead.

The maintenance chief had called his own death correctly.

But the manner it had been accomplished . . . Ed couldn't help but see this attack as an act of desperation.

Only people with a massive secret to hide would take the chances these people took.

And he was as determined as ever to find out what that secret was, or he and Wren would never be safe.

24

————

WREN LOOKED THROUGH THE BACK DOORS INTO THE MEDICAL HOVER where Bailey and Hatch lay, watching them being strapped down onto stretchers.

"Look after them," she said to the SF officer standing beside her.

The officer gave a jerky nod, his eyes full of worry and questions. "Captain Hyt will want to see you." He glanced over at Ed, and Wren wondered if he was thinking of how Ed had fought Hyt, just like Hatch had, the first time they'd met. "He's on his way back from Nanganya right now. He should be landing in a few hours."

"We know. We'll find him." Ed sounded sincere, but Wren wondered if he was lying.

She wondered what his plan was, because he definitely had one.

He had gone to fetch her bag as well as his own—along with the Guan scanner—climbing into their damaged runner to get them. He hefted them over a broad shoulder.

The officer nodded and then jumped into the back of the hover and it raced away.

"The medic said they'll both live." Wren couldn't keep the wobble of relief out of her voice. "The head of the Protection Unit's condition is more touch and go."

Two of the Protection team were dead, and one was lightly injured. Wren thought the Protection unit man who had survived had stared at her strangely when she was crouched over Bailey and Hatch's unconscious bodies. The way he'd studied her had bothered her, although he had left for the hospital shortly afterward to have his cuts and scrapes dealt with. Maybe he was staring at her because, like Ed, she had come away without so much as a scratch.

"Let's go." Ed began walking at a fast clip and Wren caught up to him. There was not even a question in her mind that whatever they were doing, they were doing it together.

Ed held out his free hand and she took it as he broke into a jog.

"What's the rush?" she asked.

"We don't want to be here when the Protection Unit sends an investigative team."

She hadn't thought of that, but she agreed. They were targets now, and no one was safe around them. And they couldn't trust anyone in authority, either.

"Do you think they shot from space because they didn't have anyone who could get to Banks and the others in prison?" That was actually a comforting thought. They didn't have the reach they made Banks and Trish believe they had.

"Either that," Ed said, "or they didn't want to expose their mole just yet."

The relief she'd felt vanished, replaced by a ball of fear in her gut. "That's . . . not good," she said. "Because it means . . ."

"It means they aren't done, and they need their mole for something in the future. Something bigger than snipping off a few loose ends." Ed slowed as they reached the hover port building. "And if I was going to guess the identity of at least one of their plants, it's that Protection Unit officer who was lightly injured."

Wren pulled on his hand to slow him even further. "You think he's involved?"

"He kept far enough back that he wasn't seriously injured in the strike, and he was watching us. I think he saw the silver shield your nanos used to protect us." Ed took them down the side of the port building, along a walkway, and then they joined the steady stream of people coming and going from the transport hub.

"Maybe he saw the shield, couldn't work out what it was, and that's why he was acting suspiciously. It doesn't necessarily mean he's caught up in this."

Ed shook his head. "I'd be prepared to accept that, if he'd come over and asked us. He didn't stop staring at either you or I once after we came out from under the runner. Then he pretended to go to hospital."

"Pretended?" Wren realized she had lost sight of the man when the medical hover arrived.

"He didn't seek medical help when the hover arrived. Instead he walked off the same way we have, around the side of the building." Ed was talking softly to keep their conversation private, and she moved closer to him.

He let go of her hand and looped his arm over her shoulder, tucking her in close. "You know, it occurs to me this is where we first met."

"Are we pretending to be a couple again?" she asked him.

"No. We're not pretending."

She thought about it, happy to stay where she was against his side.

"You're saying the constant shoot-outs, laser strikes and deep space rescue has done your wooing for you?" she asked.

He snorted out a laugh. "Maybe I am."

"You're sure this isn't ..." she wet her lips, "my nanos talking?"

"I'm sure."

He *did* sound very sure, but then her nanos were top grade tech.

We are not influencing him, they told her.

Except, they had before, and who knew how long it took to shake something like that off. And as Ed said, this *was* the place they'd done it. The place they'd met.

"Wren." Ed pulled her out of the stream of pedestrians into a small laneway that ran between two buildings. Someone's back gate opened out onto the lane and they had grown a climbing plant up it, its tiny yellow flowers releasing a sweet perfume into the air. His tone when he said her name was exasperated. "I am speaking for myself."

She looked up at him, into eyes that were dark and steady.

She had the feeling he would carry her until he dropped. He had already proven he would throw himself in front of laz fire for her. Walk out on the line in a deep space debris field to grab her.

He had her back.

She didn't know of anything sexier than that. Although his broad-shouldered, long-legged frame and blunt, stark features really did it for her, too.

"Then I guess we aren't pretending," she said, and found herself pressed up against the sweet-smelling flowers, being kissed.

She softened in his hold, pressing closer, sliding her hands up his shoulders and behind his head to hold him in place. When she drew back slightly, she felt breathless.

"Aren't we running for our lives?" she asked.

"Sweetheart." He kissed her again, a quick nip of her lips. "We've been running for our lives since we met."

Well. That was actually true.

She went back in for more, but the sound of someone in the courtyard behind them brought them to their senses and they slipped back into the walkway, joining the pedestrians headed for the heart of the city.

"Are we going to see Hyt?" she asked.

"Yes, but we're taking the back door again."

That made sense.

If no one knew where they were, no one could shoot at them from space.

25

Defense Headquarters was wild.

Wren guessed someone shooting at an SF runner at the hover port from space, while two battleships looked on, would do that.

They were in the secret passageway in the Gate, and the offices that had been empty before were now in use. All except Velda Shanïha's. That lay in darkness, so she was obviously not in the building, not just elsewhere in a meeting or out for lunch.

She glanced over at Ed, who was watching a senior administrator in her office, talking on a screen to General Baccal and a battleship captain, who stood respectfully behind him and to his left.

"This makes us look like a joke," the administrator was saying.

"We are aware of the blow to our reputation," General Baccal said, voice stiff. He angled his head to the captain standing behind him. "Captain Goa can tell you how this happened, and why neither she nor Captain Rendra could do anything about the attack."

Captain Goa stepped forward, shoulders rigid. "The ship is similar to one we've seen footage of a few times. At the Cepi disaster, over Parn during the bombings, and as recently as over Fynian a few months ago. It matches the description of a couple of ships that are a collaboration between the executives of the old Core Companies that ruled the breakaway planets of Garmen and Lassa, and the Caruso. They're amazingly fast, they can pinch to the black quicker, and they have a powerful laz cannon. But they also have some tech that makes them incredibly hard to spot.

"They used the freighter line to hide as they shot numerous times at the freighters our teams were inspecting, destroying one completely, then they went quiet for an hour. They then took numerous shots at the observatory station, went back into hiding among the freighter line again, and then finally took a shot at the prisoners an SF team had brought down to the hover port from the obs station, moved extremely quickly to a second point, fired one more time, and then they fled. They got some distance from Aponi, then pinched to the black. It happened in less than two minutes."

The administrator frowned. "Who did they fire on the final time?"

General Baccal shook his head. "We're looking into that right this minute. Somewhere to the north, between Nanganya and Demeter. We'll send through what we have as quickly as possible."

"Not another hover port?" the administrator asked.

Baccal shook his head. "The middle of the mountains. Perhaps they were shooting at a hover, as that's the approach most pilots take to come in to the Demeter hub, but we don't know yet what happened."

"And this ship that managed to sneak past the best battleships we have, it's a collaboration between the Core Companies and the Caruso?" The administrator sounded tired. "When was this first noted?"

"When Arkhor took Garmen back under the auspices of the Verdant String Coalition, followed shortly by Bodivas doing the same for the second breakaway planet run by the Cores, Lassa." The general answered. "Both Arkhor and Bodivas saw the ship or ships, and one was also spotted a few months earlier than that, when a ship matching its description destroyed the ruins on Cepi."

"I wasn't in Defense during that time," the administrator said slowly. "I only heard about the details through public comms, like everyone else." She shook her head. "I must have missed this information in the notes I was handed when I took the job." She waved a hand, suddenly impatient. "Never mind. How likely is it that this ship will return and make another attack?"

"It may try to return," Captain Goa said. "But our systems did a scan of the signals just before they took their shot at the runner at the hover port, and we know what to listen for, now. They won't find it so easy to drift past us and cause trouble again."

"I hope you're right, Captain." The administrator rubbed at her temples. "Because with Velda Shaniha on her way back from Nanganya, I am tasked with informing the public about what happened."

"What are you going to say?" General Baccal asked.

She leaned back in her chair. "I think the truth is all that will suffice right now."

The general gave a nod, and after a moment, the administrator's screen went blank.

Velda Shaniha was in Nanganya.

Wren wondered if she'd gone with Ethan Hyt, or had had to follow him for some reason. It explained the dark office, anyway.

Just as she thought that, a light flickered down the passage, coming from the direction of her office, and surprised, Wren headed there, wondering if Velda had already returned.

They had hoped to speak to her while they waited for Ethan to return from Nanganya, and give a debrief of what they had learned since they'd last seen each other.

Wren came to a stop, and she couldn't help the gasp that escaped her. She didn't think she was loud, but the noise brought Ed jogging over.

They both watched two figures moving through Velda's office, using small lights to illuminate her desk and the stack of drawers to the side.

"When's she due back?" one whispered to the other.

"I was told not for a while, if at all. She was returning from Nanganya with the captain of Demeter Special Forces, and our friends managed to cause some travel issues for them."

"What are we looking for? Her files will be online and secure."

"We're looking for any notes she may have made the day she and Captain Hyt had a meeting with Wren Thorakis and Ed Zeneri. No one saw them come in, but one of our people saw them leave her office, and soon afterward, they were sent up to the observatory. Velda Shanïha would have had to approve that big of a disruption to shipping, but no one can find any files on her system about what led her to agree to it."

The lights played over her desk, but after a few minutes, the two men seeded a few listening devices and then left empty-handed.

After the door closed, Wren waited for a moment, then turned. "The second, mysterious shot. That was them 'causing travel issues' for Velda and Ethan."

"I'm afraid so." He ran a hand along her arm, and his touch in the gloomy darkness was comforting.

"They may be dead." She forced herself to say it.

His lips brushed her forehead. "Ethan Hyt is too stubborn to die. With luck they missed, or their runner is simply down. The general said the military is looking for them, so they'll have help soon. But for now, it looks like we're on our own."

That was okay, she was used to being on her own, and now she had Ed at her back. "I'm a bit tired of having these people do whatever they like." She examined the fury growing inside her, and found both she and her nanos approved.

"I'm with you there." Ed stepped back, set the Guan scanner down on the floor for safekeeping and started walking to the exit. "Let's go stop them."

Sounded like a plan.

26

ED AND WREN FOLLOWED ONE OF THE MEN WHO'D BROKEN INTO VELDA'S office via the secret passage, only stepping out into the open when the passage ended, and they had to risk going into public to keep after him.

The other man had stepped into a large, open plan office and stayed there, but one seemed to be leaving, and Ed was very interested to see where he was going.

If they were going to stop their enemies, they had to find out who they were, first. And like Wren, Ed was tired of reacting and defending.

They had been proactive up at the obs station, scanning the freighters, but whoever they were up against proved yet again they were prepared to take insane risks and be extremely aggressive in order to advance their strategy.

Which made him think they were desperate. This whole thing smacked of a last chance scenario.

Which begged the question, last chance at what?

Everything pointed to this being a plot conceived by the former Core Companies of the breakaway planets. They were adrift now, could call no place home since the VSC had asserted their control of

Garmen and Lassa and were actively seeking the old company directors for a long list of crimes. They'd since tried to interfere on Faldine, and even on Fynian, but both of those were peripheral planets or moons, vassals rather than major VSC planets.

Aponi was a major VSC planet.

But it was also the most remote, and the closest to Caruso, the planet most hostile to the VSC, and who the Core Company executives had definitely made a bargain with before, when they'd held control over Garmen and Lassa.

If they were going to go big, and try to grab a VSC planet, Aponi was the obvious target.

And damned if he would stand for that.

He'd lost his home planet once before. He wasn't going to lose another.

The man they were trailing walked down two flights of stairs and then stepped out onto the mezzanine level, taking the massive escalator down to street level.

He was in a hurry, which made Ed hope he was off to report his findings to his handler.

He only walked a short way down the street, less than a block from the Gate, and then crossed the road and entered a small cafe. Ed took Wren's hand, giving it a happy swing as if they had all the time in the world as they crossed after him, and then slowed to a stop near the entrance.

Wren bent as if to tie her boot lace, and when she straightened she shook her head. "It's too small of a place for us to go in after him. He'll see us."

Ed shifted, had a look himself. He was glad they only had their bags, and he'd left the Guan scanner in the secret passageway. It was unique enough that it would have drawn far too much unwanted attention.

Their quarry was standing at a counter, talking to someone, and then he turned and headed back out.

"I'll watch what happens here, you follow him," Wren murmured as they turned their back and slowly walked away, heads together, as the man ran back across the road.

Ed didn't want to separate, but he accepted this was the logical course of action.

"Meet back at the house," he said, bending to give her a quick, hard kiss, and then he turned and jogged across the road, keeping the man in view.

When he glanced back, almost reflexively, Wren was gone.

She was so far from helpless, he forced himself to focus on what was in front of him, and he came to the decision that it wasn't going to work to let this traitor go back into the office, as it appeared he was planning to do.

That would be more time wasted, more time treading water. More danger of exposure.

This asshole was going to tell Ed what was going on. Right now.

He took a few bigger strides, which got him level to his man, and then he put an arm around him and shoved him into the narrow alley that ran between the Gate and the building next to it.

The man had let out a strange squeak when Ed made his move, and now he looked down at the laz Ed held at his throat and back up with very big eyes.

"You've come to my attention," Ed told him. "Hunting for notes in Velda Shanïha's office and talking about how she's been taken out, along with Ethan Hyt, will do that."

"How . . . ?" he could barely get the word out.

"Velda is a suspicious sort. Do you think she didn't set eyes and ears in her own office before she left?"

The man blinked rapidly, as if suddenly realizing the depth of his trouble. "I was caught on *comms feed*?"

"Oh yes." Ed gave him a slow smile, wishing he really was on comms feed, but making him think he was was almost as satisfying.

"I'm . . . done." He looked around wildly, as if he expected to be murdered any moment.

"Depends what your understanding of done is," Ed told him. "Banks, the head of maintenance on the observatory, was killed by a nearspace laser strike at Demeter's hover port. I think your friends tried to do the same to Velda Shanïha and Ethan Hyt, didn't they? That would be too easy an end for you, in my opinion. Imagining you locked up for the rest of your life will do for me."

"Locked . . ." The man looked like he was going to faint. "I thought . . ." He swallowed. "You think I'm a traitor?"

"I know you are. You're involved in killing Protection Unit officers at the hover port and trying to kill Aponi's head of Defense and Demeter's head of Special Forces. What would you call that?"

He seemed to be having trouble getting his brain to work. "I do them favors, but I haven't personally . . ." He blinked again, sucked in a breath. "I'll make a deal. I'll tell you everything."

Ed jammed the laz a little harder into his throat. "You'll tell me everything anyway."

WREN MOVED into the small cafe, aware her nanos had altered her features very slightly.

Chances were not strong that the man behind the counter would know who she was, but just in case he did, he would hopefully not recognize her.

"Can I get some jah?" she asked, settling onto a stool close to the counter. She hadn't had anything to eat or drink since they'd taken the runner back down to Demeter, and she suddenly realized she was running on empty.

She helped herself to a glass and poured herself some water from a jug, then tapped her code into the payment device the man held out to pay for her jah.

She had been keeping careful watch on him since she'd entered the little cafe, and she guessed she had interfered in his plans, if his look of aggravation was anything to go by.

"We're closing in ten minutes," he told her, voice a little harsh.

"That's fine." She said it with a sunny smile. "You can give me the jah in a takeaway cup. I have to get back to headquarters, anyway."

"You work at the Defense Headquarters?" he asked casually as he ground up the jah and tapped the holder on the side of his jah machine to level it out.

"Yes. I suppose you get a lot of us in and out, you're so close to the building."

He gave a cautious nod. "Did you hear about what happened at the hover port?"

"Just what everyone else has heard, no inside data," she said, keeping her voice light and a little disappointed. "Quite shocking. I'm looking forward to hearing what Velda Shanïha has to say about it."

"Is she going to make an announcement?" he asked, head coming up as he poured her drink into a cup and handed it to her.

"I can't see how she won't," Wren said. "Everyone needs to know what's going on."

"I had heard from some of the other staff that she was in Nanganya." He said it carefully.

She took the cup and started walking backward toward the door. "Even if she's in Nanganya, she can still make an announcement." She said it as if she thought he wasn't very bright. "She's Head of Defense for the whole of Aponi."

She let the door close behind her, then stood on the pavement, as if to wait for the traffic to clear, and heard him come up behind her, close the door and lock it.

When she glanced back, he'd set the sign to Closed and was walking to the back. She watched him disappear into the back room, and as soon as he was gone she walked casually down the street, looking for a good place to wait without being seen.

She found a large pot full of thriving plants, and sat on the little box beside it. The spot kept her out of sight, but she would see him when he exited the alleyway.

She had barely settled in when he passed by. He didn't so much as glance in her direction.

She got to her feet and walked after him, keeping well back, sipping on her jah, impressed with how good it tasted. She hoped he didn't do anything that would necessitate her having to run and spill it.

He kept a steady, fast pace, though—head down, shoulders hunched.

None of these people looked happy with their betrayals, she realized. Everyone so far had seemed deeply conflicted.

Whatever they were part of, they didn't like it.

Which made her wonder why they were cooperating. If it was similar to the freighter captain they'd caught, then it was blackmail. Which would explain the deep unhappiness, she supposed.

The special forces soldiers who'd transferred down from Nanganya and had attacked them at Ethan Hyt's apartment behaved as if they had actually bought into the plot, but they were the only ones so far.

The man was heading in the direction of the hover port, but before he reached the main intersection he turned off to the right, and Wren found herself in a long street with warehouses on either side—storage for the goods being traded on and off planet.

She felt a sudden surge in anticipation. Could they be headed to the warehouse that was storing whatever it was their enemies were trying so desperately to hide?

Up ahead, she noticed a few boxes stacked almost in a staircase up the side of a building the cafe owner had just passed, and her nanos urged her to use them to get up onto the roof and follow her quarry from above.

It was a good point.

If the cafe owner looked back now, she was the only person he'd see. They were alone on the street and she guessed the laser strike at the hover port had closed things down for the day.

She accelerated, running silently toward the boxes and then leaping up. Four big jumps and she was on the roof, moving down a solid beam that ran along the front of the building.

The jump from one warehouse to the next was easy. There was only enough room between each one for waste disposal services access and a fire exit.

She caught up to her man quickly and slowed so she was walking just behind him.

He turned at the first intersection he came to, and for a moment she feared he would cross the street and she would need to find a way off the warehouse she was standing on.

But instead, once he was around the corner, he stopped, faced the building she was standing on, and knocked.

A door opened, and he stepped inside.

Wren turned to look at the roof, hoping for a way to peer inside, or at least listen to what was being said.

The roof had a steep pitch, like most buildings in Demeter. They needed it to deal with the torrential rain they got each year.

She walked up the slope, careful to be as silent as possible, and eventually she stood right at the peak, hands on hips, and admitted defeat. There was no way to get a look inside.

She moved back down to the side entrance the cafe owner had used, just in time to see him slip out and close the door quietly behind him.

She watched him go, wondering if she should keep following him, but eventually decided seeing who else was in the building would be more useful.

She crouched down and then sat cross-legged, settling in mentally for a long wait, but the door opened again almost imme-diately.

She rose up to her feet, and saw a woman with hair caught low on her nape in an elegant bun, her clothing dark and sophisticated.

Wren followed her back toward the city from the roof, then stopped to wait for her to get a bit ahead before she jumped down the staircase of boxes, in case she made a noise.

The street was empty but at least it was growing dark. Still, if the woman turned around and saw Wren, she would know she was being followed.

When the woman was far enough ahead, Wren quietly dropped to the ground and then sprinted to the corner.

The woman was gone.

Wren kept herself pressed against the wall, aware that she would give herself away if she ran into the street to look for her quarry. She searched for a few more moments, wondering if it would be worth doing that, anyway.

But patience rewarded her. She caught sight of the woman, finally.

She had crossed to the other side of the street and the long shadows of dusk had hidden her as she stood very still, looking into the window of a building a little way down from the corner.

Was she really interested in what was in that window display, or had she picked up that someone was following her, and was waiting to catch their reflection in the glass?

Suddenly, though, as if she was nervous, the woman straightened her shoulders and moved a little to her right, walking up a few steps to the door of the building. Wren expected her to touch the comms set on the side of the door but instead she simply pulled it open and disappeared inside.

Wren waited for a while, watching the shadows lengthen, and then finally she crossed the street and walked past the window.

It was a fabric shop, which looked like it had been closed for a few months at least. There was dust on the inside of the window, and the rolls of fabric on display had fallen over, lying in a haphazard fashion on the wooden floor.

Interesting.

She kept going, speeding up as soon as she was out of sight.

The sooner she got home, the sooner she and Ed could go back to the warehouse and break in.

27

———

Ed was already back.

As she ducked under the vines and slipped through the courtyard door, he was waiting for her at the top of the kitchen steps.

She slowed as she crossed the small, shadowed courtyard, suddenly shy for reasons she didn't quite understand.

He stood casually, leaning against the doorjamb, his gaze on her, his big body blocking the entrance almost completely, and when she reached the bottom of the steps, she looked up at him.

"Come here," he said, and suddenly she couldn't move fast enough.

She jumped, her nanos giving her the strength to go straight up, and Ed grabbed her out of the air, pulling her flush with his body.

He walked back into the house and flicked the door closed behind them with his foot, spun and set her down on the kitchen table.

As he stepped between her legs, she reached up and hooked her hands around his neck, pulling him down so she could kiss him.

He made a humming sound as his hands reached beneath her shirt and lifted it up, tossing it over her head when he got it off her.

"I'm forced to say that we don't have a lot of time," she murmured against the hot, salty skin of his throat.

"I'm aware." It didn't seem to give him pause, though. He grabbed her trousers and she lifted her hips up to make it easier for him to slide them off.

It obviously wasn't giving her pause, either. She smiled.

He studied her as he stepped out of his own trousers and threw his shirt in the same direction as hers. "What's the smile for?" he asked.

"Us." Her amusement dried up at the sight of him, naked in front of her. She leaned back on her elbows, suddenly languorous. She lifted her eyebrows at the way he stared at her.

"Come here," she said.

THEY MAY NOT HAVE HAD a lot of time, but they made full use of what time they had allowed themselves.

Ed glanced at Wren as they strolled along the street, headed for the hover port. Her thick lashes were lowered, and he realized how desperately he wanted to know what she was thinking. He felt a sudden, overwhelming urge to stash her somewhere safe and not let her out until this was all over.

He could almost blame her nanos, but he knew the strange tightness in his chest was a hundred percent Wren.

She sensed him looking at her, turned her face up to his, and gave him a blinding smile.

He felt something shift inside him, and reached for her hand.

"Any news on Ethan Hyt and Velda Shanïha?" she asked, threading her fingers through his own. "I forgot to ask."

Ed shook his head. "Guttra, Hyt's second-in-command, is a friend, and he told me the military are still trying to find their runner. Seems like the laser strike only clipped them. There is very little debris, so the runner itself may be mostly intact. They're hopeful."

"Did Guttra ask us to come in for a debrief?" Wren asked.

"If he'd thought about it, he might have, but he's too busy dealing with Hyt's disappearance. He's probably going out to lead the search for them tonight, so we'll be dealing with Lieutenant Bartam while he's gone."

"And Bailey and Hatch?" He could hear the fear in her voice.

"Stable. They'll make it."

She let out a sigh of relief. "So what was the name of the creep you interrogated?"

He smiled. "The creep's name was Grayson. I called Violet Fann and played his confession to her. She was very interested in talking to him, so I'm guessing he'll be in custody by tonight."

"But he didn't know much?"

Ed shook his head. He'd been beyond frustrated when he'd realized the little traitor really didn't know anything useful. "Just that he got his orders at the cafe, and passed the information he acquired back at the same place. He did give me a list of people he was told to spy on. It tells us who we can trust."

Wren gave a nod. "That's something. And Violet Fann will also arrest his co-conspirator, so between them, she can at least work out how much damage has been done. Did Grayson say what information he was looking for?"

"Aponi's defense arrays positioning and military protocols in the event of attack." Ed's voice was dry.

Wren stopped dead, looked across at him in horror.

"I know," he told her. He had felt the same when he had put it together. "When I pressed Grayson, he said he was told it was trade related. That the Verdant String Coalition's time was coming to an end, and Aponi was going to be first in line."

"First in line for what?" she asked.

"I think he meant in line to leave the VSC."

"Like a breakaway planet? Like Lassa and Garmen? That isn't going to happen," she said. "Why would he even think that was better?"

"I think he was promised some things he can't have under VSC laws." He recalled the strange, almost sick light in Grayson's eyes, and guessed whatever it was, it wasn't going to be anything sanctioned by a planet that was part of the VSC, or even those that were VSC allies. "So yes, exactly like a breakaway planet. We know now what things were like on the breakaways, and that would fit with what I think he was hoping for."

"Like sexually deviant stuff?" Wren suddenly got what he was alluding to. She focused on his expression and her eyes widened in dismay. "Like that freighter captain?"

"Yes." He said it slowly. "Just like that. Seems we've found one of their recruitment tools."

"I really don't like these people."

They'd been headed in the direction of the hover port, but Wren slowed their pace, and now she turned to look down a dark street.

"Here?" he asked, voice low.

She gave a nod. "It was deserted this afternoon. It should be even more deserted now."

They kept close to the buildings and the deeper shadows as they made their way toward the warehouse. With the hover port nearby, even without much street lighting, the sky was brightly lit and the ambient light made true darkness impossible.

Wren slowed again, and pointed to a building a little way ahead. "That's where the woman went in."

It was not exactly derelict—Aponi didn't allow any building to get in an unsafe state—but it had clearly not been an active concern for some time. The only reason for that would be if it had been bought by a company and then left deliberately unused.

Ed wondered what the chances were it had been bought roughly two years before. Around the same time he was being manipulated into resigning.

He pulled his comms unit out of a pocket and tapped out a quick message to Violet Fann. "It would be interesting to know who owns this building," he said.

"And what else they own," Wren agreed.

They had decided to leave the building the woman had entered until the end, if they had time, and they made their way to the warehouse.

Up ahead, at the port, he could hear the sound of hovers. The warehouses at that end of the street would be close to the back of the hover port, and Ed guessed they were loading up a freighter.

This warehouse, though, was absolutely silent and dark.

Wren walked straight to the door, ran her finger through the laslock and pushed it open.

They were inside in seconds.

Ed closed the door softly behind them and pulled out the small light he always carried with him.

He held it high, trying to get a sense of what was inside here.

The place smelled strange, almost sweet and musky.

Crates were packed in neat rows, to about head height, in a grid system. The warehouse was almost full.

Wren had come to a stop as soon as she'd stepped inside, and when he swung the light in her direction, he saw she was standing, eyes closed, chin slightly lifted, sniffing the air.

"Explosives," she said.

He felt a visceral chill, took a careful breath. "What kind?"

"I don't know." Her tone, when she opened her eyes and looked at him, was frustrated. "My nanos tell me the composition of the chemicals we can smell is highly explosive."

That was good enough for him. "There are two ways we can go," he said. "We can slip out of here and set up a watch to see who comes and goes. Or we can call in the SF teams now, and see what exactly what we're dealing with."

Wren put her hands on her hips. "There are advantages to the first approach," she said. "But I vote for door number two."

"Why?" He agreed, but he wondered what her reasons were.

"Because they need to be rattled. They need to feel hounded. And they need to lose access to this arsenal. So far they've shown no limits to their behavior. They'll shoot from space, they'll taunt battleships, they'll try to assassinate people by manipulating the head of the SF teams. I want what's in this warehouse to be made useless." As she said that, she turned to look thoughtfully at the crates.

"What?"

"We could maybe have the best of both worlds." She walked over to a crate, put a hand on top of it, and went very still for about five minutes. When she lifted her gaze to his, she looked a little smug, as well as a little tired. "Well, they'll never use this stuff again now."

"What did you do to it?"

"The electronics are dead, and the chemicals have been slightly adjusted, so they are useless."

Ed looked around the warehouse. "There's too many for you to do all of them. And I'm guessing it takes a toll."

She hesitated, turned to study the whole space, and then gave a reluctant nod. "All right, then. Stick with calling in the SF teams."

Ed used his light to illuminate the freighter label on a few of the crates. Each one was different, but after he went a little further down the row, they began to repeat. It seemed they had a regular fleet of ships that had brought these crates in a few at a time, and they'd had two years to fill this warehouse.

This was a very long game.

"Custom and Excise will need to be invited, too. There's enough evidence here to keep someone busy for years." He was amazed at the arrogance necessary to keep the labels on the crates, but then, they'd never been caught before. Or they'd used it to keep their suppliers quiet and cautious. If the warehouse was discovered, the freighter captains would know they would be implicated.

"What about the woman?" Wren asked. "We can call this in to Protection and SF, but we should be the ones to go look through that building she went into."

He was pulling his comms unit out of his pocket as she spoke and he paused, gave a nod. If there was anything to be learned, he'd rather they be the ones to learn it.

Paranoia wasn't a feeling he was used to living with, but looking around the warehouse, it was clear these people had put a lot of time, effort and money into this operation. They would have put people in place to protect their investment.

Right now, Wren was the only person he trusted completely.

"Agreed." He lifted his comms unit and got in touch with the person Guttra had told him was in charge while he and Hyt were unavailable. "Lieutenant Bartam, I have found something I think you'll be interested in."

28

Wren stepped into the hall, Ed right behind her, and what little street light illuminated the space disappeared as he closed the door silently behind them.

There was a faint light coming from above, and her eyes adjusted to reveal a large entryway with a sweeping staircase to the right.

There was a faint scent of perfume in the air, and she guessed it was from the woman she had seen come in here earlier.

The woman had been reluctant to enter the building this afternoon, but she was here often enough that her scent lingered.

Wren looked left and saw double doors that probably led through to the fabric shop visible from the street. Ed started up the stairs, and she followed him, her nanos on high alert.

She heard the rumble of a big hover coming down the street, and went very still. It had to be the Protection Unit and the SF teams Ed had called in, moving toward the warehouse.

Ed stopped and turned at the sound as well, and she rose up a step to get level with him.

"If people are here and they heard that, they will have looked out a window. They'll know something is up," she whispered in Ed's ear.

He gave a nod, but there was no hesitation in him as he continued on to the next floor.

The dark purple gleam of jarram wood on the landing was visible in the glow of a small wall sconce, and they both stilled at the sound of a voice behind one of the doors set along a short passageway.

It sounded like a woman, and as Wren got closer, her nanos helped her make out the words.

"I was right. There was someone following me from the warehouse this afternoon." The woman's voice was low and rich, her accent not Aponian. "They must have followed Vim when he came to deliver his message. It's possible they followed me when I left. The whole operation is blown."

"You shouldn't have come straight back here if you thought you were being followed." The man who answered was curt.

"I had no concrete reason to suspect I *was* being followed. It was a feeling I've had many times before that's come to nothing. I've gotten used to living like this." Her voice was just as curt, as if she didn't like being criticized. "I received word today that Salisas hasn't come home for two nights. Do you know where he is?"

"No. I'm the one who told management he was missing. He didn't come in yesterday, and that's not like him. You think he's the one who ratted out the location of the warehouse?"

"I doubt it. I've kept away from the secondary warehouse because I agreed that it was best not to draw any attention to it, but when I heard Salisas was missing, I walked past it yesterday evening. Had a look inside."

"So they might know where the second one is, too?" The man sounded outraged.

"No, because the address I have for it is wrong. The warehouse I broke into isn't ours."

"You sure you wrote down the correct address?" The man asked.

"That's what you're going with?" She sounded disappointed. "Where is it, Pontia? What's going on?"

Pontia sighed, as if aggrieved. "Just another layer of security, is all, given its importance. Someone up top knows where it is, obviously;

they pay the rent on it. If they say I can, I'll tell you. If Aponi Defense has found the primary warehouse, though, we need to get out of here before it blows."

The way he said it made Wren go very still.

She touched Ed's shoulder. "Boom?" she mouthed.

He gave a quick nod, taking out his comms unit to tap out a message for Protection and the SF teams.

While they'd been inside it, they hadn't found anything that would indicate the whole warehouse could be set off, but the SF explosive experts would be checking for that before anything else.

"They'll be coming here next," the woman said.

"So hurry."

There was silence, and when it went on longer than a minute, Ed shoved at the door, and they both peered inside.

It was empty and completely dark.

Wren stepped into the room, and as she did, a light came on. She blinked, looking around for where the two could have gone, and saw the wall to the left was slightly angled.

She shoved at it, and it swung open easily, showing a staircase that went up at a sharp angle.

They both heard the whine of a hover from above.

She raced up the stairs, Ed on her heels, but by the time they reached the top the hover was lifting up and away.

A man lay, panting, to one side of the hover pad. It looked as if he'd been shot. Wren guessed it was the man the woman had addressed as Pontia.

"She shot you and then left you here for us, did she?" Wren asked as she jogged toward him.

Pontia bared his teeth at her. "There's a lens pointed down the hidden staircase. We saw you coming up as we got to the hover. She decided I wasn't moving fast enough."

Wren circled him as Ed lifted his comms unit to speak to Lieutenant Bartam about the hover heading over the city. "Where are you from? Not Aponi."

"Arkhor." The man looked ill, which was unusual for anyone in the VSC. Access to high level med tech was available to everyone.

"What's wrong with you?" She crouched beside him and reached out, but her nanos wouldn't let her touch him with her own fingertip.

Just before she made contact, a tiny silver probe extended out.

"You have an unknown infection." She wanted to shuffle back, but her nanos told her it wasn't contagious, and so she kept up the contact. "Where did you get it?"

"A pit of unrelenting horror." Pontia spoke in a whisper, and she wondered for a moment if he was a little insane.

If it's unknown, then he caught it on another planet, her nanos told her. *A place no one else in the VSC knows about.*

"Another planet," she said, and he blinked at her, as if trying to work out how she knew that, and then he looked up over her shoulder.

Ed had come to stand behind her.

"Where is this planet?" she asked.

"Doesn't matter where," Pontia said, looking away. "No one in their right mind would ever go there. It's . . . the most terrible place I've ever seen. Everything there is nasty. From the flowers, to the insects, to the animals—" He shook his head. "The monsters."

Ed bent a little, gave her a questioning look. "He's ill," she said. "Unknown infection, caught on a mystery planet."

"Too medically interesting to get checked out?" Ed guessed. "Maybe there would have been too many questions?"

Pontia gave a reluctant nod.

"Well, the med techs will help you now." And being denied medical care because your very body would raise questions your bosses didn't want answered might lead to some resentment.

Like giving the incorrect address for the secondary warehouse.

Unless he was telling the truth about it just being another layer of security.

The sound of footsteps running up the stairs was clear, and Lieutenant Bartam and a small team ran toward them.

"Where did your friend go?" Wren asked, keeping the nanos in contact with Pontia while her other hand waved in the direction the hover had taken.

He opened his mouth to say something, stuttered, and then turned to look at her. It seemed as if he was struggling against himself.

She should probably feel bad about forcing him to speak, but she thought of the laser strike at the hover port and shoved all guilt aside.

"She's headed for our freighter at the port, is my guess. She tried to kill me. She thought she had." He gave a grimace that Wren guessed was meant as a smile. "She waited for me to tell her where the other warehouse was, and when I did, she shot me."

"But you lied?" The nanos were picking that up.

He gave a wheezing laugh. "I lied."

"No honor among conspirators?" Wren asked.

Pontia shrugged. Shook his head. "I was never an equal partner, just a drone. She was with me on that planet, but if she'd gotten sick, they'd have found a way to treat her."

"Aren't you afraid she'll come back to find you when she works out you lied?" Ed moved a little and crouched beside Wren, blocking the silver of her nano's probe from view as Bartam reached them.

"Who've we got?" Bartam sounded like she was in the mood for good news.

"One of the people responsible for the warehouse. Pontia. He's been cooperative with his answers so far," Wren said. "Maybe question him while he's in a talkative mood." She rose to her feet, and Ed did the same.

"What's wrong with him?" Bartam didn't automatically reach down to grab him.

"Whoever these people are, they found a new planet, and this one apparently picked up something bad for his health there," Ed said. "I'd be very interested to learn where that place is."

Bartam turned to stare at their prisoner, and gave a slow nod. "I'm sure everyone will be. Where are you two going?"

"To the—" Before Wren could finish her sentence, the warehouse blew, a sheet of blue-green flames shooting up into the sky like a geyser.

Everyone on the roof turned to look at it in stunned silence.

The noise it made was indescribable, and Wren put her hands over her ears to dull the sound.

Their prisoner stared at the sky, face slack.

Bartam ran to the edge of the roof, shouting into her comms unit.

Wren couldn't see how anyone who'd been inside could have survived. These people may have taken yet more victims.

"What's in the second warehouse? More weapons?" Wren asked Pontia, stepping back to his side and crouching down. She grabbed his wrist—strange infection be damned. She would get a truthful answer.

Her nanos agreed.

He swallowed. "Yes."

He suddenly looked up at her, horror in his eyes at his own answer. "I need some water, I'm not well."

Wren stepped back as Bartam pulled out a water bottle and handed it over. Pontia took it with trembling hands. He took a long drink, and then knocked it over as he went into a seizure.

"He's taken something. He's trying to kill himself." Bartam slammed him down on the ground, forcing his mouth open, but it was too late.

He curled up, made a strange, guttural sound, and then died.

Wren stared down at him.

Had she done that? By forcing him to answer, had she frightened him so much he'd taken his own life? Or was he more afraid of his former colleagues?

"These people are prepared to take their secrets to the grave," Ed said, his gaze serious as it met hers.

Bartam took out a small device, pressed it against Pontia's neck and then let out a sigh. She slowly rose up and turned to look at them, her lips a hard line. "He said there was another warehouse?"

"Then killed himself before he told us where."

It was almost impossible to imagine there was another cache this big, but one thing Wren was done with was underestimating their enemy.

"Casualties from the explosion?" Ed asked Bartam.

The lieutenant hesitated, then shook her head. "None. They tried a high pulse frequency before they entered, and it just went up. No one entered."

"We did," Ed murmured. "We had a look around."

Bartam gave a nod. "That's not lost on me. You're lucky to be here."

"Lieutenant, any word about Bailey and Hatch?" Wren asked.

"They're still unconscious, but stable." Lieutenant Bartam's tone was stiff.

She didn't know Wren, and she didn't trust her yet.

There was nothing Wren could do about that right now.

"Time is wasting," Ed murmured, taking a step toward the stairs. "We'll be in touch, Lieutenant." He gave Bartam a sketchy salute.

"If you find out anything about the other warehouse, that's priority," Bartam called after them.

Pontia's partner thought she knew where it was, and Wren guessed that's where she'd head as soon as she picked up her freighter from the port.

Wren ran faster.

29

———————

The hover port was still on high alert after the laser strike, although Wren was sure at least one of the battleships was parked directly over it in nearspace.

No one's reputation would withstand a second strike.

The freighter section was not at full capacity, and Wren couldn't help but grin. "We've unknowingly made our lives easier," she said.

"How's that?" Ed asked. He picked up her amusement, and was looking at her with a gleam in his eye.

"There's a line of freighters waiting to land in nearspace, but we delayed them with our scans, and then the laser strike delayed them even more. So there are half the number of ships for us to check."

"There's still a lot." Ed stopped, looking down the neat row of freighters lined up on the loading docks.

"She's on her own, so I'm guessing it's a small rig." Wren studied the candidates, dismissing anything too big.

"True," Ed murmured. "And there she is."

A woman in a dark gray flight suit walked across a slender docking arm, head down, and entered a code to gain access to one of the smallest freighters in the line.

Wren and Ed sprinted toward it, hitting the docking arm as it started to whine, warming up to retract.

Their weight stopped the process, and the system reset.

Thank goodness for safety measures, Wren thought, slapping a hand against the small keypad on the freighter's entrance. Her nanos did something to it—from the burning smell, something permanent —and the door slid open.

Ed went first, laz in hand, and she came up behind him, grabbed his jacket in her fist, and tugged him back.

He looked over his shoulder at her, face both confused and irritated, and she held his gaze with a steady look. "She has a laz, remember. She shot Pontia."

Ed frowned, and then Wren let her nanos shimmer into the silver bands at her wrists, and he moved up against the wall of the passage, and with a sigh, let her go first.

She followed the short corridor to the front of the ship, and the flare of laz fire lit up around her as she stepped into what on a bigger ship would be called the bridge.

Her nanos deflected, and they had to have been thinking about it, because they deflected the shot directly back at the woman, and she went down.

The rebound isn't as strong as the original shot, they told Wren. *But it's strong enough to do some harm.*

"That's some laz protection," the woman said, curled up on the floor, holding her arm.

Ed moved past Wren and scooped up her dropped laz.

"We knew you were armed, we had a few words with your friend near the warehouse," Wren said.

"My friend?" she frowned. "Ah, Pontia. That's not how he described our relationship, surely?" She compressed her lips.

"And you are?" Ed asked, holding his laz steady.

"Evette Linao," she said. "And you're Wren Thorakis and Ed Zeneri. You've been quite the disruptive force, haven't you?"

"Pontia said you were on a monster planet with him."

Linao gave a bitter smile. "They did to my beautiful battleship exactly what they nearly did to your runner this afternoon. Shot it to bits from nearspace. While we were on-planet. Without any way of getting home."

Wren blinked. That was not what she had been expecting. "Why?"

"My ship had been damaged. The inhabitants of Fjern, the planet we stumbled across, they had strange abilities. Such a mix of backward tech and almost . . . magic." She shook her head. "They caused a runner to crash into the front end of my ship and it started to burn. There was no way we could take off, and more of the Fjerna warriors were coming. So, rather than leave our tech behind, they decided to destroy it, whether my crew and I were clear or not."

"Fjern." Wren said the word softly. "What do the Fjerna look like?" She imagined something like the other sentient beings the Verdant String had come into contact with; the Caruso or the Hathr.

Evette Linao shot her a look. "Just like us. Seems the ancestors didn't just land on the planets in the Verdant String. One of the motherships crash-landed on the monster pit that is Fjern. And the people it was carrying survived." She tilted her head to one side, looking at Ed. "But they've developed more than just blue hair and a tendency to secrets."

"What's different about them?" Ed asked, and while he sounded calm, Wren sensed he was insulted by Evette Linao's comments about his almost extinct people.

"They say they were given some kind of tech called gyra. A technological advantage created by our original ancestors, because they were headed for less accommodating sectors of space. The gyra are strictly controlled, given to hand-picked warriors, and when those warriors need to protect their people—which is all the time—they bulk out to fight the monsters that are constantly trying to kill them."

"Gyra." Wren didn't know why that word had such an effect on her, but she felt it soul-deep. Her nanos seemed to be vibrating with intense emotion.

"They have some ceremony to pass the gyra on, and the warriors who are chosen live in special compounds. It's archaic and very structured. But then, it's the only control they have on that wild place. Chaos is too mild a term for what Fjern is."

Bulk out, her nanos thought. *We could do that, but it might harm you.*

Let's leave things as they are. The silver shield is pretty effective, Wren answered.

Yes, they agreed. But they were intrigued. She could hear it in their tone. *We would like to talk to these gyra.*

"Pontia caught something nasty in this monster pit called Fjern?" Ed asked.

Evette Linao gave her first genuine laugh. "We were stealing ore from the Fjerna, and that necessitated actually landing on that cursed place. No one knows how he got sick, but no medicine seems capable of shaking it."

"You've been very forthcoming," Wren said, suddenly realizing she hadn't touched the woman. Hadn't needed to. "Why?"

"I'm done," Evette said, and leaned back against the bulkhead, closing her eyes for a moment. "They tried to kill me. They expect my loyalty, but they would have erased me on a far-flung planet without a second thought. Since then, I've been given nothing but boring drone work. I made the mistake of making my anger at what they did to my ship—almost did to me—very obvious. I no longer have a ship, but there aren't many of us capable of flying Razors, and the plan is to build more. At the very least, until more come off the production line and I get a new one, they need me in reserve." She shrugged.

"What are they planning to do?" Ed asked.

She opened her eyes a little, watching them through narrow slits. "I think I need to negotiate a deal," she said. "I have valuable information, and I don't fancy a long time in prison. So put me in front of someone in authority who can come up with something I'm willing to live with, and I'll tell you."

"Where is the other warehouse Pontia said is out there?" Wren asked.

She saw Linao reacted instantly, her face went suddenly blank, and she blinked rapidly. "Another warehouse?"

"Don't give us that, he told us you waited for him to give you the address before you shot him." Ed frowned at her.

"That is something tangible I have to negotiate with. Get me a deal, or you can ask Pontia." Linao took a deep breath and let it out slowly.

"Tell me how you found Fjern, at least," Wren asked, changing the subject. It might be wise to keep the fact that Pontia had killed himself from Linao for now.

"From the ancestral ship's signal," Evette said. "The same way they found the battleship on Finian."

"And on Ytla?" Wren asked softly.

Evette shot her a look, then eventually gave a nod. "The part of the ship that held the signal on the Ytla wreck was quite a way from the part you stumbled across. They'd been looking for the other part of it for a long time before they found it while they were chasing after you."

"It was only after I heard their reactions to the wreckage while I was hiding from them that I realized they were using the cult as a cover for their explorations on Ytla." It had explained so much about her captivity with them.

Linao studied her closely. "You know a lot."

Wren shrugged. "They weren't particularly careful in what they said when they had me as their prisoner."

Linao swore softly. "I knew we were taking a risk using amateurs like that, but then, we don't have too much choice anymore. All the professionals are either dead or in jail."

"Professional thugs who did what they were told on the break-aways?" Ed asked, and there was an edge in his tone.

Linao quirked her lips. "Exactly. I gather you took a few of the last ones we had left down on the streets the other night. They're in custody, and my contact on the inside says the VSC is sending someone to collect them to answer for crimes on Lassa."

"You seem to have recruited a few more here on Aponi," Wren said. "There are a few Demeter SF team members who are clearly onboard."

Linao looked away to hide her reaction.

She hadn't known they knew about that.

She may be pretending to be all about cooperation, but Wren guessed she was giving just enough to try and get a deal.

Most likely because her crimes were too numerous for anyone to be comfortable giving her a light sentence.

And she didn't miss that when she'd talked about the difficulty of hiring good thugs, she'd used the word 'we'. Like she had a say in the hiring.

If Evette Linao wasn't at the top of this food chain, she'd be very surprised.

"Where were you going to escape to?" Ed asked her after a long silence.

"I was just going to get away. Go to Faldine or somewhere where the VSC has less of a hold than the Verdant String planets." Linao hunched a shoulder.

She was lying, but Wren didn't think they'd get the truth out of her.

"Time to call Lieutenant Bartam," she said.

Ed gave a tight nod. "Agreed."

30

They stood outside, in the chill breeze.

Ed had restrained Evette Linao, but he wanted a conversation with Wren out of their prisoner's earshot, and so had moved outside to wait for whoever Lieutenant Bartam had sent to take her into custody.

They stood on the slender bridge that connected the freighter to the docks, and happy to use the cold as an excuse, Ed slid an arm around Wren's shoulder, and felt another one of those strange flutters when she curved her own around his waist, so they stood, angled toward each other. Entwined.

He had not allowed himself to become entwined with anyone for a long time.

Not, he forced himself to admit, since he had been held hostage as a teenager while his planet, Halatia, imploded, and the rest of the VSC bickered about who would take the most number of refugees.

Aponi had taken him in once the extent of the disaster became clear. A Special Forces captain called Drake had broken ranks and saved a smuggler ship of hostages held near the VSC planet of Parn —or what was left of them—and after that, the whole VSC had acted swiftly.

It was why he'd become an SF officer himself. He wanted to be in a position to do what was right, damn the consequences.

But he'd let his deep seated anger at that original rejection—that original delay—dictate his actions two years ago. Those long weeks, when he was no more than a child, held in a tiny cell on a smuggler ship, grieving his parents, as he slowly worked out help wasn't coming, had colored his whole life. And he could see how that feeling of bitterness had influenced him, and not in a good way.

He had been manipulated two years ago because someone knew how he would react. Knew they could force him out of Special Forces. That alone was as enraging as it was uncomfortable.

The breeze lifted Wren's dark hair, and it caught on the rough fabric of his jacket, lying across his shoulder and tickling his neck.

He bent his head, and she looked up at him in surprise, gave a little gasp as he kissed her.

She smiled against his lips, and was still smiling when she leaned back a little, opening her mouth to say something, but at the sound of boots on metal, she turned her head.

Two men were walking toward them, the SF uniforms they wore identifying them as the team Bartam had sent to collect Evette Linao.

Wren turned back, still relaxed in his arms, but before she could speak, light bloomed around her and she fell, pulling him down with her.

Into an abyss.

Wake up!

The nanos were shouting at her.

Wren didn't think they'd ever done that before.

It wasn't a direct hit last time, they replied, calmer now that she was answering.

Ouch, she said.

There was a moment of stillness. *Very ouch,* they said. *We did not have time to form a shield.*

Ed? she asked.

Still unconscious, they told her. *Lying behind you.*

She rolled a little, bumped into his back.

The warmth of his body against hers calmed her. She could hear him breathing, now that she was listening.

Her hands were restrained behind her, but not too tightly. Her feet were shackled, too. She guessed Ed was trussed up the same way.

We can unlock the restraints, her nanos said. *We can dissipate out of this room, but the freighter was already in nearspace when we came back to ourselves. We can only dissipate within this freighter.*

Leave the restraints on for now, she told them. There was no value in showing her hand too early.

Voices rose from the next room, and she focused her attention there. She could feel a slight tremor beneath the floor she was lying on, a clear indication they were flying, just as her nanos said.

"Bartam will be hunting us soon, if she isn't already." The man who spoke was close by, and Wren guessed he was standing on the bridge.

She turned her head, but there was no way to see beyond the narrow room she and Ed had been tossed into.

"We're blown now. We insisted on being the two who came to arrest you. The fact that we haven't checked in, that the freighter is missing, and that Zeneri and Thorakis are not responding, means Bartam will know she's got a problem." The second man who spoke sounded vaguely familiar, and Wren wondered if she'd been introduced to him when she'd come in to headquarters for her interview with Ethan Hyt.

"*I* didn't call you in, so don't get up in my face." Wren recognized Evette Linao's voice immediately. "I'm not saying I'm not grateful that I'm not going to jail, but it wasn't my call to blow your cover."

"Who do you know at the top, that you always get special treatment?" the first man asked.

"Who says I know anyone at the top?" Linao asked.

"Everyone. Because you miraculously survive time and again, no matter what you say or do." The second man's clothing rustled, as if he was pacing.

"I can fly the Razors," Linao said. "And that's the answer to all your questions. We are down to two pilots left from the original number and only one Razor between us. They can't afford to throw me away right now. That would leave them without a spare pilot. Why do you think I've been parked looking after a warehouse on Demeter for the last six months?"

"And if they train up a new pilot?" The first man asked.

"Then I'm expendable," Linao answered.

Something about the way she said it made Wren sure she was lying. If her guess from before was accurate, Evette Linao *was* someone at the top. Rubbing shoulders with the lower rungs, either because she liked it, or because she wanted to keep an eye on them.

"If you were going to leave Pontia behind, why leave him alive? He talked, from what I hear." The second man sounded close, like he was leaning against the wall close to the door.

Interesting, Wren thought. The news hadn't gotten out that Pontia was dead.

"Pontia wasn't fast enough." Linao's contempt was clear. "If I hadn't left him, I'd have been caught, too. He's been ill since Fjern, and he's only gotten worse in the last few weeks. And as it happens, I thought I had killed him. I was in too much of a hurry to double-check."

"I heard Bartam's freaked out over what he said about Fjern," the first man said. "About the idea of another VSC planet."

"I'd like to see the VSC try to deal with Fjern," Linao said, scorn dripping from every word. "I was a prisoner on that planet for a week, and had to work at a mine site there for months before that." She shuddered. "They're welcome to it."

"It can't be that bad?" It sounded as if the second man pushed away from the wall.

"The monsters are massive and voracious, and the people who live there have to stay in walled cities just to be safe. It's more backward than Kalastoni was when the rest of the VSC found it, mainly because they have to fight to survive being eaten every day. They have some interesting vehicles and hovers, though." Linao's voice changed pitch, sounding thoughtful. "We tried to steal one, which was our undoing. It was dropped onto the nose of the Razor and caught on fire."

"Pontia told Salisas that there are warriors there that change shape to fight the monsters?" The first man sounded hesitant, as if he couldn't quite believe the rumor.

"They call it the gyra," Linao said. "Some kind of tech from the Ancestors. That's the myth, anyway. Given how otherwise backward the tech is there, I'm inclined to believe it. No way they came up with something so sophisticated themselves. The story goes they were given it because they were headed to more dangerous reaches of space, not the mild and verdant planets of the String. It was supposed to be something to protect them. My guess is nanotech of some kind. But it's nothing like we've got now."

"What does it look like?" The man close to the door asked.

"Don't know. The warriors who are chosen go through a ceremony to receive whatever it is, and then go through training. And somehow, these gyra help make them a larger, more ferocious version of themselves to fight the monsters."

"Sounds . . . almost unbelievable."

Linao laughed. "I barely believe it, and it was my life for months." She paused. "Get ready, we're far enough out now to speed up."

"The military might be watching Ytla," the first man said. "Captain Hyt definitely passed on suspicions about what's happening there up the chain."

"To Velda Shanïha? Because she's most likely dead." Linao sounded absolutely calm.

"Maybe to Velda Shanïha, but also to the generals. This isn't contained." The second man sounded sure about that.

Wren felt a lift of hope.

"Well, our orders are to take Wren Thorakis to Ytla, and as you've already pointed out, I'm skating close to the line as it is, so I'm going to be a good little soldier and obey orders this time." Evette Linao's voice was amused. "Hang on, now."

Wren felt the sudden clutch of nerves, and then the weird pulling sensation as the freighter went into high speed.

She had hoped to never see Ytla again. Looked like that was a wish that wasn't coming true.

31

———

Evette Linao was an excellent pilot.

Wren had to give it to her.

They had made good time to their destination, and when they were close, they'd latched on to the back of a supply freighter headed for the battleship which sat between Ytla and RTS004, the gas giant Ytla orbited, keeping the tiny ship within the freighter's signature.

As soon as the supply freighter had crossed the meteor field that lay between Ytla and RTS004, they slid away and followed a cluster of falling rocks that flared as they crashed through the atmosphere of the tiny, habitable moon.

With a quick burst of power, the freighter followed the meteor shower in, keeping so close to the rocks that Wren adjusted her estimation of Linao's piloting abilities up another notch.

She was only able to see the pilot's brilliance because she and Ed had been dragged onto the bridge, the better for Navar and Fenton to watch them, and from her position on the floor, she had a view through the large front viewport.

Navar looked familiar to her, but Wren couldn't remember where from. She had to assume she had met him in passing or simply noticed him while she was in SF headquarters. She had never seen Fenton before.

The freighter shuddered, and Wren slid along the floor as the whole ship tilted. As the angle changed, she caught sight, at the top of the bridge viewport, of the gas giant that Ytla orbited, a swirl of cream, brown and gray.

"That was easier than I thought," Navar said as Linao switched on the engines completely and began to fly downward toward Ytla's surface.

Wren saw Linao's lips twist up in contempt, and couldn't say she blamed the woman. That had been many things, easy wasn't one of them.

"How did you know about that supply freighter, and why didn't the navigator tell anyone we were riding their tail?" Fenton asked.

"Do you think I was in that warehouse patrolling the aisles?" Linao asked. "I was sitting in the office researching everyone involved in supply and support entities to the military. There are enough people with secrets to hide to suit our purposes. I know the exact position of all the battleships in Aponi's territory, and I knew when that supply freighter was leaving. I got confirmation about it this afternoon."

"How did you get all that? And the names of the people you researched?" Navar asked, and for the first time, Wren heard a little fear in his voice.

"We had two informers in Planetary Defense. They had access to that information, although I'm assuming either one or both of them are blown, given that the warehouse was discovered."

"You're sure that supply freight navigator didn't tell someone anyway, and they're just watching us now, to see what we do? It seems incredible they didn't notice us." Fenton was less willing to believe they'd gotten away with it, although, sadly, Wren thought they had.

Linao was just that good.

"They didn't notice us. I went to a great deal of trouble to make sure they didn't." Linao leaned forward in her chair, watching the panel in front of her. "My instructions are to land about an hour's walk from Har Met Vent headquarters. They'll meet us halfway, which is apparently where they think the wreck is located."

"Crazy bastards. I wish we could do this without them." Navar sounded aggrieved.

Suddenly a light went on in Wren's head. Navar had been part of the team that was busy kitting up at the SF camp on Ytla to rescue her, when she had stumbled in on her own.

That's why he was familiar.

"You do know that they aren't really crazy?" Linao looked over at him, her contempt clear this time. "They're just pretending, so the VSC leaves them alone."

"Some of them might be pretending, but they've attracted some interesting followers for real, as well." Navar shook his head. "I've had to deal with them, so believe me, I know."

He wasn't wrong.

Wren didn't like thinking about her time in the Har Met Vent camp, but there were definitely people there who had bought into the tenets of the cult.

She didn't know what most of those tenets were—no one not in the cult did—but some of it had to do with rites they believed had been carried out on Ytla a hundred years before, by a small group of settlers from Aponi whose outpost had been wiped out by disease before anyone knew they were even sick.

"Should these two still be so out of it?" Fenton suddenly asked, and Wren had to force herself not to tense up.

She'd been watching things through half-closed eyes, and, worried Fenton was focused on her, she let her whole body go limp as Linao piloted the freighter into a sudden right bank.

She closed her eyes as she fetched up against a wall.

Ed's body bumped up against her, so she lay caught between him and the wall.

She let her forehead rest on his back, soothed by the heat from his body.

"Check their breathing," Linao suggested.

With a huff of annoyance, Navar left the bridge, then returned to crouch beside them. She heard something make an electronic ping and with a grunt, he rose to his feet. "They're fine. But I'm not carrying Zeneri if he's still unconscious when we land."

"We have a hover stretcher, I think," Linao said. "We can put them on that."

That suited Wren. She'd rather save her energy.

We can dissipate when we land, her nanos said.

Not without Ed, she told them.

She felt their hesitation, and then the sudden agreement. *Not without Ed.*

Wren knew the moment Ed came to.

They were lying together on the hover stretcher, backs to each other, but his fingers twitched against hers and she curled her little finger around his for a moment before releasing it.

Their little group had been walking for slightly more than the half hour Linao had estimated, and Wren guessed they must be close to the meeting place with whoever was coming from the Har Met Vent.

The two SF soldiers were taking up the front and rear of their group, with Linao walking beside the hover in the middle.

Something up front caused them to slow down, which had happened a few times before as they negotiated around an obstacle, but this time, Linao's body language told her it was more than just a large fallen tree or a rocky outcrop.

"Renard," she called, voice cool.

"Is that Captain Linao?" Renard's voice came from close by.

Wren shivered at the sound of it. She had hoped never to see or hear from him again.

"It is. Lower your weapons." Linao moved forward, and Wren wondered whether she should continue to pretend to be unconscious or not. She didn't like the thought of Gy Renard standing over her while she lay bound on the ground.

He had hit her, starved her, and had threatened her with worse if she tried to escape.

She had escaped anyway.

But the feelings of helplessness had left a deep impression. She never wanted to feel that way again, and yet, here she was.

Not quite, her nanos said.

You're right. She immediately felt better. *Not quite, at all.*

"You've got my little escapee there, I see." Renard's voice rose a little as he must have caught sight of her.

She couldn't quite read the tone of his voice.

"Open your eyes, Thorakis." Linao put the cold end of a laz against her throat, and Wren opened her eyes. "You, too, Zeneri. I know you're awake."

Ed stirred beside her, and she guessed he had also decided it was better not to be seen as helpless right now.

Although being conscious only made them slightly less helpless than they'd been before.

"I'm not happy to be back on Ytla." Wren kept her voice flat as she sat up, looking around to locate Renard and his two henchmen. She'd never caught their names when she'd been held by Renard in the ill-maintained hut, but she recognized them well enough.

"Bad memories?" Linao studied her face, and she must have seen more there than Wren intended to show. The captain turned to Renard. "What did you do to her?"

Renard's sneer held for a moment, but his eye contact with Linao finally cut away and he gave a one-sided shoulder shrug. "Nothing. She's fine, isn't she?"

"She wasn't fine when she got to the SF base," Navar said, his gaze flicking from Wren to Renard.

"We're supposed to be a crazy cult. We had to rough her up a little," Renard said. "We needed to be believable." He flicked a hand. "And she was out in a storm for days, as well, remember. Not all of it was us."

Linao watched him for another beat, then seemed to shake her disgust off. "This wreckage is somewhere close?" she asked.

"Apparently." Renard narrowed his eyes at Wren. "My people stumbled on it while trying to recapture her, but then they had to leave it to chase after her, and when they came back this way, they couldn't find it again. That's why we argued against the plan to eliminate her in Demeter, and why we requested that someone bring her here when we were told she'd been captured." He glanced over at Linao. "Of course, I never dreamed she would be brought to us by such an exalted leader as yourself, personally."

"I read the request." Linao chose to ignore his sarcasm for the moment. "But what I can't understand is how that can be." She shook her head. "You honestly can't work out where it is, when you've had months to do so?"

"My people found it in a raging storm. They took a quick look around, then went after our escapee again, and all the landmarks were gone when they came back later." Renard tilted his head. "We aren't able to use tracking devices, remember? It was forbidden because it could lead the Aponi military or the SF teams to the site."

Linao's expression told Wren she felt nothing but contempt for Renard's incompetence. Then she turned her ire on Wren. "Let's hope you remember the way."

It was hard not to take her words and tone as a threat.

She exchanged a quick glance with Ed, but that was the wrong thing to do, because Linao suddenly turned to study Ed. "You're very quiet all of a sudden."

Wren had noticed that herself. He'd shut himself down, tight as he could. She couldn't read him but he didn't have nanos to help him recover, and maybe he was letting them underestimate him into the bargain.

"I was hit with a laz strike." Ed's voice was hoarse and choppy, which made her sure she was right. He was sitting slightly stooped over on the hover, hands bound behind his back like her, legs bound at the ankles. He looked like he was still in pain.

It reminded her she could probably act a lot more injured than she felt. At the very least have them think her too weak to run.

Could we give Ed a boost? she asked her nanos. *Transfer some of you across?*

The response was so visceral, she couldn't help but wince.

We are a single entity now, they told her. *We have been together too long. We go to no one else.*

Linao glanced at her as she rubbed her temples, then turned to Ed. "You can stay on the hover."

She turned to Wren. "You're not going to have that luxury, no matter how bad you feel." She stepped forward and released Wren's ankle restraints, and Wren slid off the hover onto the ground.

She bent over, as if in pain, hands still secured behind her back. She straightened slowly, as if every movement hurt, and stared straight at Renard. "I bet they did find the wreck again," she said. "No way they didn't. It was big. I wasn't even looking for it and I found it. They've probably been stripping it all these months, and now they're going to pretend there's nothing there when we reach it."

The sidekicks moved restlessly, as if they'd like to come at her.

"She right?" Navar asked.

Renard studied her. "Revenge. I can respect that." He gave a shake of his head. "No, she's not right. But I wasn't very . . . nice to her when I had her, and she's stirring you up against me in retaliation."

"How was it she found the wreck and you didn't, when that was the only job you had after you found the first half of the ship?" Fenton leaned back a little, arms crossed.

"Pure luck," Renard said. "The second site is over three thou away from the part of the ship we did find. We never imagined the whole thing could have broken up over such a large area, especially into two such big, distinct pieces."

There was silence, broken only by the soughing of the wind. Cold and cutting, it was far worse than she'd had to deal with when she'd escaped. The weather then had been wild, dangerous, even, but the temperature had been a lot higher. It had been the end of summer, whereas now they were going into the beginning of winter.

Wren shivered. It seemed to snap Linao out of whatever she was thinking.

"Let's go." She was standing by the hover, and she set her laz against Ed's neck and made eye contact with Wren. "I understand there is very little here to motivate you. If I was in your boots, I'd be asking myself why I should cooperate. If we'd brought you here on your own, that would be a problem for me, but unfortunately for you, you weren't brought alone. Your friend here will get another laz strike if you don't cooperate. Do I make myself clear?"

Wren turned her back on Linao, held out her bound wrists. "Very clear. I'll need my hands free."

There was a moment of hesitation, and then Linao came forward to release her.

"Thank you." Wren faced them again. "Where's that trash pit you call cult headquarters?" she asked Renard.

He raised an eyebrow. Pointed north east. "The camp is that way."

She looked in that direction, studied the rocks and the withering grasses. The way north east rose up to a low hill, and she remembered running down a slope as part of her escape. She started walking toward it, brushing past Ed deliberately as she went.

He thrust his bound legs out, barring her way. Exchanged a look with her.

Telling her with his eyes not to sacrifice herself for him.

She leaned toward him, pressing her hand against his cheek. "It goes both ways now," she told him softly.

Navar grabbed the back of her jacket and hauled her away.

He is lucky he isn't touching your skin, her nanos said.

Even if he did, we couldn't do anything, she warned them. *There is no safe way out right now. We have to wait.*

She didn't look at Navar. He needed to underestimate her, just as they were underestimating Ed, and she couldn't hide the contempt that she felt. So she looked down and pretended fear, instead.

"Stop wasting time," Renard warned her, and Navar gave her a little shove.

She let herself pitch forward, putting out her hands to break her fall, as if the shove had been harder than it was.

"You're the ones wasting time," Linao snapped out. "Fuck's sake. Stop getting handsy with her and let's get on with it."

Oh, Linao *definitely* didn't just know people in high places, Wren decided when she got to her feet and brushed the dirt off her hands. She *was* people in high places.

They had one of the top bosses in their midst.

There was suddenly no doubt in her mind.

She straightened her jacket and started walking, very deliberately brushing past the hover with Ed sitting on it.

She ran a hand down his arm as she went, in defiance.

No one touched her again.

32

———

The surroundings looked familiar, but Wren had been running for her life when she'd come through here, and during a storm, as well.

There had been a few breaks in the weather, and she'd escaped in the early morning hours, so it had been during daylight hours when she'd stumbled across the wreckage.

To the right, the nanos told her. *It's just through the trees.*

She stopped, and thinking she needed water, Linao passed her a bottle.

She took it and drank, taking her time.

"How did Renard and his group know I was here on Ytla, and that they should kidnap me, specifically?" she asked as she screwed the lid back on the bottle. "Was that just coincidence?"

"Renard and his people had found those carvings months before, but they hadn't found the other half of the wreck, and they needed more supplies. The scientific team had arrived a short while after them, and their arrival complicated things by making supply drops difficult. Our contact on the supply freighter couldn't drop anything off for them in secret anymore." Linao had taken out her own bottle of water and was drinking. It didn't look like she was going to give anything to Ed, so Wren walked over to him.

"At least let him have his hands in front of him," she said, and after a pause, Linao nodded to Fenton and he released Ed's hands from behind him, and restrained him with his hands in front.

Once that was done, Wren handed him her water.

He hesitated, looked up at her.

She gave him a fierce look back, and with a tiny quirk of his lips, he took it.

"Thanks."

Wren watched as Linao packed her bottle away, and decided to prolong the conversation. "So Renard told Navar where to find the carvings, so they'd have a civilian to kidnap? Why not kidnap one of the scientists?"

"That *was* the plan. They thought Special Forces would allow the scientists access to the carvings and they were going to take whoever showed up to check them out," Linao said, flicking a look at Navar. "But someone up the SF hierarchy had a personal grudge against someone on the scientific team and refused to let them look at it. Insisted an SF consultant be called in. You were the lucky person."

"Politics," Navar said, and spat.

"Why not kidnap someone from the teams?" Ed asked. "Why bring a civilian into it at all?"

Renard gave a snort. "Because they wouldn't have waited for a few days for the storm to pass to rescue one of their own team members," he said. "Navar could argue it was too dangerous to bring a civilian through that weather, but one of their own? They wouldn't have waited, and we needed time to get the supply drop organized."

"But I *was* part of the SF," Wren said.

"A consultant. Not a team member." Navar shrugged.

That had come through, loud and clear, Wren thought. It was why she trusted no one on the Nanganya teams any longer. She'd thought she was part of the group. She had been shown very clearly that she wasn't.

"That puts you in your place," Linao said, an edge to her voice, as if she sympathized with Wren. "So, how sure are you we're going in the right direction?"

"Everything here looks familiar," Wren said, letting her gaze sweep past the trees her nanos said were a landmark. "Maybe we need to slow down now?"

There was no way she was showing them the wreck. She had gotten the sense she and Ed were dead the moment their usefulness was up.

The early winter dusk was already creeping up on them, though, and she wondered what the plan was for where they were spending the night. Darkness was falling swiftly, and the clouds on the horizon were a nasty bruised purple.

As if she'd just noticed all this herself, Linao turned suddenly to Renard. "Did you bring any gear for us to sleep out?"

He lifted his head in disgust and shook his head. "No."

It was obvious they hadn't, so Wren didn't know why Linao had even asked. To point out to him that it was his fault, probably, rather than hers.

This was looking less and less well planned by the moment.

They hoped she could find the wreckage, but if they'd been looking for it for all the time she'd been away from Ytla, how did they think she'd be any better at finding it?

"We provide your supplies, we're offering you a place in our arrangements," Linao said. "You're the ones who know this terrain, the distances, and what equipment we need and I expect a little advance warning about those things." She was holding her laz now, pointing it right at Renard. "Are we going to be trying to get back in the dark?"

Renard stared at the laz. "I know what happened to your last fake cult set-up. The one on Cepi?" Renard said. "Don't think I don't know you'd do the same to me when I've served my purpose."

Linao looked at him for a long moment. "Cepi didn't go to plan. We put people in place who made some very strange decisions. Some of it wasn't their fault, I grant you, but some of it was. We were operating on the very edge of the blade there. There were very real time limits that made it tricky. If there had been another way, we'd have gotten them off Cepi, rather than blown it all up."

"That was back in the good old days, over a year ago now, wasn't it?" Ed spoke for the first time in a long time. "When Garmen and Lassa were still breakaway planets and your Core Companies still controlled money and influence."

Linao looked over at him, and there was some anger in that look. "Yes. So you can imagine if we were desperate then, how much more desperate we are now that we no longer hold Garmen and Lassa."

"Now that you're hunted," Wren said.

In response to that, Linao shifted the angle of her arm, pointing the laz at Ed's chest. She flicked some setting on the side. "Unless you make some progress in the next minute, your Halatian friend here will be killed. I've upped the settings." She flicked out her comms set and looked down as if checking the time.

Wren didn't want to cooperate, because like Renard, she felt they would be killed when their usefulness was over, but it was better than being killed right now.

"I said this place looks familiar, didn't I? Those trees look like some I might have gone through." She pointed.

"Go look," Linao told Navar and Fenton, and they jogged away.

There was silence for long minutes. Ed held himself still, but he was more watchful now than recuperating.

Renard, obviously sensing he no longer needed to worry about a laz blast to the chest, took out some water and drank, and his two sidekicks did the same.

A shout rose up from deep within the trees, and then Navar came jogging back. "She's right. It's there." He looked over at Linao as if waiting for orders, and she flicked her gaze behind the sidekicks as if to tell him to take up the rear. He gave a nod, and then they all went into the forest.

The wreckage was less than a five minute walk away.

Well done, she told the nanos. *I think you saved Ed's life.*

Linao had kept her laz on Ed, but when they stepped out into the long, wide scar the wreckage had carved for itself all those hundreds of years ago, she let her arm drop.

It looked different to how she remembered it, but the weather had been wild and she'd been running for her life. She'd caught glimpses of a massive, rotting hulk of metal, but now she could see just how big it really was. And this was only part of the original ship.

Steel girders rose like the ribs of a gigantic beast from the ground, and over time, sand and foliage had covered the base, so it looked as if it was planted in the ground—some strange, organic structure.

A forest had grown up around it, or it had landed in the forest, which had slowly reclaimed its space, with the canopy of the massive trees completely hiding all sight of the wreck from above.

Wren glanced back, checking to see who had eyes on her and Ed, to see if they could maybe disappear into the brush, but Renard was looking straight at her.

"How?" he asked.

"I thought I recognized the trees," she said, with a shrug.

"This is what your people found while they were here?" Linao asked, gesturing, and Wren looked over to see a small pile of items set in the lee of one of the curved metal girders.

Renard glanced back to his side kicks. "Kine?"

The dark-haired one nodded. "Looks about right."

"He was one of the people chasing Thorakis?" Linao focused on the unfortunate Kine.

Kine lifted his chin in assent.

"Kine and Crach were both there," Renard said. "Made sense to bring the two who had already been here."

She eyed the men for a beat then turned to Wren. "Where were you?"

"Hiding." Wren waved her hand vaguely. "I could barely see my hand in front of my face, the rain was coming down so hard. And I didn't see anything like that," she said, looking at the pile of equipment they had stripped from the wreck instead of looking for her.

"Besides, we shot you, didn't we?" Kine said.

She shook her head, because there had been no sign of the shot by the time she'd reached the SF base on Ytla. It had been a glancing strike, but it had been a strike, nevertheless. "Came close, but you didn't hit."

"I got a hit signal," Kine insisted.

"Maybe you hit the edge of the wreck where I went to ground," she said with a shrug. "Ask Navar. I didn't have any laz wounds on me when I got to base."

"That's true. But you weren't in great shape, in spite of that. Three days on the run with no food took its toll." Navar wasn't paying attention to her, he was staring at the wreckage, face alight with awe.

"She looked the worse for wear?" Linao asked, and something about the question caused the banked fear in Wren to whoosh to life.

"Of course." Navar looked over at her at last. "She was running for days through rough terrain in wild weather. She was close to collapse."

"How quickly did she bounce back?" Linao asked.

Navar shook his head. "They took her off planet straight away, to the med unit of the Ern, the battleship that was patrolling this part of Aponi territory."

"I wonder what those medical records will say?" Linao asked.

Wren met her suspicious gaze. "I imagine you can intimidate or bribe someone to have a look." She twisted her lips. "What are you getting at, Linao?"

Linao looked like she wanted to explain, but also didn't, because of their audience.

She suspects about us, the nanos said.

Yes. Wren wondered how. It sounded like the warriors who carried nanos on Fjern transformed bodily, which was nothing like how it worked for her. Were there others in the VSC who, when they'd found a wreck, had also found the nanos that went with it?

The last place a wreck had been discovered was on Fynian, a habitable moon just like Ytla, and before that, it had been Faldine, the new planet the VSC was establishing. There had also been the ghost ship the Raxians had found even longer ago. An ancestral battleship just floating in space. What had happened to the nanos that might have been on those vessels?

Also, she recalled the Protection Unit soldier that Ed was sure had seen her silver shield when the observatory maintenance team had been killed. He could well have passed that information on to Linao.

In the distance, the sound of rumbling grew solidly louder, and Wren turned in that direction. "Looks like a storm," she said.

"A couple of tents would be handy right now," Linao said, shooting a look at Renard. "Is there a place to find cover in the wreck?"

"Yes." Kine moved forward, walking down the line of metal ribs and then disappearing from sight.

After a moment Linao started after him, her laz still pointed in Ed's general direction as the stretcher floated along with her.

Kine was pulling back branches that had been blown against a large opening, and Crach stepped up to help him. After a moment, Fenton joined them.

When they'd cleared the entrance, Wren could see a room with a floor of soil and leaves. The ceiling was low, but Wren guessed the original floor was several feet lower than it was now, and that a few thousand years of wind had slowly filled in the space with debris.

The first hard, stinging raindrops began pelting down, and they all moved inside. It was instantly warmer. Calmer.

Better.

"Why didn't you store the equipment you found in here?" Linao asked, irritated.

Kine waved at the door. "Because while I could see there was a room beyond, it was just myself and Crach, and we didn't have time to move the branches. Given the weather, it would have been a wasted effort anyway."

She stepped to the doorway, looked out at the rain that was now sheeting down. "How long will this last?"

Renard gave a shrug. "All night, most likely."

"We're no more than an hour from our freighter. I'm not spending the night here." Linao turned back to study them. "I'll go get the freighter and land it as close as I can. We can use the hover stretcher to load the artifacts directly into the bay. I don't like leaving them out in the weather like this."

"They've been out in weather like this for thousands of years, if this really is an ancestral ship," Renard said.

"It is." She didn't explain how she knew, but Wren guessed Evette Linao was not used to explaining herself to anyone. She looked over at Navar and Fenton. "Watch our two prisoners. I'll be back in just over an hour."

She ducked out and disappeared almost immediately.

"Well." Renard leaned back against a wall and then sank down to his haunches, looking out of the door as if to be sure she'd gone. "She's not too friendly, is she?"

Fenton and Navar refused to respond.

"Got nothing to say?" Kine asked them, speaking without being spoken to for the very first time.

"We're SF teams, man," Fenton said. "We've heard about her, but we only met her this morning for the first time. We hardly know a damn thing about her, except she's in charge."

Renard gave a snort of derision. "Fine. And what about this one?" He gestured to Ed, who was still sitting on the hover stretcher, arms still restrained in front of him, quietly watching everything. "Who's Thorakis's friend?"

Renard didn't know who Ed was, Wren realized. And he hadn't asked until Linao was gone, even though he must have been dying to find out.

"He's SF teams, same as us," Navar said.

Wren was interested that he didn't elaborate, didn't say Ed had only just rejoined, and as a specialist, not a soldier.

"A Halatian in the teams? Don't they try to make sure you lot don't get so much as a boo boo on your knee? Being part of the teams would be too high risk, wouldn't it?" Renard was watching Ed with interest.

Ed looked coolly back. "No. That would be discriminatory."

"So why are you here? Wrong place, wrong time?" Renard persisted.

"Why are you so interested?" Fenton asked, stepping in front of Ed, as if to shield him from Renard's questions.

And then Wren got it. They didn't want to talk about Ed, because some time before her nanos had woken her up, Linao, Navar and Fenton must have had a conversation about how they still had a use for Ed when it came to the Guan scanner.

Linao's threat to kill Ed had been a bluff.

And as she couldn't know where it was, because it was in a hidden passage in the Gate, she might well need Wren, too. As motivation for Ed to talk.

Something had changed since they'd tried to blow her and Ed up on the space observatory. Maybe now they had Ed as a prisoner, they thought it would be handy to have his skills with the scanner for themselves.

She had done her part. Had led them to the wreck.

Her role was finished.

Now they were going to use Ed.

Which meant they'd definitely flip things around from now. Hold the laz to her throat to get Ed to cooperate.

And just like she had, so would he.

So they had better find a way to escape.

Soon.

33

Ed had thought his usefulness to their enemies was in his relationship to Wren.

The two of them had revealed too much. Shown their attachment too clearly.

She would do what they asked of her to save him, and they knew it.

But now, as Fenton blocked Renard and his two men from looking at him, Ed realized it wasn't strictly true that that was his only value.

And the only other thing he had to offer was the Guan scanner.

Pontia said there was another warehouse, that he'd lied about its location, and then he'd killed himself.

Even though Linao didn't know of Pontia's death yet, she would soon enough. And either way, she'd need his scanner to find it.

Which meant she needed him.

"What's the big secret?" Renard asked Fenton. Ed could just see his head, tilted to the side, as if trying to look around Fenton.

Fenton said nothing, and neither did Navar.

"All right," Renard said, getting comfortable against the wall. "All you've done is make me more interested, but so be it."

He was baiting them, Ed could see, and enjoying himself while he did it.

Silence fell as they settled down to wait for Linao to return. The rain was still pounding down, making it hard to talk anyway as it drummed against the metal.

As usual, his gaze came to rest on Wren. She was looking out at the silver wall of water, her expression contemplative. She sensed him looking at her and turned, sent him a quick, secret smile. He had the feeling she was about to do something.

Then she stood up, almost panicked, hands scrabbling at her heart. "I feel strange. Like I can't breathe . . ."

She fell to the ground, choking, and Fenton, Kine and Crach all moved toward her.

Ed instinctively did the same, but Navar gripped his shoulder, and he felt the press of a laz against his shoulder blade.

"What is it?" Renard asked, also crouching beside her as she rolled onto her side, gasping.

"Maybe a side-effect of the laz strike?" Fenton asked, looking back over his shoulder at Navar. "A heart attack?"

"Could be," Ed said, as he saw Fenton's palm press against Wren's forehead.

Fenton rose to his feet, moved back a little and leaned against the wall, his face a little slack.

"What is it?" Kine glanced up at him, and put his own hand against her forehead.

He pulled it back instantly. "She's burning up."

He shuffled to make room for Renard, who was looking down at Wren with a suspicious frown. "She has a fever?"

"Feel," Kine invited, then sat down beside her, the same slightly blank expression on his face as Fenton was wearing.

Renard hesitated. Ed had to give it to him, he was wary, and he was right to be, but he couldn't work out what the trick was, so he touched the side of her face, grimaced.

"She *is* hot. What setting were you using when you hit her?" He glanced over at Navar.

Navar shook his head. "It was medium-range. Enough to render them both unconscious."

"Maybe too much for her. Especially as she's been doing some serious walking since you arrived, looking for the wreck." Renard stood. "Put her on the hover stretcher," he ordered Crach.

Crach scooped her up, and Ed saw Wren's hands flop, her fingers making contact with the bare skin of Crach's wrist.

Ed jumped awkwardly off the stretcher to give Crach access and shot a look at Navar, gesturing with his tied hands to his ankles. After a moment's hesitation, Navar bent to unshackle him and they both shuffled back as Crach laid her down.

Crach moved away, backing into the wall and then sliding down it to sit with his legs extended in front of him. He closed his eyes as if he was going to sleep.

Navar reached out a hand out to see how feverish Wren was, and gave a start when his fingers touched her face.

"Do we have a med kit?" he asked.

No one even answered, and without commenting on that, Navar moved back to the wall next to Crach and leaned against it, crossing his arms over his chest.

She had enthralled them all.

Wren sat up, and Ed extended his tied hands to help her off the stretcher. She grasped his arms at the wrists and his restraints fell away.

He kept his face neutral, but he couldn't believe how easy that had been.

They walked out into the pouring rain, Ed taking his lead from Wren, keeping his movements easy and flowing.

As soon as they were out of sight, they ran.

"That was inspired," Ed said, finally dropping her hand so they could go single file through the narrow path between the bushes.

"It will only last a few minutes," she said. "But I don't think either of us wants to be there when Linao comes back."

"No." He wondered what Linao would make of what happened. What the men would make of it, too, come to that.

"She already thinks I have the nanos," Wren said. "This will confirm it."

"Maybe," Ed said, holding a branch back for her as they worked their way deeper into the forest. "But she can't know for sure, and none of those guys will admit they just sat down and watched you leave. None of them."

She made a sound at the back of her throat, as if she wasn't convinced, but he was. They were not going to confess to being manipulated.

Certainly not to Linao. She already thought they were lacking.

"We should head for the scientists' camp," Wren said. "They don't have amazing security, but they do have some to protect against the Har Met Vent, and they hate the SF team leader on Ytla, Lieutenant Trent. They'll hide us without a second thought."

"Why do they hate him?" Ed saw the path widened up ahead, and paused so Wren could jog up next to him.

"He wouldn't let them study the carvings, although we know now that wasn't Trent, it was someone above him. But Trent was pleased to deny them. He acted like they were weaklings who couldn't handle a bit of trouble when they called the SF teams in to help them with the Har Met Vent. Professor Tai was very insulted. She's organized, careful and cares for her people. She thinks Lieutenant Trent is a condescending oaf."

"How do you know all this?" Ed asked, amused.

"I was in the same runner up to the battleship with her, after I rescued myself. She was going up to complain about Trent, and she and I got on very well."

"Well, you couldn't have been feeling too friendly toward Trent by then yourself." Ed wasn't feeling too friendly toward him, either. "Is Trent still here?"

"I think the base was shut down and they're back in Nanganya. They only came out to help Professor Tai, and the plan was to leave after I rescued myself."

Causing mischief elsewhere, Ed thought. He hoped they weren't amongst the crews looking for Ethan Hyt and Velda Shanïha. The

Demeter captain and the Head of Defense would be in even more danger, if that was the case, because at the very least, Trent had been compromised.

"Did you pick up that Navar was on Trent's team when I got back to the Ytla SF base?" Wren asked him.

"I did. But it looks like he's in the Demeter team now. I wonder if he transferred over with Mornes and Jenik, the two who tried to kill Hyt at his apartment?"

"He might have come across earlier, because I'd have thought Ethan Hyt would have been suspicious of him, transferring across at the same time as those two. You'd think he'd be suspended." Wren paused. "And Fenton is obviously not a transfer, he's from Demeter."

"This goes deep." Way deeper than he could believe. He hoped they had finally reached the bottom of it, but he had a feeling there were probably a few more surprises to come.

The rain suddenly stopped, almost as quickly as it had started. It was already getting dark, and the cloud cover didn't help, but it was a massive relief when the hard, cold drops ceased.

Wren stopped, and he turned to her.

Her hair was plastered to her head, her face glowing with exertion, and for some reason, the silver circlet and the silver wrist bands were back on her.

She saw his gaze go to them.

"Protecting my face and hands from sharp branches," she said, with an almost embarrassed shrug.

He reached out and pulled her to him, and for a moment they stared at each other.

Then he bent his head to kiss her and they stood, still, calm, and quiet, for a long moment.

Until the sound of a freighter overhead forced them apart.

"She's back." Wren didn't release him. Instead she rested her cheek on his chest.

"How far is Professor Tai's camp?" Ed asked.

"I actually don't know. The professor told me it was about a day's hike from where the SF set up their base, but she said she might move to their base after they left, as it was a better spot." She looked over her shoulder as they both heard the freighter come down to land.

"How did you find the SF base that first time? I didn't think about it before, but now I'm on the ground, I can see how hard it is to navigate."

"The mountain," she said.

He turned, keeping one arm still around her, and saw the top of the mountain rising above the treeline.

"The base was at the foot of that mountain. That's the one thing I knew for sure. I kept it in my sights, and though I went wrong a few times and had to double back, I had somewhere to aim for."

"And it took you three days." Ed wondered how long they could keep out of Linao's clutches. Especially as she had the freighter.

"I was weaker then, and I know the better routes now." Wren lifted her shoulders. "It will still probably take two days, though."

"Then let's go." Ed didn't say it, because he knew with the two of them working together, they could do plenty of amazing things, but the chances of them making it to the mountain were not good.

And Linao would know that was the first place they'd head for.

34

The roar of the freighter overhead was by now a familiar sound.

Linao was hunting them from the air, and most likely the men were searching for them on the ground.

It was fully dark now, and that had helped when they had to break cover and run to the next patch of forest, but it was also slower going, moving through thick foliage with no lights.

Linao would surely have to pack it in soon, but so would they.

Even with her nanos, Wren was tired, and while Ed moved as if he could run all night, she suspected he wouldn't say no to some sleep, either.

"There." Ed had slowed down in front of her, a tall silhouette in the afterglow of Linao's disappearing freighter, and now he stopped, pointing to a small rocky outcrop she hadn't noticed because of the trees surrounding it.

"I think there's a ledge up there." Ed moved to the base of the sheer rock face, and began climbing one of the trees growing up beside it.

If there was a ledge, they'd have somewhere relatively safe to rest, so Wren followed him, and when she reached the branch above, he was crouched on a small shelf, hand out to grab her.

She grasped his hand and stretched out her leg to bridge the distance from the tree to the outcrop, letting Ed haul her to him.

They fetched up against cold, wet stone, then bent and wedged themselves under the overhang, finding a narrow strip of dry rock.

It was still cold, but if it started raining again, as it had done on and off as they'd run, they'd be out of the weather, and no one could easily sneak up on them here.

The freighter wouldn't be able to see them, either.

"It's perfect," Wren said.

"So perfect." Ed grinned at her. "Forget a warm bed, a hot shower, a nice meal and maybe some Wren-made cake. This beats everything."

She snorted out a laugh. "Well, it does." She leaned against him, and he shifted so he could get his arm around her shoulder.

The sound of shouting stopped their banter dead, and Ed slowly lowered them both down, so they were lying flush to the rocky floor, as invisible as they could be.

The trees that crowded around the base of the outcrop were thick with foliage, and though the shouts had stopped, Wren could hear the sound of someone walking through dead leaves, and then coughing.

"Don't get sick." It was Navar, and Wren guessed he was talking to Fenton. He wouldn't care if Renard or the two thugs got sick.

"I've got some meds. But I'm done for tonight," Fenton answered. "There's enough cover here, we could light a fire. The ground under that tree there is still completely dry, despite the weather."

There was silence for a bit, and Wren thought she heard the sounds of branches being dragged.

"Linao isn't going to be happy," Navar said.

"Fuck her. And I think you're wrong. She needs sleep, too. She can't keep running that freighter up and down. They've obviously holed up somewhere, and there's too much ground to cover to work out where in the pouring rain in the middle of the night."

"Agreed." A moment after he spoke, Navar's comms unit chirped.

"We've found a place out of the rain. We'll be setting up camp." He didn't say anything else.

"Confirmed." Linao's answer was slow in coming, but Fenton had been right. She couldn't keep going.

"Well, shit." Ed breathed in her ear. "This is awkward."

She swallowed a laugh. "But not so awkward we can't sneak past them and steal Linao's freighter," she whispered back.

Ed went still behind her, as if she had absolutely shocked him. "I like the way you think," he whispered at last. "But she'll sleep in the freighter, is my guess."

"We took her out in the freighter before. We can do it again." She believed that absolutely. She also didn't think they'd get off here free and clear any other way.

"Hey." The voice that called out sounded like Kine. "You packing it in?"

"For tonight." Navar answered.

"Thanks for letting us know." Kine made no attempt to soften his footsteps as he walked into the little copse. "It's pretty dry." His surprise was clear.

"We just let Linao know we found a good spot," Fenton said, almost as if he was trying to smooth things over. "Look for dry firewood."

Kine grunted, but although she couldn't see over the lip of the ledge, Wren could hear more branches being dragged.

Slowly, all the men found their way to the spot, and it didn't take long for firelight to bloom below them.

The freighter had clearly turned back, and the roar of its engines was almost unpleasant as Linao found a spot very close by to land.

Wren guessed she'd stay put, but ten minutes after she'd landed, she made an appearance.

"I brought dinner."

Well. It seemed the woman wasn't totally heartless. Wren tried to picture her deciding to inconvenience herself to bring food from the freighter to the men, and cynically decided it was to keep up morale, rather than that she cared if they went hungry or not.

Her own stomach gave a faint grumble at the thought of food, and Ed rested a big, warm hand over her midriff.

"Same," he whispered in her ear.

The sound of packages opening drifted up, and Wren realized Linao had taken it a step further and was going to eat with the men.

"This terrain is more forested than I realized," Linao was saying. "It's hard to see what's going on below."

"I think they've found a hidey-hole somewhere and are waiting out the night and the weather," Navar said. "We could be way ahead of them, rather than trying to catch up."

"That would be annoying," Renard said. "But it's possible. I think they're ahead, though. She will take him to the old base."

"She knows that's the first place we'll think of. What about the scientists? Would she go find them?" Linao asked.

Navar shrugged. "I don't know if she even knows where their camp is. I don't. They moved after we left, because Renard and his friends knew where the old one was, and they didn't feel safe there."

"We only prodded them to stay in character," Renard said, a laugh in his voice. "Although it was fun while it lasted. I was hoping Professor Tai would be the one to go look at the carvings so we could kidnap her. She said some very hurtful things about us, and I imagined her, all frightened and alone in the hut we built to put our hostage in, but then Trent insisted on an artifact consultant, and we got the fiery Wren instead."

At his words, Ed's arms tightened around her, and whether it was the nanos, or just her own intuition, she knew if he could do it without ruining their plans, he would have killed Renard right then.

"The same hut Wren escaped from?" Linao asked.

"The storm ripped the roof off," Renard said, sounding regretful. "We weren't exactly working with the best materials. Which I'm sure you know, given you're the ones who provided them."

Linao said nothing for a beat. "We've given you an excellent deal, Renard. You get a new home on Aponi, you get to stop running from the Arkhoran authorities, and you get enough resources to live a life of luxury. A few months of hard living is surely a small price to pay."

"You said that before, how lucky me and my crew are, but while you've obviously got people in influential places, who can pull the right strings, you surely do not have the whole of Aponi on your payroll. I'd say most of the good citizens of Aponi will resist your efforts to take their home from them. Living without looking over my shoulder for Arkhoran authorities will be good, but I have a feeling that will be replaced by having to watch my back just walking down the streets of Demeter."

They planned to take the whole planet of Aponi?

Wren actually heard roaring in her ears, and she knew her mouth had fallen open.

"Fuck. Me." Ed obviously felt the same. "I was thinking way too small."

They surely couldn't be serious, but Wren had to admit they'd underestimated these people too many times.

Linao wouldn't say what the plan was when they'd arrested her, had pretended to be using it for leverage, but Wren had guessed some kind of smuggling operation. She never would have guessed the former Cores thought they had a pathway to taking a planet that was part of the strongest coalition in their part of the galaxy.

The six other planets, plus the new vassal planets, would be mobilized to take it back.

And the Cores would know it.

Which meant they thought they had a way around it.

"It's the Caruso who worry me." Crach spoke, and it was as if the ledge they were lying on tilted.

Wren twisted her head to look up at Ed. Even in the darkness she could see his shock.

The Caruso were involved?

"The Caruso should worry everyone." Linao spoke into the silence that had fallen at Crach's words. "But they need trivolun, and Aponi has the biggest deposits, and because it's the furtherest planet out, it's the easiest to take."

"And you think the VSC will just let them take it?" Renard gave a laugh. "Like they didn't let them take Lassa and Garmen?"

"No, but the Caruso are prepared to keep the VSC at bay this time. They've been eyeing the trade routes that run from the VSC to the other planetary groups and the independent planets since the VSC established themselves as the heavy-weights of the sector. The Caruso like to think they're the heavy-weights, and they're ready to muscle in and show that they are." Linao cleared her throat. "I'm aware it won't be easy, and I think the Caruso overestimate themselves somewhat, but the Razors have proved themselves almost unstoppable."

"The Caruso came up with them?" Kine asked.

"It was a collaboration between some of the engineers in the Core Companies of Garmen and Lassa, and the Caruso. But the Caruso built them, as we couldn't do it with the VSC watching. We were given the first group off the production line. The Caruso were happy to let us take the risks, but it worked out for us, too. The VSC will find it hard to take Aponi back once we have it."

"And how will you take Aponi?" Renard asked. "The government isn't going to go quietly."

"We have a stockpile of weapons—enough to bring down the Protection Unit headquarters, SF headquarters, and the Department of Defense. After that, we'll have some Caruso troops to help keep control."

Except, they didn't have the stockpile of weapons any more. Which was why Linao was so desperate to find Ed.

And she was being careful not to fill Renard in on the reality of the situation.

"We have to get off this moon and back to Demeter," Ed breathed.

That was an understatement.

"How many Razors are there now?" Kine was asking.

"We've got one left and the Caruso tell us they have three. The Caruso used up all their tivolun deposits to make them, so we need to take Aponi and secure the supply before we can make any more."

"Why are you doing this?" Renard asked. "Why not take on a new identity and live a quiet life somewhere? The VSC authorities will probably never find you."

Linao gave a laugh. "What kind of life is that? We needed a place to set up business again."

"You had that, though, and you ruined it." Crach's tone was bitter. It made Wren wonder if he knew what he was talking about from personal experience.

"Which breakaway were you from?" Linao asked.

So she'd heard it, too.

"Lassa," Crach admitted. "I hid after the Bodivas took control. That's where I saw how the Caruso do things. Because you and your Core Company friends had a deal with the Caruso then, too, and it didn't go so well."

"We made mistakes," Linao said. "But that's done. The reality is we need to set up elsewhere, and we've searched long and hard for an alternative. We found a new planet, with trivolun deposits, but it was too dangerous to operate there. Before that, we took a hard look at Faldine, but it's too difficult to mine there with the magnetic fields. Aponi ended up being the best option." Linao sounded exactly like the top boss Wren guessed she was. "We already had contacts on Aponi, because two years ago we tried to buy up some trivolun deposits, and were setting up a network. It made Aponi an even easier choice."

"And lucky us, to be invited along for the ride," Renard said, and there was more than a touch of sarcasm in his voice.

"We can afford to be generous," Linao said, perfectly serious, although Wren suspected she was yanking Renard's chain as hard as he was yanking hers.

The one thing she did know—she and Ed couldn't afford to wait a moment longer than necessary.

They needed to get off Ytla, and let the Aponi know what was about to come down on their heads.

35

WREN LIFTED UP, TRYING TO SEE WHERE EVERYONE HAD CHOSEN TO sleep, but the leaves on the tree in front of them were too dense, and they blocked all view.

Their pursuers had been asleep for at least two hours, and she and Ed were both ready to go.

She got on her hands and knees and then edged back to give Ed room to move, waiting for him where the outcrop was closest to the tree.

She could jump it, but that might make some noise, so she waited for him to step across, one foot on the ledge, the other on the thick branch, and pull her over.

She made her way down the trunk first, keeping silent, her nanos humming in anticipation.

The fire was glowing, and four men lay around it, close enough to get the benefit of the heat it was putting out. They had heard Renard offer to do first guard watch, and Linao had gone back to the freighter.

Wren noticed she had not extended the invitation to anyone to join her.

Neither had anyone asked if they could.

The men lay so close to the tree she had just climbed down, she could have touched Navar if she crouched down and extended her arm.

Ed dropped silently down beside her, and tensed when he saw how tight things were.

Wren relaxed, letting her nanos steer, and began to pick a path through the sleeping men.

Ed followed directly behind her, stepping where she stepped.

The moment they were out of the circle, and out of the fire's glow, she felt a bloom of elation.

We like doing things like this, her nanos told her. *Since we chose you, life has been more interesting.*

Before that, you were sitting around a wrecked spaceship for two thousand years, Wren teased them. *I could do nothing more than bake cakes all day, and life would be more interesting.*

She felt their amusement thrum through her.

Ed tapped her shoulder and pointed to a light visible through the trees.

The freighter.

Linao had landed just beyond the copse, and given the rain had started to fall again, Wren was grateful for how close it was.

They moved through the trees toward it, and she kept watch for Renard. There was no sign of him, and something about that made her nervous.

She needn't have worried. Renard was standing at the entrance to the freighter, talking to Linao.

She was making him stand in the rain, not giving an inch to let him inside.

They were arguing.

And then Renard struck, shoving Linao hard and forcing his way in.

The door shut behind them.

She and Ed glanced at each other.

"Not sure whether this is better or worse," Ed said.

She wasn't either. But it was the reality they had to deal with, and she jogged to the freighter, touched the lock pad and waited a moment after the door opened, just to see what was going on inside.

The passage was empty, but there were sounds of a struggle further down, coming from the tiny bridge.

She stepped in, with Ed right behind her.

The freighter was warm, and it was glorious to be out of the wind and rain.

Wren used her hands to push back her hair, squeezing out the water, and her fingers encountered the circlet on her forehead as she did so. She lifted up her arms in surprise and saw the silver bracelets were back on her wrists.

She hadn't even felt them.

Because they are part of you, her nanos told her. *No laz fire will touch us again.*

She could get behind that.

Ed had gone still, and she turned to see what was wrong.

He was watching her, eyes hooded.

"What is it?" she whispered.

He shook his head. "Sounds like Renard is winning the fight."

She turned her attention back to the bridge, and decided Ed was right. Linao might be doing her best, but Renard was much bigger.

She got to the end of the passage and looked into the room just in time to see Renard step back, Linao lying at his feet.

He was holding a laz in his hand, and as he hadn't had one that she could remember, she guessed he'd taken it away from Linao and used it on her.

He started at the sight of her, and then gave a smirk. "Oh, you make it so easy."

"Do I?" Wren asked. "Thanks for disabling Linao, you can leave now."

Renard's gaze flicked over her shoulder, where she knew Ed was standing.

"Bit harder now I'm not restrained and I have a friend along, isn't it?" Wren asked.

"We were playing a role," Renard said, slowly, as if he thought she had trouble comprehending his words. "Sure, I maybe had a bit too much fun with it, but you were always going to go back home in one piece." He frowned. "What's with the weird jewelry?"

Wren looked down at the bracelets. "Weird? They're great."

She looked back up. "Now, hand over that laz, please." She walked toward him, hand extended, and he grabbed for her, his big hand clamping her wrist as he spun her up against his chest, so she was facing the door. Facing an extremely calm Ed.

He leaned against the doorjamb and crossed his arms over his chest. "Anytime now. I don't like his hands on you."

"You think she can do—?"

Behind her, Renard dropped like a felled tree, hitting his head on the corner of the control panel as he went down.

Wren winced. "Ouch."

"I could see what you were going to do, but let's try something different next time," Ed said, a little grumpy. "Like no physical contact."

"Got you." She smiled at him as he grabbed Renard's ankles and dragged him out. She looked down at Linao, and considered what to do with her.

When Ed came back, she raised her brows. "Keep as a prisoner, or dump on Ytla?" she asked.

He pursed his lips thoughtfully. "My gut says keep. They'll swoop down and get her if we leave her here. She's right at the top of this, and all her protestations about being done with them is a flat-out lie."

"Agreed." She went to find restraints, came back and shackled Linao, then pulled her into the small change room next to the bathroom.

"Let's go."

"I hope you can fly this," Ed said, with a sudden quirk of his lips. "Because I can't. I'm only licensed for petrals, which are single-passenger craft."

She looked down at her hands, flexed her fingers. Looked up at him in surprise. "Apparently, I can."

He gave a laugh, throwing back his head in delight. Then he reached out and took one of her hands, kissed her knuckles. "First time, though?"

She nodded. "I hope you like living dangerously."

He kissed her knuckles again. "I most certainly do."

36

THE BATTLESHIP WAS GONE.

Ed stared out at the empty space around Ytla and tried to process it.

"Where did they go?" Wren sat at the controls, calmer now than she'd been when they'd first taken off.

She'd given him a wide-eyed look as she'd touched all the right buttons and danced her fingers over the screen in front of her, cute even while being possessed by nano tech.

He was ridiculously smitten.

The nanos had been wasting their time and energy enthralling him when he and Wren had met, because he couldn't see another path for them except the one they were on, no matter what had happened.

Wren finally seemed to be accepting that, too. She was no longer flashing him quick, nervous looks, just in case he wasn't making decisions completely on his own.

"Maybe the Caruso popped their heads up, and the battleship went to have a look?" If the Caruso were coordinating with the Core Company execs who were behind this plot, then drawing the battleships away from Aponi while they tried to take the government made sense. Except . . .

"They've done it too early, if the location of the second warehouse died with Pontia." Ed knew Evette Linao didn't know the location of the warehouse—that's why she needed him and his scanner.

But maybe one of her colleagues had since discovered it, and moved ahead with the plan without Linao.

That wasn't a good thought.

"Pontia surely couldn't be the only one who knew where it was," Wren said.

"You'd think so, but Linao definitely doesn't know. She must have worked out Pontia lied to her while we were still unconscious after Fenton and Navar hit us at the hover port. That's why she was hoping I'd find it for her." Ed braced as Wren turned the freighter toward Aponi. It was a bright globe ahead of them, and she accelerated to the highest speed the freighter was capable of as they headed for home.

"Can you get hold of Bartam?" Wren asked.

Ed moved to the comms unit, sent out a call. It was connecting, but they'd have to wait for a reply, as there was always a long delay on in-space comms from small, private spacecraft.

The unit signaled an incoming call by the time Aponi was clearly visible in the viewport.

"Ed." Bartam's voice was faintly distorted.

"The soldiers you sent to the hover port shot us, released our prisoner, and took us to Ytla, Lieutenant," Ed said.

Whatever Bartam responded was garbled. Then: "Fenton and Navar?"

"Didn't catch the first part, but yes, Fenton and Navar are compromised."

There was a faint screech from the unit and then nothing. Dead air.

Ed had a bad feeling about it.

He stepped up to the viewport, but Aponi looked as serene and beautiful as ever, green and blue and brown.

To the left, he saw a strangely-shaped vessel moving through the debris field that surrounded the half-destroyed observatory. It took him a moment to recognize it as a magnetic scooper, distorted by all the pieces of debris that had latched on to its sides.

"Our comms unit is working," Wren said, her fingertips touching it. "Whatever cut Bartam off is coming from below."

"I figured." Ed turned his attention back to Aponi. "They've taken out Department of Defense comms, is my guess."

That's what he would do as a first step to take over Aponi.

And whatever they'd done to lure the battleships away had worked, but those battleships would only be useful against the Caruso attack. They could do nothing about what was happening below.

And the genius of taking both Ethan Hyt and Velda Shanïha out of the equation became apparent. Because if the head of the SF in Nanganya was compromised, as they thought he was, Hyt and Shanïha were two of the most senior heads of defense on Aponi who were not involved in this plot.

There must be senior military officers who were clean, too—probably most of them were—but it only took a few.

Ed thought about the military base beside the hoverport, the five floors of the Gate that the military occupied. And wondered if any of it was still standing.

From the corner of his eye he saw a flash of movement, and then Wren leaned over the controls, and the freighter began to drop straight down.

"What was that?"

"I think it was a Razor." Wren spiraled them toward Aponi.

Ed tried to look, to get a better idea of where the threat lay, but the freighter was moving too fast now, and pointing down.

"We have a good bargaining chip, at least." He struggled over to the small room off the bridge, and saw Linao was awake and watching him from the floor where he'd attached her to a bolted down table with restraints.

The whole freighter was angled down and he had to work to get himself into a chair in front of the comms unit. "We have Evette Linao in our custody." He spoke using the open channel. "Shoot us down, and she dies with us."

Wren let them fall for a moment or two more, and then pulled up. "They've backed off." She looked over at him. "I'm guessing they'll want to make a deal for her."

"Head straight down to Aponi. We've got nowhere to go up here. Once we land, there are possibilities."

She gave a nod and pointed them back on their extreme descent.

"Hold your position."

Ed looked across at Wren as the order was barked through the comms. She shook her head, and he nodded in agreement.

"No."

What were these people going to do? Shoot anyway? So far, they'd kept Evette Linao alive. He didn't think they were going to stop now.

"You happy we risk this?" he asked.

"Oh, yes." Wren kept their descent steep and fast. "We stop and let them board, we're either dead or you're scanning for weapons and I'm walking around with a laz to my throat to make you cooperate. No thanks."

There was no hail from the hover port as they came into Aponi nearspace, and Ed could see a pillar of smoke coming from the city in the last light of the day.

Demeter lay sprawled out across the peninsula, the sea that surrounded it on three side dark and choppy. The mountains and forests to the north looked cool and green, but the columns of black and brown smoke said all was not as well as it should be.

Wren saw the smoke, too, and he heard her swear softly under her breath.

"This is actually happening." She glanced at him. "They've taken the comms, and maybe the hover port." She looked down at the instruments. "I can't tell whether it's safe or not to land."

"I'm guessing the military base will still be secure, even if the comms are down. Try to land there." Although Ed was worried someone with an itchy finger might just shoot them as they came in.

Wren adjusted the trajectory a little and the smaller launch pads of the military base came in to view, lights shining bright in the growing darkness. Smoke from the city drifted across the landing field and was reflected in the spotlights, turning the air hazy.

As they dropped down, Ed saw a unit of soldiers running out, armed with the big, cannon-like laz the military used to down spaceships.

He saw a few lifted onto shoulders, but no one shot them. Yet.

Wren landed and began shutting the engines off.

"I'll get Linao and go out there, calm them down while you power down," he said. He unclipped their prisoner from the table, and secured the restraints behind her back, taking her to the door and opening it.

He stood beside her, hand raised. "I'm Ed Zeneri from Demeter Special Forces," he called out.

A soldier motioned him with a hand to come, and so he pulled a struggling Evette Linao out onto the small bridge that had extended from the bay platform. The soldiers were waiting in a line, laz raised at the freighter.

"My partner is in there, shutting down," he said. "Wren Thorakis."

He recognized the captain in charge of the unit immediately. It was Captain Darnell, the head of the unit that had helped them search the freighters in the customs queue when they were up on the obs station.

"Darnell," he said, giving a brief salute.

"Zeneri. It's never boring with you." Darnell returned the motion. "Wren Thorakis can fly?"

"Lucky for us, or we'd still be on the run from our kidnappers on Ytla." He pushed Linao forward. "Whatever's just happened down here to cut off your comms, this woman's part of the group behind it."

"Is that so?" Darnell studied Linao carefully. "I'll accept your prisoner as payment for using our port, Zeneri."

Ed shrugged. "We didn't know if the hover port had been taken or not."

"They tried and failed," Darnell said, glancing over at Linao. "But they managed to do some damage. And the Gate's top floors are more or less destroyed."

That was better than Ed had guessed when he'd seen the smoke from the city center.

He turned back to look at the ship. The engine was off now, so he couldn't understand what was taking Wren so long.

He took a step toward it, and with a breath-crushing sizzle, a laz strike from high above hit the freighter. It exploded, throwing everyone in near proximity to the ground.

Ed went deaf as pieces of the ship flew around him, some of them on fire.

When he stumbled to his feet, he could feel blood leaking from a cut on his arm, could feel the ache of his back where he'd been slammed into the ground, but he only had eyes for the freighter.

Which was gone.

It was nothing but a collection of pieces.

Wren.

Wren had been in there.

His knees gave way, and he crashed back to the ground. Then he turned and looked over to where Captain Darnell was helping Evette Linao to her feet.

She sent him a quick look, and while he expected a smirk, he didn't see one.

This had been a little too close for comfort for her.

"Did you have a way to tell them you were safely out before they destroyed the freighter?" he asked, moving toward her.

She pursed her lips, not answering, but she had to have had a way to do it. They wouldn't have risked her after everything else they'd done to keep her alive.

"Whoa. We need this one alive to answer questions." Darnell was watching him.

Ed turned his head to look at the captain.

"Seriously, Ed. She's our only link to these people. And you look . . . dangerous." Darnell began to move backward, his grip on Linao tight.

"I'll take him to get patched up by a med tech," one of the soldiers said.

Ed turned back to what was left of the wreck, felt the shout that was inside him building up.

He'd only just found her, and now she was gone.

37

WREN STAGGERED AGAINST A VINE-COVERED WALL, DISORIENTED AND confused.

What—?

Dissipated? Had she dissipated?

Yes.

Her nanos sounded as freaked-out as she felt, and she leaned back against the wall, realizing the scent of the flowers was familiar. Was this . . .?

The place where you and Ed kissed recently, her nanos confirmed.

What happened? All she remembered was hearing a strange sizzle, and then— *The freighter was destroyed? Like the Protection Unit hover when we came back from the obs station?*

We realized just in time, the nanos answered.

Gratitude swamped her. She could have—would have—been dead without them.

Their response was shy pleasure, and she slid down to sit on the ground, nestled amongst the vines in the narrow alley, still trying to get her body to feel like her own. The shadows were deep this late in the day, and she felt safe and hidden for the moment.

Her nanos had dissipated her close to the hover port, so she could get back quickly.

Ed? she asked.

He was outside. We hope he is unharmed.

He would think she was dead, though.

She put herself in his shoes and forced herself back to her feet. She needed to get back there.

She started walking, joining the stream of people walking to the hover port, the stiffness and nausea making her slow, but as she got going, she felt her muscles loosen and she began to breathe easier.

She wondered why the Cores had risked their Razor to shoot at the freighter, knowing Evette Linao was a prisoner. And then she staggered a step or two, as she remembered what she had discovered just before the laser strike.

She came to a stop.

A strange file had caught her eye as she was shutting down, and she had opened it. Had sat in astonishment as she processed the contents.

There was raw trivolun stored in the mystery warehouse, along with the rest of the weapons. The desperation to find the location that Pontia had hidden was as much because the Caruso refused to risk a full-on confrontation with the Verdant String Coalition without some trivolun as proof of goodwill between the parties, as it was a need for the weapons themselves.

The Caruso wanted to test the ore, to be sure it was the grade necessary for their needs. The file mentioned that they had threatened to leave the Cores to deal with the fall-out if they didn't get it soon.

She had just started to copy the file onto her comms unit when . . .

They were monitoring the systems? They had to have been, to react so quickly to her discovery of the file.

They wouldn't have struck unless they'd known Evette Linao was no longer in the freighter, though. So someone at the military base was in their pocket, and had confirmed she was clear.

That wasn't a shock, she admitted to herself as someone bumped her in passing where she stood on the footpath, and she began moving again. But it was a good reminder. She would be better served going into the base quietly, and keeping out of sight until she found Ed.

No sense letting the Cores and their spies know she had survived.

ED LET the soldier steer him away from the wreckage and from Linao. He looked down at his hands, and realized they were fists.

That woman had called down death on Wren, and he had to fight the instinct to inflict even a small measure of retribution on her.

A med tech began patching him up, cleaning his wounds and sealing the cuts on his arms and face.

"You were lucky," the tech told him.

He didn't answer. He wasn't lucky at all.

When the tech moved away, Ed turned back to look at the wreck, and then frowned as something was jammed into his side.

He looked down, and saw it was a laz, pressed against his ribs.

"You and me are going to walk out of here, nice and slow." The soldier who'd taken him away from Captain Darnell patted his shoulder. "And you're going to look like it's completely voluntary."

"Another one," Ed said. The anger he felt, the white hot rage at these people who kept selling out Aponi, penetrated the fog he'd been in since the freighter was destroyed.

"Another one," the soldier said, grim-faced. "How many have you met?"

"Way, way too many," Ed told him. "It's getting ridiculous."

"Well, that's too bad." The soldier steered him toward the building behind the launch pads. "I'd rather not be doing this, but I don't have a choice."

"Sure." Ed let himself be led. He was feeling nihilistic now. He had nothing to lose, and it would be interesting to see what this asshole wanted from him. "Looking for the warehouse, are you?"

The soldier slowed, glanced over at him. "I don't know why they need you, and I don't want to know. Let's just keep things quiet, all right?"

"Right." Ed sent him a sidelong look. "The fact they can't find the warehouse with the weapons they need to take control of Demeter is not relevant. Got it."

"What do you mean? They blew up the Gate and almost took the hover port." The soldier's voice rose a little.

"I'm guessing that was with weapons that just came in recently, after me and my Guan scanner left the obs station, and they were able to sneak them in." Ed knew what they'd had in the warehouse that had gone up in flames, and the attempt on the hover port would not have been unsuccessful if they'd had access to that kind of weaponry.

"I don't want to know." The soldier pushed him a little harder, and he stumbled, reaching out a hand to steady himself against a pillar.

The soldier had brought them to the covered walkway built against the side of the building. The pillars that held up the steeply pitched roof were carved with the names of those who fought in various conflicts, and he felt the engravings under his palm.

"What is it?" The soldier's question was sharp, and a little worried.

Ed looked up, happy to be making him so nervous, and looked straight into Wren's eyes.

She lifted a hand to her lips, then moved back behind a pillar, into the shadows.

He stared, trying to work out if he'd imagined it.

Wren . . .

She must have crouched down, because when she peered out again, staring at him with worried eyes, she was low to the ground.

He bent over, hands to knees, just to drink in the sight of her.

She had dissipated. He shook his head, slowly straightening up. Her nanos had gotten her out in time. He hadn't even considered . . .

He drew in a deep breath.

"You need to keep moving." The soldier was looking around nervously.

He grunted an affirmation, began walking again. Speech was beyond him right now.

He forced himself not to look to his right when he passed the pillar she'd been hiding behind, but he guessed she would need to dissipate out of the military base, because the security was heavy.

Given the burning wreck behind him, he couldn't blame them.

But that didn't have any significance to him any longer.

He could breathe again.

"What the fuck is wrong with you?" The soldier hauled him toward the checkpoint that let out onto the street. "You better keep your mouth shut."

Ed grunted again. That wouldn't be a problem.

38

———

There had been blood on Ed's clothing.

Wren leaned against the building opposite the military base, getting over her third dissipation in less than an hour, and waited for him to come through the checkpoint.

The soldier who had clearly been holding a laz on him before, now looked like he was supporting Ed as they left, pretending to be helpful.

So that's who was the inside informant at the base.

She stepped into the flow of pedestrians behind them, trying to see if Ed was injured from the way he walked, but he seemed all right.

His cuts had been treated, she saw now, but he was moving slowly.

When he stopped and leaned over his knees again, she felt a leap of worry, until he turned his head a little to look behind him, and locked gazes with her for a moment.

He was making sure she was there.

She felt a weight lift off her, and kept only a few people between them all the way until they reached the warehouses behind the hover port.

When they stepped into a dark recess beside a building with a clearly neglected frontage, she let her nanos help her find a quick way onto the roof and carefully moved to the edge, crouching down to see what was going on below.

"You got him. That's good, Kaleb. You can go now." The man who spoke had a gritty voice, and he stepped out of the shadows from a large back entrance that looked like a loading bay, and held the laz in his hand directly at Ed's chest.

"This is the end if it, Opek," Kaleb said. "I've done everything you asked for. I don't want to hear from you again."

"Of course." Opek chuckled and Kaleb hesitated, then disappeared back onto the street, the stiffness in his posture telling Wren he wasn't a total idiot. He knew Opek would contact him without hesitation. That there was never going to be an end to it.

"One day, one or more of them will get tired of being dangled from a piece of string and bite," Ed said.

"That might have been a worry before, but the end is in sight," Opek said. "We'll be in charge soon enough, and there will be no need to pull strings any more."

"Things aren't going too well for you," Ed said. "You haven't managed the big takeover you were planning."

"I hear we have you to thank for that." Opek's voice dipped a little. "Still, I can appreciate a good adversary. You didn't give us as much trouble two years ago. It was a surprise when you started making things hard for us all this time later."

"You shouldn't have tried to kill me," Ed said. "That kind of thing tends to make me annoyed."

Opek barked out a laugh. "Yes, well, obviously we didn't employ someone with the ability to get the job done. Strange how fate works, because they've been dealt with for their error, yet, here I am, grateful they didn't in fact succeed because we need you alive more now than we needed you dead then."

"You're looking for Pontia's warehouse," Ed said.

Opek was silent for a beat. "Now, how did you know that?"

"Because Pontia told us about it just before he died. And then suddenly Evette Linao was very interested in me as soon as Wren found the ancestral wreck for her and she was no longer useful. It wasn't difficult to work out the thing that made *me* useful is my ability to use the scanner."

"The ancestral wreck?" Opek almost choked on the words. He drew in a deep, deep breath, pinching his nose between thumb and forefinger. "I see."

"Didn't tell you about that? What do you think Evette Linao was doing on Ytla?"

"It doesn't matter." Opek shook his head in a sharp movement. "Just tell me, where is the scanner?"

"At Defense Headquarters. Also known as the Gate. Which I think you blew up." Ed didn't hide the edge in his tone. "That was careless of you."

Another long silence. "Fortunately it looks worse than it is," Opek said. "Only the two upper floors were badly damaged."

Wren remembered Ed setting the scanner down in the secret passageway beside Velda Shanïha's office. That had been on the third floor. And there were eight.

It should be all right.

"Lucky," Ed said.

"I'll have someone fetch the scanner and bring it here. Where is it?" Opek reached for his comms unit.

"Locked up in Velda Shanïha's office."

Opek swore. "Where?"

"In her safe, I think." Ed shrugged.

Opek moved away, the laz still pointed at Ed, and he had a conversation with someone over his comms unit, voice hushed.

"My contact says that can't be right. You're lying." He came closer, and his grip on the laz was tighter. "You had the scanner when you left the runner at the hover port."

"The runner your lot blew up?" Ed asked.

Opek waved that away. "We have vision of you carrying it as you walked away. And while the word is you did go to Defense HQ after that, you couldn't have given the scanner to Velda Shanïha for safe-keeping, because she wasn't there."

"I went to her office, looking for her, and decided to leave it there." Ed lifted his hands.

"Her office was searched. There's nothing there that could possibly be the scanner. Where is it?" Now the laz was up against Ed's throat. "I won't ask again."

"I hid it." Ed eased back a bit. "Your contact won't find it."

"Then you and I will go and get it."

Wren could see this was the last thing Opek wanted to do. There would be increased security at headquarters after the attack, and while the building wasn't too far away, it was going to take time.

Ed lifted a shoulder. "You're the one holding the laz."

"Yes." Opek bit the word off and stepped back, waving Ed down the short alleyway toward the road.

The time had come.

Wren sprinted silently along the roof, dropped down to the ground, and pressed herself against the wall.

Ed walked past her, and a moment later, Opek, a stocky man all dressed in black, followed.

Wren came up behind him, rested her palm against his neck, and then stepped back as he slid silently to the side.

Ed had her in his arms seconds later.

They stood, pressed tight against each other, and then Ed breathed in a deep breath.

"I swear I can smell the flowers from that vine where we first kissed." He buried his nose in her hair.

"That's where my nanos dissipated me." She held him tighter.

"The romantics." He kissed the top of her head.

She could feel him trembling a little.

"I'm here. I'm safe."

"What took you so long in the freighter?" He still had a firm hold on her, and she relaxed into it.

"I found a file in the system. Linao must have been reading it while we were on Ytla. It seems the missing warehouse doesn't just contain weapons. There's a stockpile of trivolun there, too. The

Caruso want it before they take any more action against the VSC. Sort of like a down payment."

"That explains the desperation." He rubbed his chin on the top of her head and finally stepped back with a sigh. "So what's the plan?"

"I was thinking . . ." She looked up at him. "If the Caruso are so keen on getting that trivolun, let's give it to them."

39

"There." Ed's voice was a low rumble. "I see it."

They were standing on an empty street in the warehouse district, the pyre of smoke from the Gate burning behind them.

The black smoke was illuminated by the searchlights of runners circling the building, and Wren could smell the oily, nasty stink of it in her clothes and hair.

At least sneaking into headquarters via the secret passage, grabbing the scanner, and sneaking out again had taken less than ten minutes.

And now it had paid off.

"The one with the gray door?" she asked.

"Yes."

They approached cautiously, Wren keeping watch as Ed used the scanner to check for what and who might be inside.

"I don't think anyone's in there," he said when they reached the door. He took the scanner off and shook out his shoulders.

Wren touched the lock and her nanos went to work, opening it in seconds.

They slipped inside and as the door snicked shut behind them, she became aware of the smell.

"Ugh." She stopped, not wanting to put herself any nearer the source of it.

Ed grimaced. "Someone died here."

Her nanos tickled her face, and suddenly there was a silver mask covering her nose and mouth. Ed glanced over at her, gave a nod.

"Good idea." He shrugged out of his jacket, wrapped it around the lower half of his face.

They moved again, walking down a central aisle, where boxes that looked similar to those they'd found in the other warehouse were stacked on either side.

At the back, neatly sorted into short rows, were large, sealed bags that looked like they contained rocks.

"The trivolun." Wren barely glanced at the stockpile, turning in a slow circle instead to find the source of the decomposition.

She spotted a boot sticking out from the end of an aisle, and moved over to it.

She gagged a little at the sight of the body. At least her nanos ensured she couldn't smell it any more, but the sight alone . . .

She turned away, breathing deeply.

"Don't look," she told Ed, who was crouched beside the ore. "It's bad."

"Who is it?" he asked.

She shrugged. "Maybe the missing Salisas that Pontia and Linao were arguing about when we first found them in that house?"

"You think Pontia killed him?" Ed straightened up.

"Who else? Pontia said he'd reported him missing, but he was in charge of this warehouse. Maybe Salisas found out Pontia was hiding the warehouse's location?" Wren wondered what had been going through Pontia's mind. He'd clearly felt abandoned, and maybe resentful at getting sick in the course of working for the Cores, and then being unable to get help because of where he'd picked up his bacteria.

This was his revenge, and she wasn't going to complain. It suited her perfectly.

"So what now?" Ed asked, resting a foot on one of the ore bags.

"Now we find an explosive in here we can put in these bags."

THEY HAD DRAGGED Opek off the street and back into the recessed area by the building's loading bay after Wren had felled him.

Wren didn't know how long he'd be out of it, but she said the nanos thought he would probably be awake by now.

Awake and unhappy, Ed had no doubt.

"I really don't like this." Ed crouched down and peered around the corner, but the outside lights were off, and there was no sign of the man or anyone else.

"They want this so badly, even if they're suspicious, I don't think they'll turn our offer down." Wren shoved one of the bags of ore that was slipping off a hover pallet back in place. They had taken three of the warehouse hover pallets and loaded them with all the trivolun. Then they had piloted them down the streets to the building where Ed had been taken earlier.

She was probably right, but Ed was not used to standing back, and this plan meant he'd have to do just that.

"I'm coming after you if something happens," he said. He hefted the massive laz he'd taken out of the warehouse off his shoulder and held it one-handed.

"I'll let you know if I need help." She put a hand on his arm. "I have a lot of tricks up my sleeve."

He blew out a breath, gave a nod. "You do."

"Here's one. Tell me how well it works." She closed her eyes, and lifted her chin a little, and before his eyes he saw the thin silver of the nanos crawl over her face, changing its shape, the curve of her lips, the angle of her brows, and then switch back to her normal skin tone.

She looked completely different.

"That's . . ." he shook his head. "I wouldn't have known it was you."

"See? Tricks," she said.

She blew him a kiss and then moved around the corner, the hover pallets following behind her.

He crouched back down, watching as she was swallowed by the shadows as she walked toward the building, but when she got as far as the loading ramp a light switched on.

She lifted a hand to shield her eyes, and kept going up the ramp.

The door opened before she reached it, and Opek stepped out, the laz back in his hand. "Who are you?"

"I got an order to deliver this stuff." Wren lifted her comms unit, checked it. "You aren't expecting it?" She looked at the laz as if just noticing it. "Whoa. Is that real? I've never seen one outside of the Protection Unit."

"Oh." He looked at the weapon and slid it into a pocket. "Sorry. With the attacks on the city and everything, we've been a little jumpy."

Wren nodded, but she took a step back, as if she was freaked out.

"Who's the sender?" Opek asked, waving at the delivery and then edging forward to have a look at what was on the pallet.

"Salisas, says here." She said nothing more, and when he didn't respond, she stepped back. "Look, if the address is wrong, I'll just take it back and we can sort it out later."

"I am expecting something," Opek said slowly. "Can I check what's in one of the bags to make sure it's the right thing?"

She played the uncertain delivery drone perfectly, moving nervously, checking her comms unit again. "Only if you can close it up again like it was."

He must have nodded, because Ed saw him crouch down beside a pallet and Wren said nothing.

He stood suddenly. "All's in order. This was the delivery I was waiting for. When did Salisas bring it in to you?"

Wren checked her comms unit again. "Two days ago, but we were affected by the attack on the hover port the other day, and everything got backed up. We're working through the backlog now. That's why I'm delivering so late." She looked around. "So who's going to unload? This is a self-unload order."

"I need to check, just a moment." Opek backed away and disappeared into the building.

Wren turned around to face the street, and he thought she might have sent him a wink.

Opek returned and Wren slowly turned to face him.

"I need to use these hover pallets to transport the delivery to another location."

"Oh, no, no, no, no." She shook her head. "I've got to get back with these, make another delivery."

This was not in the plan. Ed realized now they hadn't even considered how the ore was going to be transported after they delivered it.

That was a big mistake.

"I'll have to insist." Opek smiled but his hand went to his pocket and he drew out the laz again, holding it by his side. "I'm alone, and the delay has caused major issues. This shipment needs to be delivered elsewhere as soon as possible."

"Elsewhere?" Wren asked.

"The far end of the hover port," he said.

Ed almost couldn't believe it, but these people had been brazen from the beginning, taking chances, going further than anyone would have guessed.

For the Caruso to land at the hover port, even if it was at the far end of the facility, away from the trouble they had caused near the buildings, was staggering.

Wren was right. They were desperate for this to go ahead.

"I can't do it." Wren pretended not to see the laz and turned away from him. "If you don't have anyone to unload, I'll have to take it back to the office and you can arrange for pick up tomorrow or another day."

She started walking away, and the hovers bobbed after her.

"Stop." The shout was angry, and just a little panicked.

Wren stopped, turned slowly back. Took a step back as if in shock and fear at the laz leveled at her chest.

Opek walked up beside her. "Sit down there. You can collect your hover pallets later."

Wren sat, and the man tapped what Ed guessed was a destination into the lead hover pallet's control system and started to walk toward Ed and the street.

The hover pallets didn't move.

The man turned back, looked at them. "Why aren't they following?"

Wren shrugged. "Because they're coded to me. Saves time."

Ed wondered what Wren was doing. She'd coded the hover pallets to her, and she could disengage them any time. She obviously wanted Opek to take her along.

He didn't like it, but she obviously had a plan, and he had to admit he didn't.

"Shit." Opek hesitated, then gave his shoulders a shake. "You're coming with me." He went to her, hauled her to her feet. "Let's go."

As Ed followed them toward the port, he realized that if the Caruso were actually landing in Demeter to collect their ore, then they thought the Cores had more control over the city than they actually did.

Ed wondered what the Cores had done to convince them of it, and then decided he didn't care.

The two sides deserved each other, and he would be happy to see them both go down.

As long as they didn't take Wren down with them.

40

THE HOVER PORT WAS STILL IN CHAOS.

The building had been damaged in one corner, and there were rescue services clearing rubble and med hovers congregating near the front of the building.

As Wren walked beside Opek, she looked over at the mess and the wounded being treated on stretchers.

"How is the freighter you're expecting going to land in the middle of all of this?" she asked. Opek was still holding the laz on her, but she'd been cooperative, and he was less jumpy now than when they'd started moving.

"They've got permission to land right at the back, where they won't be in the way." Opek kept the pace as fast as the hover pallets would go, keeping to the edge of the landing pads. The back area where he was headed was all but in darkness, the way illuminated only by the pallets, blinking a warning that they needed a recharge.

Even though the distance the pallets had had to travel hadn't been that much, the journey they'd made was taking its toll on their energy levels. Given they were warehouse hovers, she was impressed they'd made it this far.

She and Ed had imagined they'd be secretly following along

behind Opek as he transported the ore some other way, to a very different location.

Using the hover port was a bold move.

"Hope we make it," Wren said, with a nod toward the emergency light.

"We have to make it," Opek said, as if he could will it so by pure resolve.

She didn't respond.

Her nanos boosted her hearing, and she caught the faint scuff of Ed's boots on the ground behind them.

She caught the faintest rev of an engine, although it was difficult to see anything in the darkness, and then the ground beneath her feet trembled a little as something heavy set down up ahead, and she guessed a Razor had just landed.

One of the pallet hovers cut out early, powering down and landing softly on the ground. The other two continued on beside her, and followed her all the way to the side of the sleek black ship.

As soon as they came to a stop, she stepped away, but Opek reached out and grabbed her arm.

"Sorry. You need to stay."

She hadn't planned to go anywhere, but it was better if he thought she was still a delivery person caught up in a bad situation.

All the better to control him.

She pulled at her sleeve, as if to free herself from his grip, and got the fabric high enough that they were skin to skin.

By the time the back ramp on the Razor was open, she had him in her thrall.

She decided it would be better to keep Opek silent.

She waited for the Caruso soldier who strode out to reach them. He almost faltered a step at the sight of her, then gave a nod which Wren returned. "There you go," she said, with a wave at the pallets.

"What about that one?" The Caruso soldier spoke broken Aponi as he pointed to the pallet that hadn't had the energy store to make it all the way.

"The battery died," she said. "It's not too far, though."

Beside her, Opek opened his mouth as if to speak and then, with a push from her nanos, clicked his teeth together.

The Caruso gave a grunt, waved a big, gloved hand, and more soldiers jogged out to start moving the bags.

They cleared the farthest pallet first and then the other two with quick efficiency, hauling the bags to the rear ramp.

Wren stood by Opek's side, taking in the ship, taking in the Caruso, who were much taller and wider than she'd realized.

The natural plating on their faces, like organic armor, made them so different from the Verdant String natives, but still, they were bipedal, with arms and legs. The two groups looked more alike than not.

"Satisfied?" Wren asked.

"You were late, but if grade is high, this will be acceptable." The leader stopped to talk to them again, his presence intimidating as he loomed over them both, a bag of trivolun in his hand.

Her nanos needed to activate the timer in that bag, and hopefully it would then arm the one closest to it, and so on, until the whole ship was full of activated explosives.

She finally let Opek speak, in order to get things moving: "We'll expect to hear from you, then."

We have a problem, her nanos said. *We cannot activate the timer remotely. You have to touch the bag. You have to touch each bag.*

That . . . would be difficult. Given they were almost all loaded in the back of the Razor.

"Not so quick." The leader spoke slowly in answer to Opek's dismissal, his grasp of the language clearly not fluent. "You don't have control of Demeter."

She was going to have to dart forward, touch the bag. And hope when it activated, it sparked the rest of the explosives in a chain reaction.

"No, we don't," Wren said, eyeing the distance between herself and the bag. It was only a couple of steps. "It was never going to be easy. But I'm sure we'll get there, and the rewards should more than make up for it." She waved a hand at the back of the Razor to remind him of the ore that had been loaded.

"You said you had control." The soldier looked toward the building at the other end of the port. "What good is deal without it? The ore can only come to us if you in control."

She saw the moment his body language changed. He flung the bag behind him, toward the Razor, and moved to grasp the big weapon slung across his chest, lifting it up.

For a split second she thought he was aiming it at her, and then she realized it was at someone behind her.

As she spun on her heel, her heart leapt to her throat, frightened it was Ed that he'd spotted.

It was not.

"Who are you?" the Caruson asked.

"I'm Vim Handras, Evette Linao's assistant." A man walked into the ring of light spilling from the back of the Razor, hands raised to show he was unarmed.

It was the cafe owner she'd followed to the first warehouse.

He looked over at her as he came even with Opek, and she could see his mind spinning. She looked nothing like she had when she'd ordered some jah from him, so he had to be wondering who she was.

Her hand was still on Opek's arm, and her nanos picked up Opek's dislike of Vim, his annoyance with having to do Vim's bidding, and his surprise that he'd come to the hover port, where he could have potentially been caught by Defense or the Protection Unit.

"What's happening, Opek?" Vim asked.

At last, Wren could focus back on the bag of ore that had been tossed but it was no longer there. One of the Caruso had taken it into the Razor.

We should have realized we had to touch—

No, Wren said. *This was a plan put together in moments. Mistakes will happen. You cannot be all knowing. Let's rather focus on how to get around it.*

"We were discussing why you lied about controlling Demeter."

The Caruson soldier finally dropped the barrel of his massive laz to point downward.

Vim shrugged his shoulders, as if to release tension. He glanced over at her and Opek, looking for clues from them as to what was going on. He cleared his throat. "There have been a few problems. But as long as you keep nearspace free of VSC battleships, we'll have the time and space we need to win."

Wren studied Vim, and wondered who he actually was. Not a cafe owner, obviously. That was just a convenient front.

"We don't like lies." The Caruson began backing away, and then reached out suddenly, moving faster than it seemed possible for someone of his size, and grabbed Wren by the front of her jacket.

She was lifted up and spun, and found herself held against the Caruson's chest.

From the sides and from behind, she heard the sudden hum of the massive Caruson weapons powering up.

"You are Evette Linao," the Caruson told her.

Well.

She glanced at him. "Actually . . ."

"She's not Evette." Vim took a step forward, looking shocked. "Evette is . . . unavailable right now."

"That's what we were told when we asked to speak with her. But then a woman appears with the ore. In charge. You looked to her when we asked about the lies, as if waiting for her to answer. This is Evette."

Wren remembered Opek had made a call, and she should have asked herself who to. Should have touched Opek before they got here to find out what had been said.

Clearly Vim had been put in charge in Evette Linao's absence, and these Caruso had wanted to speak to the boss.

Maybe that's why Vim had come in person. To smooth things over.

"Let her go." Ed's voice came out of the darkness, and he stepped into the ring of light, laz raised.

All the weapons swung his way.

"More proof of your identity," the Caruson said. "You came with protection."

She locked gazes with Ed for an instant, wishing she could let him know this turn of events might just suit them very well. Then she looked back over her shoulder. "You need to get moving," she said to the Caruson. "This isn't exactly a safe place for you."

"No." The Caruso soldier's voice was short. "But yet you told us to come here."

"Where else could you have landed? And the ore was stored nearby. If you go now, you'll get away fine." Wren kept still in the soldier's grasp.

"We'll go now, and you will come with us." The Caruson began to moved backward toward the Razor.

"What do you want in exchange for her?" Ed asked, voice clipped.

"She comes with us. We will get accurate details about take over of Aponi."

Wren had to admit it wasn't a bad plan, if she'd actually been Evette Linao. They would have a really strong hostage in exchange for getting truthful updates.

As she was dragged back, she caught Ed's gaze again. "Remember the flowers," she called to him. "And don't hang around."

In case there is a very big explosion. Which hopefully there will be.

He narrowed his eyes, fury lighting his expression, but he gave a sharp nod.

She willed him to back down. She might be able to enthrall the one who was holding her, but she could do nothing about the other eight, and they were all pointing weapons at Ed.

There was no way for him to fight them without taking numerous hits.

"No more talk." The Caruson tossed her inside as if she weighed nothing, and she was forced to roll, fetching up against one of the pallets and rapping her head.

Ow.

She pulled herself into a crouch and watched the rest of the soldiers jog inside and settle into jump seats.

This ship moves fast, her nanos told her. *Maybe too fast for us to dissipate while it's moving.*

So she had to set the explosives and then dissipate before they took off.

So, right now.

She rose to her feet and began to touch each bag as she rounded the pallet.

"What are you doing?" The lead Caruson was inside now, and the ramp was closing up.

"I'm counting the bags." She kept going, moving to the second pallet and letting her fingers flicker over each sack.

"I don't trust you. Get away from them." He stepped forward, but while his hand went to the butt of his big laz, he didn't engage it.

Probably couldn't fire it in the ship.

She moved a little faster, backing into the third pallet and touching the first few bags.

He lunged at her, and she twisted away, hands out to touch bags as she went.

They came to a stop on opposite sides of the last pallet, and his face was like thunder.

He didn't know what she was up to, but he knew it was nothing good.

She had touched enough that it didn't matter if she hadn't got them all. She lifted her hands up.

"Fine. I'll stop." Then she ducked down, out of his line of sight.

Now!

She heard the engines scream as the pilot revved for take off, heard a shout and looked to her left as the Caruson rounded the pallet, violence in his eyes.

As he grabbed for her, she felt the faintest tingle as his hand brushed her arm and then fell sideways as vertigo gripped her and the world spun away.

With a gasp she came to leaning against the vines in the alley, looking up as a dark shadow shot up into the air.

Five, four, three, two, one . . . her nanos counted down for her.

There was a moment of nothing, and then the sudden, heart-jerking boom as blue and purple light erupted from the Caruson ship.

The sound of pounding boots pulled her focus from the sky and she turned to see Ed sprinting into the narrow laneway.

"Wren, I swear." He grabbed her. "I've already told you I'm easily stressed."

She grinned against his throat. "I won't do it again."

"I'll keep you to it." He shuddered, and his grip tightened even more.

"It was close," she admitted, tilting her head up to watch the flaming pieces of the ship fall down all over the hover port. The emergency sirens were screaming into the night in response. "That Caruson saw me dissipate."

"He won't be doing anything about it now," Ed said, turning with his arm still around her to look up.

"No. But Vim and Opek are still there. Or hightailing it back to their headquarters."

"No." Ed shook his head. "They're lying on the ground, hit by my laz fire. I sent Bartam a message to let her know where to find them."

"It feels like every time we think we know who they all are, another few pop up."

"They have to be getting to the bottom of the pile by now," Ed said. "And they've lost the Caruso. You made sure of it. The trust between them is broken and their ore is gone."

"Do you think we saved the planet?" she asked, feeling a little loopy with fatigue and euphoria.

"Yeah, I think we saved it." Ed tugged a flower from a vine and stuck it in her hair. "And I think we need to celebrate."

She sighed as he kissed her. "Let's go home."

41

Lieutenant Bartam and Captain Darnell looked across the table at them. They were seated stiffly, uniforms neatly pressed.

Violet Fann leaned against the wall, her uniform dirty and stinking of smoke, her face smudged, with a thin cut along her cheek.

It was late morning, as she and Ed had slept in, and everyone here seemed annoyed with them.

"You want to tell us about the Caruso?" Bartam asked.

"We already explained." Ed pushed his chair back to stretch out his legs.

"You found information about the ore. You loaded it with explosives and delivered it, and when the Caruso took off, you activated the triggers." Darnell sounded both angry and admiring.

"And it never occurred to you once to contact me? Or any of us?" Bartam asked.

"You were all dealing with the fall out from the attack, and at least one of Darnell's people was a traitor, and certainly two of yours were," Wren said. "We also suspected a member of the Protection Unit. So it was safer for us to do it without mentioning it to anyone."

There was a beat of silence.

"That's . . . not unreasonable." Violet Fann rubbed at her fore-

259

head. "And it worked. We've got a burning hulk instead of a Razor, at least ten dead Caruso, and if Ed and Wren are right, the partnership between the Cores and the Caruso is dead, or at the least very much weakened."

"We noticed the battleships were nowhere to be seen." Ed didn't make it a question, but he looked over at Darnell and then Bartam.

"There was an incident." Darnell's face looked like it would crack, it was so stiff, and Bartam's eyes narrowed.

"The Caruso lured them away?" Wren guessed.

Violet Fann pushed away from the wall. Shot her a wry grin. "Something like that. I'm sure the full details will come out in time." She flicked a smile at Darnell, but he was staring at his clenched fists.

Wren guessed the military were in the middle of a shake-up. They had cruised along happily for a long time, but now they'd reached the pointy end of things. They needed to up their game.

And from Darnell and Bartam's expressions, it was a painful process.

"What's happened to Evette Linao?" Ed asked.

"She's in custody. She wants a deal for her freedom before she talks." Darnell rubbed at his hair. "The head of the military is considering it."

"She's one of the heads of this whole enterprise." Wren leaned forward, elbows on the table, suddenly furious. "She will lie."

Violet Fann shifted. "Is she? That's interesting."

"She can fly a Razor, but that's not her only value." Ed added his voice to hers. "If I were to guess, I'd say she was the daughter of a Cores exec. She likes the thrill of mixing with the people they've duped or coerced and those on their payroll, pretending to be one of them while she spies on them. It must have been very useful to the top bosses. But she's gotten away with too much, been rescued too many times. People have noticed that she never gets left behind, when everyone else does."

Wren remembered the questions Fenton and Navar had asked Linao in the freighter on the way to Ytla. They had definitely known she wasn't in the same category as they were.

"I think she's even more than that," Wren said. "I think she'd moved up the ranks from high-level fixer, mixing with the dregs so the high-ups feel like they know what's being said about them, to decision-maker. She felt no hesitation in killing Pontia and leaving him. Her regret was that she didn't have time to make sure he was dead. She spoke to Gy Renard on Ytla as if she was involved in the deal they offered him. And I think she was."

"So she's playing us?" Darnell asked. "To what end?"

"She's hoping to give her people time to rescue her," Ed warned. "She's drawing it out, and while you ponder the deal you're going to offer her, they're working out a way to get her out."

"I'll pass your insights up the chain," Darnell said, and Wren had a horrible feeling it would do no good. Somehow, Evette Linao was going to slither out of this mess, as well.

Wren reached out a hand and brushed Ed's arm to get his attention, then dragged her chair back with a screech and stood.

Ed's gaze met hers and he stood with her.

"Where are you going?" Bartam's voice was snappish.

"To visit Bailey and Hatch," Wren said. "You aren't holding us, are you?"

There was an uncomfortable pause.

Then Bartam sighed. "All right. As Lieutenant Fann says, what you did worked." She shook her head. "I don't like suspecting my whole team, wondering who could be on the other side."

"Join the club." Darnell sounded grim. "We've taken Kaleb, the soldier who forced Ed away from the military base, into custody. He's claiming coercion."

"I think a lot of their contacts have been coerced." Ed moved with her to the door. "Which means you need to watch the people looking for Velda Shanïha and Ethan Hyt carefully. Some might be out there looking to silence them permanently."

Bartam winced. "I did consider that. Guttra is keeping an eye on the searchers. So far, there seems to be no sign of Ethan or Velda."

"They can't have vanished," Ed said.

"No. Maybe they're hiding. Maybe they've worked out not

everyone out there can be trusted." Bartam lifted her shoulders. "We need them back."

It was a depressing end to the meeting.

Ed took Wren's hand as they walked to the hospital, which helped to lift her mood.

She glanced up at him. "When you said 'unnecessary' to the nanos, when you rescued me from the obs station, you were telling them they didn't need to influence you. You were already all in."

"Yes," he said, giving her hand a gentle squeeze. "And when you said 'it works both ways now' when Evette Linao was holding a laz to my throat, you meant the same."

"I'm glad we got that cleared up," she said, and gave their joined hands a little swing.

"Me, too," he said. "The stress was killing me."

She pressed her forehead into his arm and laughed.

He looked down at her. "I'm going to have to go back up and walk the line."

She knew it. The Cores' plan may have been disrupted, but they had been working on this for years. They had people on Aponi, and freighter captains under their control. Ed had to scan.

"Need an artifact consultant while you're up there?" she asked. She would go work on the ancestral spaceship on Ytla when this was over. But no one would be doing anything serious there until the current crisis had passed.

Ed pulled her out of the stream of foot traffic, up against a wall. "I need you, no matter what your role." He tilted his head, a flicker of a smile teasing the corner of his mouth. "Although a cake-making artifacts consultant is always handy."

She twined her fingers through his.

His face was suddenly serious. "I never felt truly at home on Aponi. I've realized that some of that's on me. But you give me a sense of homecoming, a peace I haven't felt since before Halatia was destroyed."

She lifted their joined hands, and like he often did to her, kissed his knuckles. "I moved around a lot as a child, then ended up back here—a planet I never even knew—after my parents were killed. My childhood experiences made it easy to mirror that same way of life in my work, to never put down deep roots. Now I understand my parents' sense of home was each other. And I was missing that. Until I met you."

And us, her nanos reminded her.

And you, she agreed.

"Let's go check on our friends." Ed steered them back into the stream of traffic, and she realized that despite the unanswered questions and the potential danger they still faced, she was happy.

"If we're going to visit Hatch, we need to stop somewhere on the way," she said, "and buy cake."

To GET notification of when the next book in the Verdant String series is out (Velda and Ethan's story), sign up to Michelle Diener's new release notification list. You'll receive exclusive content, access to giveaways and notification of upcoming releases. You can unsubscribe at any time.

THE VERDANT STRING SERIES

The planets of the Verdant String, the green, fecund sources of life spanning five solar systems, comprise the Verdant String Coalition.

This is the setting for the science fiction romance series from award-winning novelist Michelle Diener.

While the people of the Verdant String know they have a common ancestor, a group of explorers who colonized the planets at the same time thousands of years ago, the mysteries of who they were, and where they came from, persist.

Each book in the series can be read as a standalone:

Interference & Insurgency Box Set | Breakaway | Breakeven | Trailblazer | High Flyer | Wave Rider | Peace Maker | Enthraller

ALSO BY MICHELLE DIENER

Science Fiction Novels

Verdant String series:

Interference & Insurgency Box Set

Breakaway

Breakeven

Trailblazer

High Flyer

Wave Rider

Peace Maker

Enthraller

Sky Raiders series:

Intended (Short Story Prequel Available Free to Newsletter Subscribers)

Sky Raiders

Calling the Change

Shadow Warrior

Class 5 series:

Dark Horse

Dark Deeds

Dark Minds

Dark Matters

Dark Ambitions: A Class 5 Novella

Dark Class

Dark Class Epilogue: Free on newsletter signup

Collision Course

Historical Fiction Novels

Traffic Warden Mysteries:

Ticket Out

Susanna Horenbout series:

In a Treacherous Court

Dangerous Sanctuary (A short story - available for free, exclusively to readers who sign up to Michelle Diener's New Release Notification List)

Keeper of the King's Secrets

In Defense of the Queen

Regency London series:

The Emperor's Conspiracy

Banquet of Lies

A Dangerous Madness

Other historical novels:

Daughter of the Sky

Fantasy Novels by Michelle Diener

The Rising Wave series:

The Rising Wave (Prequel novella to THE TURNCOAT KING)

The Turncoat King

The Threadbare Queen

Fate's Arrow

Truth's Blade

Mistress of the Wind

The Dark Forest series:

The Golden Apple

The Silver Pear

Short Paranormal Fiction

Breaking Out: Part I (Short story)

Breaking Out: Part II (Novella)

To sign up to Michelle Diener's newsletter and receive notification when a new book is released, as well as exclusive novellas and short stories, head to michellediener.com.

ABOUT THE AUTHOR

Michelle Diener is an award winning author of historical fiction, science fiction and fantasy romance.

Michelle was born in London and currently lives in Australia with her husband and children.

You can contact Michelle through her website or sign up to receive notification when she has a new book out.

Connect with Michelle
www.michellediener.com

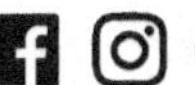

ACKNOWLEDGMENTS

Thank you as always to all the people who help make my books the best they can be. This includes Claire B. and Jo, as well as Jess W., Margaret M., Krista D., Lynn L., Cherry G., Missy W., James M., Barbara E., Monique M., and Christine B. on my ARC team.